Dewey Hill Entertainment & l

This novel is a work of fiction. Any resemblance to real people, dead or living, actual events, organizations, establishments, and/or locales are intended to give the fiction a sense of reality and authenticity. Names, characters, places and incidents are either products of the author's imagination or are used fictitiously, as are those fictionalized events and incidents that may involve real persons and did not occur or are set in the future.

Published by:

Dewey Hill Entertainment & Publishing

PO Box 32316

Charleston, SC 29417

Phone: 1-(866) 827-8477

www.Deweyhillpublishing.com

Library of Congress Catalog Card No: In publication data
IBSN-10: 0-9787274-1-X

Dedication.

Dedicated to my comrade: Gerald “Prince” Miller.

One Love, Shaborn.

Acknowledgement.

First and foremost, I must give Thanks to the Most High, for Blessing me with the knowledge, gift, and the experiences [in which I've survived] to do what I do. I've learned, from experience, how faith and belief can open any door.

Thank you, and much love, to everyone who supported my first novel "My Brother's Keeper!", which is actually still doing well in sells. I must send a thank you out to A&B Book Distributors, as well as Baker&Taylor for showing love to us Self Publishers. To my parents, Alfred Adams Sr. and Dr. Dorothy J. Adams, together the two of you has not only Blessed me with brains and good looks, but most of all, loyalty and integrity. Thank you for your unconditional love and support! Rest in peace to my grandparents, Granville & Ruth Adams, and Lonnie & Rosa Mae Brown. Also, my Aunts; Della & Prim Rose, I love you and may the two of you rest in peace.

To my brothers and sisters, I love you all, and I'm sure you all know that my loyalty is without question! Miz, it's obvious we're at the top of our game, which everyone else will see and know with the releases of our latest novels! $tack those dollars so we can take Dewey Hill & Pen Cushion to that next level!!!! My nieces and nephews are far too many to name! But Uncle Sha definitely loves you all without a doubt! And Cuz Oh [Omar 'OH' Vaughan] what can I say? You came up admiring Miz and my actions and endeavors, however, while we were both down you definitely stepped it up and represented the 'fam' to the fullest! Now, all we gotta do is make that music thing pop off!!!! We already have the best kept secret [Producer] in the game on our team! For those who don't know the name "Shim" will know it soon enough! Keep pushing out those hot ass tracks! To Debora Grant, from DG Business Management, what would I do without you? You are undoubtedly the best Accountant & Business Manager in the field, who obviously has the client's best interest at heart! You're truly a rarity, which is why I have much love for you as well. Hope Clark, your experience and consultation early on has been nothing but priceless. For that, I thank you.

Maxine, your loyalty & dedication is like no other! Well, I'm sure there are other woman out there who possess those qualities, but I can only speak from what you've shown me over the years! And for that I will forever love you...

DaQuane, you still have a lot of learning and growing to do, but I'll always love you, because you and I will forever be one and the same....remember that! Christina & Sha Born I don't get to see the two of you as much as I'd like, due to certain circumstances, but my love for the two of you is without question. In fact, much love to the entire Smith family. Rest in peace Jessica Smith, because you were certainly an Angel on earth, therefore, it's inevitable that you are one...in Heaven!!!! Ashanique, my little twin, I'm appreciative of the time you and I are getting to spend with one another these days. You are not only my little girl, but also my Heart! Najae & Antwan, I know the distance between us causes frustration, on all of our part, but it's about to get better! I promise! I love you both with all my Heart! Stacey, I know I get on your nerves sometimes, and I don't say it enough, but you are definitely the best Woman any Man can hope for to bare, and raise his children! I am indeed lucky, and so are Anthony, Najae, and Antwan! I guess you get it from your Mamma! (Smile). She too, is an incredible lady! I love you Loretta Henderson. Wanda, although we sometimes have our difference of opinions, I must admit, you've more than held it down (as a Mother), in fact, you are the manifestation of what a Woman should be. Keith Saunders, from Marion Designs, you've certainly been more than a graphic designer for my projects, because I seriously doubt that anyone, thus far, has schooled me to the ins and outs of this literary thing more than you have! Not many people, especially once they've become as successful as you have, make time for those on the come-up! However, you've done so (with me) at a time when my access and movement was very limited, for that I thank you and will always be appreciative! Not to mention, you are certainly the best in the game!!!

To my attorney Wesley Locklair, at Joye, Locklair & Powers, thanks for holding me down over the years.

Special thank you to my homegirl Queen Pen good luck on your next novel.

My "Comrades" are way too many to name! But since this is a Queens story, I gotta give love to all those who remember me and my family from South Road, Laurelton, and Far Rockaway, three places in which I've once resided, even though most of my life was spent in Brooklyn, New York. Also, much love to my homies Gerald 'Prince' Miller, C Just, Shannon, Tucker, Green Eyes Born, Robo

Just, Supreme, Lord, Divine, TaTa, ShaMeek, Jug Head, Spoon, Scar, Rufus Chico, James "Wall" Corley, Todd, Lakey the kid, and Doc…. the rest I'll continue to represent thru my ways & actions!!!!!!!!!!!!!!

MUCH LOVE,
Alfred 'Sha Born' Adams Jr.

Every **BOROUGH** ***In New York City.....***

Has Its "OWN" Story To Tell!!!!!!!!!

April 4, 1967

Kenneth Shannon was born at 1:22 a.m., at Jamaica Hospital, to Keisha and Eugene Shannon.

On the very same morning, at 1:26 a.m., Yolanda Reed gave birth to her seven pounds eight ounce male child, at Queens General Hospital, whom it was previously determined would be named after his father Joshua Reed.

Whereas, Joshua made it no secret that he'd relish, and anticipated adding the "Sr" to his name, his wife Yolanda knew that the real pleasure would come on the day in which physical contact was made, between a father and his newborn son. Unlike a joy-filled Eugene Shannon, who at that moment was holding his six pounds nine ounce son in his arms, Joshua Reed, at that very moment was confined in an 8'14 foot cell at the infamous Sing Sing Correctional Facility in Ossining, New York.

"J.R.!" whispered the 6'4", 310 pound Caucasian prison guard, at the same time using his *beat-a-nigga-down* stick, to wake Joshua, by tapping on the bars of his cell.

Although his cell was extremely dark, and the cell block was dimly lit, Joshua immediately recognized the prison guard's voice.

"White, what's up?" Inquired Joshua who was now fully awake and sitting up in his bunk. The only time he ever addressed the prison guard as 'officer' White, was when other officers or inmates were around. Even then, they kept their conversation to a minimum. In fact, Joshua's Italian friends dealt with White on the outside so, the officer's presence in front of his cell, and at such an hour, certainly dismayed the notorious street thug.

Sensing J.R.'s dismay, the huge prison guard smiled.

"Relax Reed!" He said in low tone, before adding, "I just thought I'd stop by your cell to inform you, it's a *boy*!" With that said, the smiling officer walked off.

Joshua sat there on his bunk not, at all, understanding what the prison guard was implying by what he'd said. Then suddenly, he understood exactly what White meant by that! A realization that brought a huge smile to his face! He knew one of his people made a call to the prison, or rather to White, and had him deliver the message.

As soon as the cells were cracked, the following morning, Joshua was on the telephone.

"About time you called!" Joshua recognized his wife's sister Janice's voice as soon as the call was accepted.
It was no secret that his calls were monitored and/or recorded, therefore Joshua knew he couldn't expose the fact that he'd already been informed about his son's arrival into the world.

"Is there something wrong?" He asked calmly.

"Actually, things couldn't be better," Replied a now cheerful Janice. "Well, I'll take that back, considering I've been asked to sit up in this house and await your call, while your wife and our mother get the pleasure of holding my newborn nephew!" She complained.

"So Yolanda finally gave birth to my little man?" Asked an already knowing Joshua, as the smile he'd worn majority of the morning returned to his face. “How much does he weigh? And who does he look like?”

“My mother called early this morning, to tell me Yolanda had a seven pound eight ounce boy, with a head full of wavy hair just like his father!” Laughed Janice. “Now that you’ve called I can finally get to the hospital and see him for myself.” She added, ready to hang up and be out, before adding, “Oh yeah, from what I hear, the boy’s already displaying signs of being your son!” Again she laughed when she said that.

“How so?” Asked Joshua.

“Momma also said, she thought the doctor was going to have to pull his belt off to get your son to cry!” Laughed Janice. “I think it took like four wacks on his little butt, before your son showed any signs that his little lungs were intact.”

Joshua didn’t find that funny at all, yet he held his composure.

“I can’t believe she had the baby so suddenly, I just spoke with her around 8:30 last night. What ever happened to women being in labor for twenty four to forty eight hours?” He asked.

“I guess Joshua Reed Jr. was in a rush to be amongst us!” Laughed Janice. “Now, how about you let me get down to that hospital!”

“Give my wife and son a kiss for me.” Said Joshua, suddenly remembering to ask, “Where’s Pam?”

“I took her to the Day Care this morning, my mother’s going to pick her up this evening though.” Answered Janice. “I started to call up there to that prison this morning, and ask if they’d give you a message to call home."

"Why didn't you?"

"Because your wife insisted that I didn't. She said something about not wanting to alarm you, because the prison had a tendency to pass along misinformation to the inmate, when or if a family member telephoned regarding a family emergency." Said Janice.

"And she definitely didn't want you being summoned to the Chaplain's office."

At that, Joshua laughed. He remembered telling his wife that inmates dreaded being called to the Chaplain's office, because nine times out of ten, the Chaplain served as the bearer of bad news.

"Be careful, and again, give my love to my wife, son, and your mother when you get to the hospital." "I certainly will," Janice replied, before hanging up.

"I can only imagine what a relief it must be to have *finally* dropped our little load." Mona smiled, looking down at her first born grandson whom she held in her arms. "Because Lord knows, you've certainly been *carrying* him."

Yolanda knew exactly what her mother was implying by her remark, since she had decided to continue working up until the day her water broke. As well as single handedly hold down all of her household duties, and take care of her three year old daughter Pam.

It was no secret that what Mona found most unbelievable

was the fact that, up until Yolanda's ninth month of pregnancy, she continued, each and every weekend, to take the two hour train ride to visit her husband at Sing Sing. "*Ain't no way in hell*!" Mona thought to herself. Never mind the fact that her son in law had proven to be a better man, father, and provider than most men who were *not* incarcerated. Her train of thought was suddenly interrupted when Yolanda reached out for her child.

Once baby Joshua was properly nestled beneath his mother's bosom, at the same time causing a familiar suction sound, as his hungry mouth made contact with Yolanda's right nipple, which discreetly protruded from her nightgown. Looking down at the feeding infant Yolanda replied to her mother's earlier comment.

"Actually mother, I haven't even *began* to carry our little load of joy. Right little fella?" She asked baby Joshua, at the same time gently running a finger through his head full of curly hair, before adding, "Because as soon as the weekend arrives you and I are going to dress up real nice and warm, so mommy can take you to meet your daddy. You'll love that, wouldn't you?" Yolanda smiled, before answering her own question, "Momma *know* you will. And guess what my precious baby?" She continued her one sided conversation with her feeding child. "Your daddy will love it even more! For the past nine month *your* arrival has been all that man has talked about." She laughed.

Mona however, stood beside Yolanda's hospital bed in total disbelief of what she was hearing come out of her daughter's mouth.

"Yolanda! You can *not* be serious." She stared at Yolanda as if she had totally lost her mind. “What woman in her right mind would take her newborn child, and herself for that matter, Up State to that filthy jailhouse so soon? It would be outright crazy, on your part, to do such a thing. And if Joshua had good sense, which I’m inclined to believe that he does, *he* wouldn’t even allow it!”

Unmoved and certainly unconvinced by her mother’s words, Yolanda met Mona’s stare, than spoke, “For one, I do not know what correctional facility you’ve ever visited, but I assure you the visitation room at Sing Sing is *not* filthy. In fact, that area of the prison, looks a whole lot cleaner than many of the homes I’ve seen belonging to a number of so called babysitters. And two, I do not think this is the time or place for you and I start a debate. Your being here, right now, means the world to me. Actually, *you* mean the world to me, because you have always been there for me, Janice and Pam. But with all due respect mother, so does my husband. Matters discussed, or decisions made between he and I are not even open for anyone else’s opinion. I can’t even explain how badly it affects me that Joshua’s face wasn’t one of the *first* faces this child looked into, upon opening his eyes to the world.” Yolanda sighed, looking back down at her newborn child who was no longer feeding from her breast milk, instead he was resting. “But I *assure* you, his father’s face will certainly be one of the first faces he looks into come Saturday morning, because he and I will be in the front of that line when those visiting room doors open.” Yolanda smiled at the thought. Looking up at Mona, she asked, “How about you take your grandson down to the nursery, so that your extremely exhausted daughter can get some much needed rest?"

Not appreciating, one bit, how Yolanda conveniently changed the subject Mona, nonetheless, happily reached for her sleeping grandchild. Just as she was about to let her daughter know that, although she was grown, her actions and decision was obviously foolish, all Mona could do was shake her head seeing how quickly Yolanda had *already* fallen asleep!

As Eugene stood outside of the hospital's nursery observing his newborn son while he slept, all he could do was smile recalling his reluctance to hand the child over to the on duty nurse. If he could've had it *his* way, Eugene would have held his son until the Sun rose. Yet, even he knew and understood the importance of monitoring the vital signs of a newborn baby, therefore he didn't give the nurse too much flack.

"And *I* was under the impression that *somebody* was heading home for a bite to eat, shower, and a little shut eye?" A woman's voice spoke from behind.

Instead of turning to face his wife, Eugene closed his eyes and envisioned her extremely beautiful face along with the face of his resting son, realizing that it was indeed a matter of opinion that one couldn't tell which parent a *newborn* child resembled most, because baby Kenneth was indeed the spitting image of his wife Keisha. The light complexion, the wavy hair, light brown eyes, thin nose and deep dimples.

Opening his eyes, Eugene turned to face his wife, at the same time producing his trademark white tooth smile. A smile in which countless men secretly despised, and countless women whispered how lucky Keisha Shannon was to have him.

Although his wife's hair was simply pinned up, she was without any make up, and standing before him in a pale blue hospital nightgown beneath her opened robe, Eugene knew that he was the luckiest man on earth to have such a lady.

The two of them simply stood there observing one another, no words at all being exchanged. As he took in the sight of his wife, Eugene thought back to how beautiful Keisha had been as a young girl, a teenager, and now as a woman. His woman. In fact, she was obviously one of those females who became even more beautiful with age, he told himself.

At twenty two, Keisha was still a young woman. She and Eugene were actually the same age, and had known each other almost their entire lives. As youngsters, five years old to be exact, they'd became neighbors living in the Redfern Houses in Far Rockaway, Queens. Unlike today, back then, the Redfern Houses were indeed a step up as far as better housing compared to a number of other neighborhoods in Queens. In fact, just as with other newly developed housing projects, a number of white families were prevalent.

During the late 1950's and early 60's Eugene Shannon had earned a reputation for being a jack of *all* trades! Before becoming one of the most well known and respected *numbers* runner throughout the borough of Queens, he'd worked odd jobs, hustled, as well as maintained high grades at Far Rockaway High school.

At the young age of twenty, Eugene married his childhood sweetheart, Keisha whom everyone called KeKe, and the two of them purchased a house in South Jamaica, Queens. The house was actually located on South Road and Liverpool Street.

Despite their moving, Eugene continued to receive love and respect throughout Far Rockaway, where his loyalty and generosity had not only earned him *but* raised him to legendary street status. Which often dismayed even him, whereas he knew he was still too young to even be considered an *OG*, let alone legendary status! He showed love to the children in his Far Rockaway neighborhood by sponsoring various sports, music, and picnic events. As well as contributed to the trust funds of those who showed college potential. His visits to the Elks Club, which was a neighborhood after hours type social club, always produced talk being that drinks were on *him*, the entire night, for everyone!

Early on, Eugene began his numbers operation by paying small establishments, mostly black owned bars, poolrooms, candy stores, dry cleaners, and cab stands a decent fee in exchange for allowing him to set up shop in their basements, or possibly in the back of the establishment. Some of the establishments were so neighborhood oriented and familiar with their customers, they actually allowed majority of them to play their numbers from right over the counter top. Which was especially the case with most bar owners, who certainly were not trying to hear *or* feel any, and everybody having access to the back *or* basement of their establishment, because it would undoubtedly make them easy marks for any and all would be robbers!

During the mid 1970's to 1980 Eugene's most profitable numbers locations, which was actually referred to as 'numbers hole', was a bar located on 150th street right off of Liberty Avenue, and a cab stand that was located on the Square. The 'square' was the intersection where Farmers Boulevard connected with Liberty Avenue. It was also where Eugene Shannon formally met the infamous Joshua Reed.

Back then, it was common for the true gangster, hustlers, and gentlemen to introduce and identify themselves in *full name* fashion, opposed to the aka's and bka's, regardless of what their hustles of choice or street endeavors consisted of. Most notably were Frank Matthews, Freddie Myers, Guy Fischer, Jesse Grey, William 'Bill' Underwood, Tito Johnson, Jerome Harris, Ronnie Bump, and John Freeman.

Unsurprisingly, dated articles published in such publications as Time Life magazine strived to make one believe that the whole *full name* thing, used by the hustlers and gangsters, was nothing more than a derivation and fascination adopted from the likes of Jesse James, Butch Cassidy, Dutch Shultz, Al Capone and the like, when in truth, actuality, and reality the derivation and fascination could *only* have come from the Nat Turners', Marcus Garveys', Malcolm X's', Huey Newtons', Bobby Seales', Clarence X Smiths', George Jacksons' and a *long* list of others whose endeavors and accomplishments were indeed fascinating, to say the least!

When Joshua Reed was released from Sing Sing Correctional Facility on June 13, 1971 his daughter Pam was seven years old, whereas his son Joshua Jr, who everyone called 'J.R.', was four. Although Joshua had been well connected, prior to his bid, he still found himself serving a six year prison sentence. Indeed six years was a lengthy sentence for a gun beef, nevertheless he laid down on it considering the automatic pistol found in his possession had a silencer attached to it.

A self taught automobile mechanic, Joshua found work at an Italian owned auto repair and body shop, located on Astoria Boulevard. At the time of his employment, he was only sixteen years old. A job in which he certainly needed at the time, being that he had gotten a young classmate pregnant, and needed money for her abortion.

The shop specialized in custom body work, which included equipping vehicles with hidden stash compartments. Joshua did any and all engine work. However, the *body work* he did put in for his employers, paid Joshua ten times what he made underneath an engine. As for the Italians, they didn't mine paying young Joshua *well* for his services, because he had more than proven to be their most capable hit man.

Joshua couldn't believe the money he was making to do a job he clearly enjoyed. He mainly enjoyed it because majority of his work consisted of knocking off other Italians! Even though it was against *family* rule and principle to allow an outsider, especially a 'moulie', to takeout one of their own. However,

Joshua soon realized, just as with any other family on earth, disregard and drama was inevitable. In fact, he even questioned his employer one day, regarding the alleged rule.

"Forgetaboutit!" Was the employer's response, and Joshua did just *that* with each trip to the bank. Although he realized the danger surrounding the underworld in which he'd become a significant part of, Joshua was very protective of his family. Never once did he regret marrying Yolanda Jones, who had bore him two beautiful children, and never questioned any of his actions or decisions.

Shortly following his release, it was his former employers who had provided the necessary funds for Joshua to purchase his own auto repair shop, which also served as a gasoline station. Nevermind the fact that Joshua Reed had *plenty* of his own money stashed away. The shop was located on Linden Boulevard. About a year later, he opened a soul food restaurant directly across the street from his shop. Shortly after that, he purchased the well established cab stand that was located on the Square.

It was the former owner of the cab stand who had introduced Joshua Reed to Eugene Shannon. The rest was a history in the making. A history in which few were a part of, fewer paralleled, all of New York City respected! A history involving gambling, money laundering, drug and gun trafficking, extortion, and murder.

A history in which not only set the stage for many of Queens most infamous and notorious kingpins and murderers, but also, undoubtedly and ultimately defined their two young sons.....

Joshua "J.R." Reed and Kenneth "K Smooth" Shannon!!!!

Chapter One.

"You *gotta* be kidding me right?" K Smooth asked in disbelief, as he held the telephone receiver listening to what J.R. suggested they do that evening. Once J.R. was done speaking, he added, "Listen to me, and listen to me good partner. I could care less *who* is DJing in 48 Park tonight, the risk isn't worth taking. You *know* how stupid them niggas from 40 projects be acting when they spot niggas on their side, who aren't *from* their side." Hoping he was getting through to J.R. he further emphasized his point.

"In fact, I'll give you three good reasons why I'm not trying to go to no jam over on that side. One, I'm from the *opposite* side of Supthin Boulevard. Two, if something *does* jump off, it's very unlikely we'd make it out of the park. And three, if we were to make it out of the park, it's a *long* run home!"

Listening to his partner, J.R. knew that K Smooth made some valid points. But still, the fact remained, he simply found it too hard to accept that due to geographical reasons he and his crew were basically barred from attending one of, if not *the*, biggest jams of the Summer! Which was also the *last* Summer jam, being that school was about to reconvene in less than two weeks.

Over the Summer they had been to countless school yard jams, park jams, and block parties throughout Jamaica, Queens. However, tonight's jam at 48 Park would undoubtedly be the *jam* of all previous Summer jams.

The flyers in which J.R. had seen, which were posted just about everywhere, listed Infinity Machine, the Disco Twins, DJ Hollywood, Sweetie Gee, Cipher Sounds, Eddie Cheeba and a host of other well known DJ's and MC's mostly from the Q-Borough. Even if most didn't show up, a roster such as it, would still amount to the Summer's hottest jam.

"Shit! 48 Park isn't even *connected* to 40 projects!" J.R. angrily told himself, being that the park was on the opposite side of the tracks.

"Besides," K Smooth went on. "I've already informed the rest of the crew that we'd hook up, and then head over to 153rd street." One fifty third street was one of those blocks, during the Summer months, in which the deejay equipment was brought out damn near every night.

"Anyway, what you rockin tonight?" K Smooth changed the subject.

"I don't know." J.R. replied, obviously dissatisfied with having to settle for 153rd street being their party location for the night. "I'm thinking about wearing my navy blue Lee jeans, and my navy blue short sleeve tee shirt that has 'J.R.' pressed on the front, and the 'South Road Boyz' pressed on the back."

"The Lee jeans sound cool but I don't know about the tee shirt. I mean, 153rd isn't exactly our side of town either. Granted, them niggas on the Linden Boulevard end of Supthin don't be showing out when we come through, but brandishing our *set* I think is a bit much." K Smooth expressed.

"I guess next you'll be telling how it's not safe to go outside after dark." J.R. laughed.

"It ain't even like that." K Smooth replied, "I'm saying though. We're trying to get our party on tonight, *not* our scrap on." He explained, then quickly added, "But if shit does hit the fan, I'm always ready to handle my business."

"Since you put it like that, I think I'll wear my tee shirt." J.R. laughed.

K Smooth sighed loudly, then responded, "Whatever. Just carry your denim jacket as well." Even though he knew J.R. was not trying to hear such a suggestion.

"I got you kid." J.R. said, before adding, "Let me get dressed, because something tells me *tonight* is gonna be the night."

"I'll meet you and the rest of the crew on the corner in a few. I gotta hurry up and get dressed as well, while my moms isn't here. You know how she starts talking that 10:00 pm curfew shit." With that said, the two young boys hung up. Yet, K Smooth couldn't help wondering what J.R. had meant by *tonight* being the night?

Once J.R. was dressed and ready to roll he couldn't help wondering why he hadn't revealed, to K Smooth, that he'd long ago peeped where his dad kept his arsenal of various guns stashed, and that he'd decided to roll out to the jam.....strapped. Actually what J.R. really hoped was that, when he revealed the

357 magnum to his crew they'd have a change of heart about 48 park.

As he proceeded towards the corner, J.R. noticed that he was the last man to show. Each of his boyz were dressed in their starched Lee suits, silver name plates hanging from their silver rope chains, South Road Boyz emblazoned on the front of their white tees, and ready to roll out.

The 'corner' as they referred to it, was 108th & Liverpool street, across the street sat Eddie's game room and candy store. Their crew consisted of five members, J.R., K Smooth, Cocky, Steve O, and Reese. The five of them began hanging out on the corner at the age of seven years old, each of them were now fourteen. Except for Steve O, who had recently turned fifteen, and could already pass for twenty one. At fifteen, he already stood 5'11 and weighed 182 pounds, not to mention a face full of facial hairs. All of which usually placed him in the center of his crews' joke cracking sessions. Just recently K Smooth had kicked it off when he informed Steve O, "Nigga I hope you know you *owe* me one?"

"Owe you one?" Steve O was clearly dismayed by his homie's comment. "Owe you for what?"

"For staying home from school last week."

"How the fuck do I owe you for *that*?" Steve O inquired.

"Because I sat in my window from 8:30 am until 3:30 pm, staking out your crib. That's why." K Smooth answered.

Steve O stared at his homeboy wondering if he was alright? Not realizing that K Smooth was lining him up. "How the fuck was you doing *me* a favor by staking out my crib all day?" He asked.

K Smooth smiled, then replied, "So I could get a better look at the mailman, milk man, postman, and any *other man* who stopped by, because you *damn sure* don't look anything like your pops!"

At that, the entire crew burst out laughing.

For as far back as either of them could remember, they'd been cracking jokes on one another, and *no one* [Mom, Dad, Sister, Brother, Uncle, Aunt, Grandparents], or *no thing* [House, Car, Clothes, Financial Status] was off limits! Yet, the odd thing was J.R. and K Smooth had never once cracked on one another, or their families.

"Damn, I can't wait until I'm old enough to drive!" Cocky expressed, as the crew made their way down Supthin Boulevard en route to 153rd street, which was approximately ¾'s of a mile from their block. "Because I *hate* walking!" He complained.

"Who are you telling." K Smooth agreed. "Once I'm old enough to drive ain't *no* car in the hood safe! Give up them keys, or I'm *stealing* the bitch!" He laughed, and so did the rest of his boyz.

Somewhere between Lakewood & 109th Avenue, Steve O slowed his pace almost to a complete stop, which caused the rest of the crew to look back in his direction. All he could do was laugh seeing how huge each of their eyes had become, when he reached into his Lee jacket and pulled out the bottle of Southern Comfort. After taking a long swallow, Steve O wiped his lips with his sleeve, smiled, then said, "Yeah, y'all be try'na make a nigga the butt of y'all jokes and shit, but if it wasn't for the fact that *I* can easily pass for a twenty one year old y'all jitterbugs wouldn't even know what alcohol smelled, or taste like."

Not one of the boyz argued his point, instead, they each took turns drinking from the fifth sized bottle as they headed towards the jam. It wasn't long before the five of them were pissy drunk, and not having a car or being too young to drive was *now* the last thing on their minds. However, the five of them cracked jokes on just about any and everyone they passed.

Once they reached their destination none of them could believe their eyes! Not only were there about twelve people at the block party, none of them were even dancing!

"I guess it's *back* to the hood." Suggested a visibly disappointed Cocky. "This jam is so *dead* the DJ might as well throw on some funeral music."

"You ain't lying!" Reese agreed with his homeboy.

"Word up!" Steve O slurred in agreement. "I can't believe we walked all this way for this shit! We could've chilled on the corner and got drunk."

Taking in the scenery, in total disbelief, J.R. turned his attention to K Smooth and suggested, "We're only like seven blocks away from 48 park." Then with a shrug, followed by a smile, he added, "We might as well roll."

K Smooth just stared at J.R. before turning his attention to their other three homeboys, who in spite of being intoxicated, he could tell were somewhat shook by the thought of partying in 48.

Also noticing their expressions, J.R. lifted the front of his tee shirt exposing the huge nickel plated .357 magnum handgun. He nearly choked on his laughter seeing how each of their expressions quickly changed from fear, to astonishment.

"Damn! Y'all niggas act like y'all ain't never seen a gun before!" He laughed. Once he got over his initial shock, Steve O drunkenly shouted, "My nigga! What the fuck are we waiting on? Which *way* to 48!".

Suddenly, yet swiftly, K Smooth grabbed hold of J.R.'s right arm, at the same time looking around to see if anyone else might have seen the pistol.

"Boy are you crazy? What the hell are you doing with a gun? Where did you get that thing?" Before J.R could even answer, K Smooth added, "Why didn't you tell me you were strapped?"

J.R. wasn't sure if it was due to fear, or the Southern Comfort, but *damn* K Smooth came at him with like twenty one questions! "Be easy kid! I got this!" He laughed, before adding, "I'll answer all your questions later, right now the *question* is, are we heading to 48 Park?"

K Smooth gave his partner a serious stare, and after a few minutes of silence, he replied, "I know one thing, if we *are* heading to 48, we're taking the long way. I wouldn't care if it took *seven* days to cover those *seven* blocks, but we *are* going to walk off some of this *seven* comfort." For some reason the entire crew had a tendency to refer to the alcoholic beverage as Seven Comfort, opposed to it's rightful name. "Because I'll be damned if I'm walking into potential enemy territory UTI! Gun, or no gun!"

"What the fuck is UTI?" J.R. asked.

"Under the influence. Now, which way would be the *long* way?" K Smooth inquired, more so to himself, as he turned and walked off.

Not only could the music be heard, clearly, five blocks away from 48 Park, but the remaining blocks all resembled block parties, due to the amount of people who were dancing in the streets.

"Damn! We like five blocks away and look at all these girls!" K Smooth commented. "We might as well chill out *here*, instead of going all the way to the park."

Instead of responding, his four homeboys continued to bob their heads to the music, as if in a trance, as they continued ahead *totally* ignoring K Smooth's suggestion.

The five of them had been attending block parties and park jams for as long as they could remember, yet none of them were prepared for the huge crowd in which they'd encountered once they reached their destination. It was by far the largest crowd either of them had ever seen! The park was so packed with people, no one had room to dance!

Outside of the park, people stood on anything they could. Cars, vans, garbage cans, roof tops, and some even climbed atop the park's twelve foot fence.

"Yo, isn't that Blue and some of his crew, standing over there by the entranceway?" K Smooth asked, at the same time pointing in that direction.

Blue, and most of his crew were also from the South Road side of Supthin Boulevard. However, Blue traveled most of South Jamaica, being that he was a member of the South Side Seventeen. The South Side Seventeen was a notorious street gang, which actually started out with only seventeen members, but were now like *seventy* strong!

Seeing Blue and his two partners served to ease the five young boys fears.

"What the hell y'all little niggas doing out here?" Blue asked the five of them as they made their approach. Yet, it was J.R. whom he was making eye contact with, as he made the inquiry.

"The same thing as *everyone* else is doing out here." J.R. answered, not breaking the eye contact.

With that said, the staring match ensued for like a minute longer, before Blue smiled, nodded his head, then looked elsewhere.

His two homies knew that had Blue not been fucking Pam, J.R. certainly would've caught a bad one, as a result of his attitude.

"*Some of these little niggas have entirely too much heart for their own good*!" Blue thought to himself, as he nodded his head to the music.

J.R. just stood, also nodding his head, yet thinking to himself, "*If these 40 project niggas have 'second' thoughts about bringing it to Blue, they better have multiple thoughts about fucking with me! Or any of my niggas!*" Feeling the weight of the huge pistol tucked in his waist.

K Smooth knew that his crew was among the best, in all of Jamaica, when it came to *break dancing* and the *electric boogie*. Yet he also knew that 48 Park wasn't the place to be showing out, or drawing unwanted attention to themselves. Besides, the crowd's capacity wouldn't allow it anyway.

All eyes were focused towards DJ Divine when he turned the music to a low volume, and announced, "I know you all have witnessed some of the best, of the best, take to the turntables as well as the microphone tonight. But I wanna personally welcome to the microphone three of the hottest MC's on the planet, who happens to be right out of the Q Borough!" Without any further ado, Johnny Wah, E, and Rayvon stepped to the three microphones and did their thing!

At the mention of the three MC's, J.R. knew instantly that K Smooth would be making his way to the front of the crowd.

During the earlier part of Summer, K Smooth had went to spend a week with family who lived in Springfield Gardens, at which time he'd first heard of, and observed the three MC's, along with a fourth rapper named Chucky Chuck, do their thing at a park called Monte Bello. When he returned home the four MC's was all he talked about!

"Man J.R., I'm *telling* you, these dudes were better than the Treacherous Three!" He'd exclaimed, seriously.

Just as he predicted, K Smooth had already proceeded towards the front of the crowd. "There goes to being *shook!*" J.R. shook his head, as he and the rest of the crew followed suit.

Once the three MC's were done performing K Smooth looked over at his boys with a smile on his face, and each of them certainly had to admit that he hadn't exaggerated, because the three MC's were nice *for real*!

As they turned and headed back towards the entrance/ exit way, the boys noticed a group of females from their block, one of which was J.R.'s sister Pam.

Pam's mouth literally dropped open, seeing her younger brother and his friends make their approach!

"Please tell me that my eyes are playing tricks on me?" Pam shouted in disbelief, before continuing, "What the hell are you kids doing out here? Don't you know mommy and daddy will have *both* of our asses if they knew you were out here?" Clearly upset, and looking at J.R. as if he'd lost his mind.

J.R. didn't respond. In fact he pretty much ignored her, being that her girlfriend Regina had his full attention! He'd had a crush, not to mention *countless* freaky dreams, of Regina from as far back as he could remember.

"How you doing sexy?" J.R. asked, with a smile.

Without bothering to look in his direction, Regina replied, "I'm good." Before adding, "But I really don't think it's safe for y'all youngsters to be out here this time of night, especially considering how rowdy these 40 niggas be acting."

At that, J.R. laughed and responded, "Now that I've run into *you* I'm definitely not going anywhere. I mean, what kind of man would *I* be if I didn't stick around to protect my interest?"

His question caused everyone, including Pam *and Regina*,

to laugh.

Once the laughter subsided K Smooth looked at Pam, who was like a sister to him, and said, "You sure have a lot of nerve stressing us about being out here, yet you're out here looking like Mrs. T!" Seeing all the gold on her neck, wrist, and fingers.

"Boy please! I ain't worried about none of these clowns out here, because I'm sure my baby has me in his line of sight." Pam blushed, knowing Blue was watching her every move, and certainly wouldn't let no nigga violate her.

Just as K Smooth was about to reply, the first gun shot was let off!!!

Suddenly people were being knocked to the ground and trampled over, as the huge crowd attempted to disperse in various directions!

Instinctively, J.R. took action. "Steve O block my sister! Pam tuck that fucking jewelry in! Regina give me your hand, and stay low behind me!" He barked, like a young general. "Hurry up y'all! Before this park turns into a shooting gallery!"

Once they all had succeeded in reaching the park's exit point, they noticed a dude getting jumped by at least five guys, and his two partners taking flight!

"That's my *baby* they're ganging up on!" Pam screamed hysterically, realizing it was Blue who was being ganged. "*Let go of my arm Steve O, I gotta go help him*!" She cried out, at the same time trying to break free of Steve O's grip.

Being that they'd made it out of the park, J.R. knew that their chances of making it home were good. Yet, he also realized what he had to do. Looking at Steve O, he said, "I don't care how hard she fights you, or tries to break free, don't let her go. Drag her to the block if you have to, just make *sure* she gets home safely." Turning his attention to Regina, he added, "Please don't be difficult, because my homeboys are gonna see to it that you make it back to the block safely. I'll meet y'all there shortly." J.R. spoke seriously, looking her in the eyes, *hoping* that would ultimately be the case. He could've been wrong, he told himself, but for a split second he thought he'd detected genuine concern in Regina's eyes before he turned and headed in the opposite direction.

Unbeknownst to the rest of the crew, while J.R. had been giving his instructions, K Smooth had already snuck off to help Blue.

Although there were a number of gun shots being let off in the vicinity, J.R. knew the *bark* from his .357 magnum was by far the loudest....when he'd shot the dude who was stomping Blue!!!

Chapter Two.

"I can't believe how much this school has changed." J.R, shook his head, seeing how preppy niggas were looking these days. "This use to be one of the wildest schools in New York City."

Walter E. Shimar, also known as Junior High School 142, was located on Linden Boulevard between 142nd & 143rd street. Most of Queens referred to the school as 'Shimar', pronounced shy-mer.

K Smooth certainly could not dispute J.R.'s comment, because he too had observed the school's recent transformation. According to statistics, the transformation placed the school in a more favorable light, whereas students attendance and grades were at an all time high.

According to a number of students, who'd been there awhile, the transformation was anything *but* favorable! Especially whereas, majority of them had gloated on the school's bad reputation. Shimar being one of the worst schools in all of New York City, had certainly given them bragging rights!

As he gave it some thought, K Smooth realized that his first day at Shimar, two years prior, would undoubtedly be a day

in which he'd never forget. Not only were the corridors very poorly lit for an Institute of learning, they were also smoke filled, with the smell of cigarettes and marijuana, which many students smoked openly and freely. To say that students loitered in the halls would certainly have been an understatement!
Truthfully, to K Smooth that is, most of the students back then didn't even fit the description of junior high school kids. For one, majority never attended any classes. Two, most of the male students were some of the roughest looking cats he'd ever seen. In fact, he'd bet his lunch money that some of them had been *left back* at least five times!

A lot of the female students weren't much better, especially those who were involved with the rough necks.

However, what stood out most about the school was the fact that every single window was covered with bars! An observation which often made K Smooth feel as though he was in jail! He recalled the time, in his freshmen year, he approached a fellow student and inquired, "Pardon me, but what's the deal with all the bars on the windows?"

At first, dude shot him a look as if to say, *nigga where the hell you've been*! But realizing that K Smooth must've been a freshmen, he replied, "Kid, don't even sweat them shits." Referring to the bars. "Them shits been up since last year. They put'em up right after this cat named Robert Fuller tossed this racist ass Science teacher, named Mr. Savage, outta his science class window. Which happened to be on the *fourth* floor." Dude informed him with a shrug, as if it was really no big deal, before continuing, "I don't know what happened to the kid Rob, who tossed him, because I've never seen dude after that. But they did shut down the entire fourth floor, with the exception of the gymnasium."

Although K Smooth hadn't verbally responded to J.R.'s comment, how much the school had changed, he certainly concurred with his homie's observation, because Shimar had indeed been a *wild* spot back in the day!

Thesedays, however, there were fights here and there but the violence was a lot less random. Actually it almost appeared as though most acts of violence only occurred when, or if another school, namely I.S. 8 *or* J.H.S. 172, came through to compete against Shimar's basketball team. The last time I.S. 8 visited their school they defeated Shimar's team by 21 points! Unfortunately, the victory was very short lived, whereas a number of Shimar's students blocked off the gymnasium's doors, and damn near the entire school commenced to ganging the visiting team! Not even the visiting cheerleaders *or* coach were spared an ass whipping!

It wasn't long though before Shimar's team learned, first hand, that for every action there's a re-action. Which they found out thirty days later, when *they* were the visiting team at I.S. 8. Actually, at first glance, one could tell that majority of the spectators weren't there to watch a basketball game. In fact, it was obvious that most of the crowd seated in the bleachers, and standing around were more than likely *thugs* from the school's surrounding areas, New York Boulevard, Merrick Boulevard, and 40 projects! Opposed to junior high school students.

Adding fuel to an already intense atmosphere, was Shimar's star point guard. A kid named Rodney 'Hot Rod' Hamilton, who was definitely on fire! Every shot he took was good! The closing score was 88 to 60, Shimar had won by 28 points, and Hot Rod himself had put up 58 points.

Yet, no one really had a chance to pay much attention to the score board, because as soon as the final buzzer had been set off….so was the riot!!!

The only reason Shimar's team didn't catch it as badly as I.S. 8 had, thirty days prior, was mainly because the gymnasium's doors hadn't been blocked off, nor were there any bars covering the windows!

Shimar's main casualty came in the form of Rodney Hamilton, being that he wouldn't be assisting them in the Championship, considering *both* of his legs had been broken in the riot.

"*Yes, Shimar had certainly did a three sixty*." K Smooth thought. "*But then, so had J.R.*" He told himself. Ever since that night, at 48 park, when J.R. shot at least three dudes, and kept the rest at bay while he and Blue made their escape, he hadn't been himself.

The day following the 48 park episode, K Smooth and J.R. witnessed Blue savagely pistol whip *both* of his so called partners, for leaving him that night.

"Blue, why can't I just *shoot* these two cowards?" J.R. asked, as he stood directly behind Blue, holding his father's .357 magnum at the ready.

Instead of responding, Blue commenced to whipping both dudes with the huge 45 caliber automatic.

Meanwhile, K Smooth had seen enough. Nor could he help noticing the sudden change in J.R.'s demeanor and attitude. He knew it was up to him to do all within his power, to get a grip on his homeboy, who was more like his brother.

Two days later, K Smooth approached J.R. and said, "Remember, I too, was at 48 that night." He began, looking his homie directly in his eyes. "And although we didn't have to do what we did, we *represented* nonetheless. Thankfully, we got away." He smiled. "But on the same token, *I* for one, am not trying to get on some *all out* thug shit! Running around busting caps in niggas." He paused momentarily, then went on, "I'm not surprised, at all, by how much Blue is feeling us right now. I mean, we did show him first hand how we get down for ours. But, at the end of the day, our mentalities are entirely different from niggas like Blue. He's ready, willing, and even living to die that thug shit. Yes, you've shot a nigga or two, but you can rest assure Blue will *not* rest until he puts a shell into every single one of them dudes who plotted on him. What surprises me the most, is that it even went down like that. Every nigga in Jamaica knows he's down with the *Seventeen*!" K Smooth said, shaking his head at some niggas ignorance, or rather obvious death wish. "Just as I'm sure everybody in Jamaica knows that Blue, is more than likely, next in line to be the gangs *leader* being that D.C. and Baby Boy have both gotten locked up, and Cocaine was recently murdered." He said, reiterating what was basically hood knowledge. "When Blue began dating Pam, I'll admit, I kind of dug the nigga because he always gave it to you and I from a real G's perspective. Especially when he told us that *we* were probably the only young niggas in Jamaica, who weren't repping our block. Which we couldn't dispute being that you had them Supthin niggas, Lakewood Crew, Linden Posse, Liberty Ave & Van Wyck Crew, The Junior Crowns who were under the Seven Crowns, and also niggas throughout hoods such as Laurelton where them Boom Bash niggas repped. So we decided we'd call ourselves the South Road Boyz, and rep our block. Yet, it was agreed upon that our shit would be different. Unlike the rest, we weren't going to be all about the guns, bodies, and the rest of that madness." K Smooth reminded him. "Our shit was to become them fly young niggas who weren't taking any shorts, yet we'd be more about money, clothes, and fly young hoes! Til death do us part, remember that?"

Although J.R. realized, following the park incident, that he could easily get use to putting the pistol to niggas, he knew K Smooth was right in all that he had said. From the beginning, the five of them, collectively, made a vow that the South Road Boyz would not be about, or entertain the whole violence thing. Unless, niggas brought drama to their set. He also understood why K Smooth shied away from the thought, and act of gun play, considering what had happened to his father two years prior.

At the time, the two of them were only twelve years old, and although neither boy was actually ever told what really happened, they did overhear that Eugene along with J.R.'s father

Joshua, had extended their business ventures into the other four boroughs of New York City. Just about everyone in the City knew of the two men. In fact, *one half* of the population loved them. The *other half* feared them. *All* of New York respected, the two gangsters.

Unfortunately, one late evening in August, of 1979 three young stick up kids decided to rob a neighborhood Bar & Grill, called E & J's, located on Utica Avenue, in the Crown Heights section of Brooklyn. Unbeknownst to the young robbers E & J's actually stood for Eugene & Joshua's, nor did the 16 year old who was nervously guarding the door, while his comrades emptied the register and more then a few pockets, know that the well dressed black man who had emerged from the back of the establishment, at the same time catching five shells to the face and body….was the infamous *Eugene Shannon*!

J.R. knew his father kept an arsenal of artillery, but the latter part of the story dismayed him and K Smooth, when they'd heard that Joshua flushed the three young stick up kids out of their hiding spot, and *personally* put a bullet into each of their skulls. Six years prior to Eugene's death, Joshua and his wife Yolanda decided to purchase the three family house, right next door to Eugene and KeKe on South Road. At first, Yolanda was reluctant to move out of their Saint Albans home, in which she had put so much into over the years. Even young J.R. didn't approve of the move, being that it would mean leaving his many friends behind, and he'd certainly miss his trips to Oconor park, which was actually located on Murdock Avenue and right around the corner from where he lived. In the park there was a swimming pool, playground, basketball court, and a boxing gym!

When Joshua took his wife to see the house on South Road, which he totally redesigned the structure and landscape, it was a case of love at first sight! Yolanda couldn't believe how beautiful and spacious the place was, never mind the fact that it was smack dab in the hood! They moved in immediately! Even J.R. and Pam liked the house. It could've easily been converted into a four family house, being that the finished basement, which Yolanda's younger sister Janice ended up moving into, and the attic, which Pam immediately laid claim to, were *both* basically apartments.

Shortly after Eugene's death, Joshua wanted to move both families out of South Jamaica. In fact, he already owned a little over twenty acres of land up state New York

"No way!" Was Yolanda *and* KeKe's response. The two women had become too attached to their homes, not to mention, they'd also become close as sisters.

Chapter Three.

As KeKe exited Supthin Food with her groceries in hand, and was about to turn the corner on 107th Avenue, she was startled by loud honking of a car's horn. When she looked in its direction, the vehicle's rear passenger side window slowly descended, and a woman's smiling face appeared.

Although the sun light was somewhat bothering her eyes, KeKe immediately recognized the woman's face. It was a face in which she despised, whereas it was no secret that the woman and her two sons were supplying most of the neighborhood with drugs.

"I realize it's been nearly four years since Gene's passing, and I am truly sorry for not making it by your house to extend my condolences. As for my absence at his funeral, I simply *do not* do those. I'd miss my *own* if I didn't have to be there." The lady named Nilda laughed, then added, "But I must say KeKe, you certainly appear to be maintaining. But then again, I'm sure Gene left you and the kids straight like that."

When KeKe spoke her disdain for the woman was obvious, "First of all my husband's name is *Eu*gene, and it's Mrs. Shannon *not* KeKe. I don't even know you like that, nor do I care to. As for you not stopping by my house, I assure you, you'll never be welcomed. Just as I'm glad you did not attend my husband's funeral, because I would've hated to have had to escorted you out. And lastly, what you should be *sorry* about is your obvious desire to live in luxury, by flooding the community with that poison, in which I hear you seem to relish being known for. It's actually a shame, if it's true, how those sons of yours be out here recruiting people's children, to peddle your dope." KeKe said with contempt in her voice, for the lady and her sons who were oddly named after the days of the week. "But I'll tell you this," She said, moving in closer to the car in which Nilda hadn't gotten out of. Yet, close enough for the two of them to see eye to eye. "The day I stumble across one of your glassine bags of poison, in my son's pocket or book bag, you *will* be attending a funeral, because it *will* be yours." KeKe warned, displaying a stare so cold it could have only been termed *murderous.*

The woman Nilda smiled as she held KeKe's stare, then shook her head shamefully, before replying, "People like *me* and my *sons* huh? I guess it's *not* a shame that *your* little four bedroom mansion in the hood, was modeled, remodeled, landscaped, furnished, and fully paid for as a result of those same, *other folks children*, peddling those poison filled glassine bags." Nilda smirked, then went on to drop the bomb. "I mean, it was *your* husband, may he rest in peace, who had been my *supplier* for nearly a decade!"

KeKe stood there in complete shock! She'd known about most of her husband's illegal activities, but *drugs*? She hadn't had a clue that Eugene was heavily involved in the drug business, or that he had ties to the woman Nilda. In fact, she was still standing there speechless, as the window ascended, and the chauffeured driven Rolls Royce pulled away from the curb.

"Yo youngblood, what are you doing on a block like this?" Inquired the dark skinned brother dressed in a dashiki type shirt, and coofi on his head.

At first K Smooth hadn't realized that the muslim looking dude was speaking to him, but after seeing that they were the only two people standing in the immediate vicinity, he replied, "Oh, I'm just waiting on my homeboy Cocky to come down stairs. He lives in that corner building."

"Cocky." The stranger repeated. "I happen to know your boy Cocky quite well. Yet, I can't say that I've ever seen you around here before. Do you live around here?"

"Not too far." Was all K Smooth said, not wanting to give up too much information to a complete stranger.

"I don't think I've ever heard of a neighborhood, or block called *not too far*." The stranger joked. It wasn't that he was being nosy, he always questioned the young brothers whom he'd encounter on the drug infested block. Some of whom were actually preteens.

"I've noticed you standing out here for at least twenty minutes now. Does Cocky even know that you're awaiting him?" He asked K Smooth.

K Smooth had become tired of all the questions, therefore

he snapped, "Man, what's with all the fucking questions?! If you're trying to *recruit* a nigga to sell that shit, you may have the right ploy, but you definitely have the *wrong* boy! That's exactly why I hate meeting Cocky around here! Muh'fuckers are always either trying to sell something to a nigga, cop something from a nigga, or recruit a nigga! Man, I swear I can't understand how Cocky can stand living on this drug infested block!"

The kid certainly has a filthy mouth, the stranger told himself, but nonetheless he liked the young boy's attitude. Especially his obvious disdain for the drug business.

"Listen little brother, " The stranger began, with a smile on his face. "My name, or rather let me rephrase that, my *attribute* is Allah Be Wonderful. I teach civilization classes a few doors down, at the Allah school. You can rest assure that I'm not selling, buying, or recruiting. At least not recruiting for the purpose of poisoning our people. Who, and what I am, is a poor righteous teacher. Whose sole endeavor is to enlighten, and uplift my people from this crippling blind, deaf, and dumb state of unawareness, in which majority of us presently trapped into." He explained.

K Smooth really didn't have much of a clue, as to what dude was talking about. In fact, he'd *already* forgotten his name! However, he did remember Cocky mentioning the Allah school around his way, being that the place excited him a great deal.

"Man, I'm *telling* y'all!" Cocky had exclaimed. "I can go there any day of the week and *eat* for free. Learn *karate*, and the black man's *history* for free. As well as the Caucasian, white, man's history for free. Plus, I've even been allowed to sleep there, more than a few times, for free!" The last part not really surprising his friends a whole lot, being that it was public knowledge that Cocky's mother was a dope fiend, and alcoholic, who usually allowed her dope fiend friends to take up space at her apartment.

K Smooth's attitude towards the stranger suddenly changed, as he recalled all in which Cocky had said that day.

"Is it true that you teach karate?" K Smooth asked, then quickly added, "For free?" "Yes, I do teach karate. But mostly to my brothers who attend the school." Allah Be Wonderful answered. "Actually, I've been blessed with the knowledge, wisdom, and understanding to teach *many* things. But again yes, I am very qualified to teach the art of karate."

"For free?" K Smooth asked excitedly.

"Yes, free of charge."

"What *belt* are you?" K Smooth asked, obviously still excited.

"As of two months, I'm proud to say, I'm officially black belt status." Wonderful replied smiling.

"Wow, *black belt*!" K Smooth repeated incredulously. "Have you ever had to fuck a nigga up?" He asked, with a wide eyed expression.

"Truthfully, I tried to avoid unnecessary altercations. Especially with my a likes."

"What's an *a like*?" K Smooth was clearly dismayed by the term.

"My black brothers, as well as my black sisters." Wonderful answered. "We may come from different fathers and mothers, but we're *all* alike."

K Smooth nodded his understanding, then gave an unimpressed shrug of the shoulders, being that he was more impressed by the *karate* stuff.

"What if a nigga pulled a gun out on you, do you think you'd be quick enough to take it from him?" Again, K Smooth awaited his response with the same wide eyed expression, except now he was smiling.

The brother Wonderful was also smiling, considering just minutes ago K Smooth had angrily asked *him* what's with all the questions? However, he didn't take offense, because he knew that young black minds were inquisitive by nature.

"Fortunately, no one has ever pulled a gun on me. Nor do I give people reason to. But to answer your question,,,," Was all he got to say, before he was interrupted by someone running down the block screaming frantically.

"Spread out! Spread the *fuck* out! The *gray van* is coming!" The person shouted, for the entire block to hear.

Suddenly, a different voice began shouting, "It's Carmine! Carmine's coming through! Hurry the fuck up! Carmine is in the gray van!"

All those in the vicinity using, copping, and selling drugs had quickly spread out!

The block was 150th Street, and it was famous for its 24 hour drug activity.

K Smooth didn't make a habit of hanging on the block, but then again he, like just about everyone else in South Jamaica, didn't have to….to know *who* Carmine was! His name rung bells in the streets simply because he was a cop, he played dirty, and he implemented fear into the hearts of junkies and drug dealers. Carmine was the equivalent to the Bronx's *Crazy Joe,* and Brooklyn's *Sarge* or *Batman & Robin.*

When the gray van came to a complete halt, Allah Be Wonderful and K Smooth were the *only* two left standing on the block! A realization that made Wonderful shake his head. He couldn't believe how so many of his brothers and sisters had, literally, *spread out* like roaches! What made the situation even worst, was seeing the look of *satisfaction* on the cop's face, seeing how his presence made every nigga in the vicinity run and hide.

K Smooth, on the other hand, just stood there in awe of the cop! He'd heard countless stories about the so called *super cop*, whom he'd never seen until now.

"Come on young blood." Allah Be Wonderful straightened his Universal Flag pinned to the upper left side of his shirt, straightened his coofi, then firmly took hold of K Smooth's right arm, and said, "Never mind that *devil*, lets take a walk over to the Allah school, so I can enlighten you to what's *really* going on."

Chapter Four.

"I got next!" Steve O shouted, as he and J.R. entered the school yard adjacent Public School 50. Observing Pam doing her thing, on the handball court, against a neighborhood cat named Richie.

Meanwhile, J.R. made his way over to Regina, who was keeping score from the side line. "Damn sexy lady, why are *you* playing so hard?" He asked with a smile on his face.

Regina, momentarily taking her eyes off the match, looked him up and down, before replying, "Boy what are you talking about? I'm not even *on* the damn court!"

"Who said anything about the court?" J.R. chuckled, then said, "I'm talking about *hard to get*!"

At that, she rolled her eyes. Yet, he did make her smile.

"You know," J.R. began. "My old man once hipped me to the consecutive *three smile* rule, in which he applied in his pursuit of my mother. However, I won't hip you to the *rule* just yet. But nonetheless baby girl, please keep in mind that there is smile number two." He informed her, whereas he brought about smile number one that night, before the shooting started, at 48 park. "Mind you, if or when I'm the cause of smile number three, I'll have no other choice *but* to move in for the kill."

Instead of smiling, Regina burst out laughing! She had to admit, the boy was certainly good! A bit young for her taste, but nonetheless impressive with his tongue.

"Can I pull'leaseee, get some competition over here!" Pam shouted victoriously. "First up was Richie's scrub behind. Then *this* bum," She said, referring to Steve O. "Have the nerve to bring his non handball playing ass on *my* court!" She laughed.

J.R. looked over at Steve O, who was doubled over as if he was totally out of breath, suffering from dehydration, or maybe just bent over thinking of a strategy? J.R. seriously doubted the *latter* being the case! The one thing he did feel certain of was, whereas Steve O had gotten *shut out* on the court by Pam, *he* had undoubtedly *scored* with Regina! The eyes *never* lie, he told himself.

On another note, J.R. couldn't believe how embarrassing a sight Steve O was, still standing in the middle of the handball court, hunched over and out of breath!

The situation had become even more embarrassing when Pam began shouting,

"Little boy, I hope you've learned from this ass whipping to *never* compete against a grown woman! "Matter of fact, little boy," She walked directly over to Steve O, then looked from him to J.R., then back to Steve O and said, "Let this be a lesson, that little boys need to stay in *little boy* places!" With that said, she walked over to her girlfriend Regina, who she gave a high five.

"Damn this dude!" J.R. cursed Steve O under his breath, knowing it was time to bounce. Before doing so, he looked over at Regina and informed her, "I'll be seeing *you* later, because a *laugh* and a *smile* is actually one and the same. Therefore, that laugh made number three! So, you *know* what that means." He smiled, gave her a wink, then walked off the court.

As the two young boys exited the park, Pam looked over at her home girl and asked, "What the *hell* did my brother mean by that?"

"Believe me, I have no idea!" Regina answered. Yet, unbeknownst to Pam, she couldn't wait to find out!!!!

"Yo, I still got these after school passes, for free admission to Jamaica Roller Dome." K Smooth showed J.R. the free passes to the skating rink, which was located on New York Boulevard, between Jamaica and Archer Avenue. Jamaica Roller Dome was Queen's equivalent to Skate Fever in the Bronx, and Empire Skating Rink or Skate City in Brooklyn.

J.R. looked from K Smooth to the free passes he was holding, then back at K Smooth. Realizing his homeboy was clueless, he informed him, "Boy, you better take your head out of them books, and get on point regarding what's going on in these streets." J.R. spoke as if he had street knowledge. "I guess you haven't heard that nigga Big C Lo, down with the Cooper family, got shot in the Roller Dome last week?" Neither of the two boys knew, nor did they ever see Big C Lo or any of the Cooper siblings. Yet, as in the case of *majority* of Queens, they'd certainly heard of them! As well as their influence in the streets. "From what Blue tells me, it's only a matter of time before that spot gets burnt to the ground, if the Coopers don't get their man!"

"In *that* case," K Smooth replied, ripping the free passes to shreds. "I, for one, will *not* be up in that piece when it goes down!"

"Exactly!" J.R. laughed.

"Girl, I spent the weekend at my girl Cindy's crib. You know the half Spanish one who lives in Baisley?" Pam informed Regina over the telephone. "Anyway, you're not gonna *believe* how much shit went down, in just two days!"

"Try me." Regina replied, only half interested.

Mistaking Regina's response for an attitude, Pam got quiet for a second, then went on, "I tried to call you like a million times to see if you wanted to hang out, but your answering machine kept picking up. Anyway, Saturday night we partied at the Fantasia, and when I tell you that club was packed! I mean, everywhere I looked I saw cuties, roughnecks, and ballers!" Pam was obviously excited as she spoke, "By the way, *where* were you this weekend? Even from the club, I tried calling you."

Caught off guard by Pam's question, Regina desperately wanted to tell her best friend that, she too, had a *lovely* weekend! Especially considering the two of them never kept secrets from each other, Yet, she knew that there was no way she could tell Pam that she'd spent the entire weekend, over at *her* house. In the attic, which was *her* section of the house, meaning she was in *her* bed, getting her freak on with *her* little brother! *No way*! Regina decided it would undoubtedly be best that she kept her mouth shut. But then again, she wished she could tell somebody, anybody, how thankful she was that the Reed family even *had* an attic! Because J.R. certainly knew how to make a girl scream!

"Damn, that boy *know* he can fuck!" Regina had J.R. on her mind, and a kool aid smile on her face.

Regina was only half listening to Pam as she went on about her lovely weekend.

"Girl, let me tell you, this guy named Spoon, from 40 projects, approached me in the club, then had the nerve to get all up in my space telling me how he's been scheming on *this* for a minute now. And, how all he needs is *one night* to make me forget all about Blue!" She laughed, then went on. "So,,,,,"

Meanwhile, on the other end of the telephone line, Regina was preoccupied with her *own* thoughts, "His little sneaky ass! I should've known he was lying, when he raised his right hand to God, and swore that he was a virgin! Since when do virgins make a bitch cum *that* many times? Shit, his young ass had me speaking in tongues!" Regina was smiling from ear to ear, recalling her weekend with J.R.

"Girl, are you even *listening* to me?" Pam asked. "You so quiet, I thought your ass hung up or something!"

"Huh?" Regina couldn't believe she had zoned out, not hearing a word in which Pam had said. "Oh no girl, I'm still on the line. I guess I just have a lot on my mind, that's all. Anyway, how does this *Spoon* character look?"

"See, I *knew* you wasn't listening!" Pam complained. In fact, she'd always had a problem with people, anyone, not giving her their full attention. Nevertheless, she went on, "Anyway, I'll describe him one more time." Sighing loudly, she began, "He's,,,"

"Damn, I wish I had my *own* apartment! Regina said to herself, again paying her best friend no mind. "Because then, J.R.'s little *fine* ass could stay over whenever he liked. Hell, he could even move in!" She smiled from ear to ear, suddenly her smile turned to an uncertain frown. "Then again, wouldn't that be considered *kidnapping*, or some shit? I mean, he *is* only 15!" She gave it some thought. "The dick felt *fantastic*, but I'm not feeling getting my door kicked in for nobody! Fuck all of this wishful thinking crap, he and I will just have to figure out a way to continue seeing each other, on the low low." Again, she was smiling her pretty white teeth smile.

"Regina,,,ReGina,,,REGINA!" Pam shouted into the phone.

"Pam *please* stop yelling my name. I told you I'm *still* here."

"Whatever!" Pam snapped. "I'll just call you later! Because I can not *believe* you fuckin got me sitting here talking to my damn self! I mean, the nigga Spoon is straight and all, but his ass ain't *that* motherfucking straight whereas I'ma be on this telephone talking to *myself* about him!"

"No, I'm here girl. Believe it or not, I heard everything you've said about him." Regina lied. "So, after you left the club, did you give him his *one night* to prove himself?"

When Pam giggled into the phone, opposed to responding, Regina was certain that Spoon had gotten the goodies.

"So, moving on to the *next* question. How was he?" Regina asked laughing.

"Bitch I never said I *gave* him some!" Pam laughed.

"Girl please. I *know* you! Just like I know he's the only reason you called me this morning ." Regina said, still laughing. "Fronting like you actually wanted to know my whereabouts, why I hadn't answered the phone, and how *my* weekend had been."

"That's not true." Pam became serious. "I really *did* wish you were there. Cindy and her girl friends are mad cool, but *nobody* represents the way you and I do when we're up in the place!"

At that, they both laughed, because *they* knew it was the truth.

"As we were about to leave the club, Cindy and her other two girl friends were telling me how *paid* the nigga Spoon was, and that he was a major player on Fat Boy's team. They even emphasized his status, by filling me in on the fact that Fat Boy bought Spoon a *Porche*, whereas the rest of the team he bought motorcycles." Not wanting to sound like she was all that impressed by what the girls had revealed, she added. "The only reason I gave him his *one night,* was to see if he could back up all the shit he was spitting. And girl, let me tell you,,,,"

Unbeknownst to Pam, Regina had once again drifted off into

her *own* escapade from the previous weekend. In fact, she had drifted off *long* before Pam had spoke about *who* he was down with, *what* he drove, or whether or not she'd given him his one night! No, Regina hadn't heard any of it. As she thought about it, Regina could almost *still* feel J.R.'s, alleged, unexperienced tongue teasing, and manipulating her clitoris!

"Damn!" Just the *thought* made her wanna scream! She loved the fact that he'd taken his time. Also how he allowed her to get on top, taking control, until she was content. And, after they both came, and she *thought* the love making was over, J.R. instructed her to lay on her stomach so he could eat the pussy from behind!

"And," Regina thought, with a kool aid smile on her face. "That boy ate it, as if it was his *last* supper!"

"Damn girl!!!" Pam screamed, startling Regina just as she was about to climax.

"What's wrong?" Regina was still somewhat startled.

Pam giggled, then said, "You gotta excuse me girl." Sounding, more than, a little embarrassed. "I guess I got a *little* carried away huh?" She laughed, not knowing Regina hadn't been listening the entire time. "I'll tell you *another* thing." Pam giggled, before revealing, "I *see* why they call his ass *Spoon*! You might think I'm exaggerating girl, but that nigga ate this pussy as if he was eating his *last* supper! I bullshit you not!"

"Trust me, I can *believe* it!" Regina replied, almost at a whisper, before inquiring,

"So, where does *that* leave Blue?"

Again Pam giggled, then asked, "Blue *who?*"

Chapter Five.

"I thought turning *16* meant my moms letting up a little bit! But it seem as though she's getting *more* strict, the older I get." K Smooth complained to J.R., who'd also recently turned sixteen, being that their birthdays were on the same day. "Her excuse is that, my little sister has a tendency to watch, and imitate everything I do. But I'm not buying that, because I can't see myself doing *anything* that a girl would do, therefore, I can't see my sister doing any of the shit that I would do."

J.R. nodded his head, in agreement with K Smooth's point.

"I think the *real* reason she be riding me so hard is because, she fears losing me to the streets, like she did my old man." K Smooth expressed.

Again, J.R. simply nodded in agreement.

"I can understand her concerns, but *damn* I wish she'd stop treating me like I'm a little nigga. Yet, she always tell me how I need to start taking responsibility, being that I'm basically the man of the house! Her words say one thing, but her actions are insulting." K Smooth vented his frustrations.

"I feel you on that," J.R. replied. "My moms be on that same type shit. I guess she gets it from *your* old lady, because she never use to ride me the way she does now."

K Smooth shot J.R. a look, then both of them laughed.

"Nah, for real though," J.R. began. "We've just reached that age in which *all* mothers worry. Then that shit that happened with Steve O, doesn't make *our* case any better." He pointed out.

"You ain't lying! That shit has been on every News channel in the world!" K Smooth exaggerated. "I *still* can't believe his crazy ass went and did some shit like that, in broad daylight!" He shook his head.

J.R. stopped dead in his tracks, looked K Smooth in the eyes, and asked, "What's so hard to believe about it? If a nigga raped *my* sister, I wouldn't give a fuck if I caught his ass at a policemen's ball, parade, or in Flushing Meadow Park on crowded ass Brooklyn-Queens day *his* ass will get it!" J.R. was serious, and K Smooth knew it.

"So, if you ask me, my nigga Steve O did exactly what any real nigga would have done. You have a sister, so how could you *not* understand his actions?" He asked K Smooth.

"I guess you got a point." K Smooth replied, but then added, "However, I *still* don't think I would've shot a nigga in broad daylight, in front of everyone."

Again, J.R, looked him in the eyes, shook his head, then walked off mumbling loud enough for K Smooth to hear, "I love you like a brother, but you need to get some fucking heart!"

"Girl I can not believe you're sitting up in this room, crying your eyes out!" Regina had *never* seen Pam in such a state, especially over a dude. "Spoon is not the first nigga to ever get locked up. Nor will he be the last. I'm sure he knew that *hustling* and *jail* were *synonyms*, when his ass was out here driving that bright ass candy apple red *Porche* through the ghetto!"

Pam shot Regina a cold look. "Bitch, who the fuck is *you* to be talking shit about my man?" She snapped. Then added, "I can't even *remember* the last time you had one!"

Regina started to come back with something slick, but decided to hold her tongue. The two of them sat there staring at one another, before Regina reached out and took Pam's hand into hers, and said, "Listen, you've been my best friend since Elementary school, and I did not come over here to argue or fight with you. Besides, we don't even get down like that." Regina smiled, bringing about one on Pam's face as well, before continuing, "Trust me, any nigga at Spoon's level *always* prepare himself for this type of shit. So instead of sitting on your behind crying all day, what you need to be doing is embracing the situation as best you can, and deal with the reality of it. That *reality* is that, your man is *down* right now, meaning you need to get *up* off of your ass and get down to that jailhouse, so he'll know you're *with* him!" Regina advised her, then added, "Nor will it hurt to drop a few coins in his account, before one of them little chicken heads, from the projects, beat you to it! Because I *know* you don't think that *you* were the only bitch his ghetto fabulous ass was fucking!" Regina laughed.

Although Pam wasn't feeling the *closing* of her little speech, she had to admit, Regina was right in all that she had said. Also, she appreciated her friend for lifting her spirits, at such a time. Truthfully, Regina had always been one to make excellent points, thought Pam, who also couldn't help thinking, "It's truly a shame that such a beautiful girl, who seems to have all the damn sense, can't get a *man* to save her life! And if she *does* have one, the bitch can keep a secret better than a *dead* person!"

"Cocky, what's going on kid?" J.R. asked as he made his approach. "Me, K Smooth, and Reese were just talking about you yesterday, so I thought I'd come through and check you, being that you don't come through the block anymore."

"I know man, I know." Cocky half smiled. "But trust me, ain't shit changed! The love and bond will always be in tact, til death do us part, remember that?" He laughed, at the same time extending his right hand giving J.R. some dap. "For real though, a nigga just been out here try'na bring some sunshine, to these cloudy days."

"How so?" J.R. inquired.

Cocky looked away, then returned J.R.'s stare before he began, "You know my old lady never really *had* much, therefore, she never really *gave* much. Well, except to the dope man that is." He gave a slight shrug and a half smile, then went on, "And thesedays, she lets it be known, now that I'm sixteen it's all about self preservation. In fact, her slogan thesedays is, if a nigga wanna eat, sleep, and be warm, he better kick out for food, clothing, and shelter!"

Even though that was not the situation at his house, J.R. nodded his understanding, then asked the obvious, "So, I guess you're out here slinging dope now?"

"Yeah." Cocky confirmed. "I come out early in the morning, before school, then I come *back* out on the block at around five o;clock p.m. It seems as though the junkies only *need* something to get them going, and then, something to take home in the evening. The ones you see hanging out on the block *all day*, everyday, aren't even the ones who are spending money. They're the ones out here trying to earn a bag or two, by running niggas customers. But I don't be trying to fuck with them like that, because they'll bring *anyone* to you, and lie like they've be doing business with the customer for years! The whole time it's the police he's bringing, and you're serving!" Explained Cocky. "So I definitely have my people picked."

As J.R. stood there listening, he couldn't believe how much Cocky had learned about slinging, especially in such a short period of time. But then again, he'd been around dope *and* fiends most of his life, J.R. reminded himself.

"I *hear* that it's unbelievable, how much money comes through 150th street, but it's also like 150 *plus* niggas out here trying to get it. So how is it even possible for so many niggas to eat?"

"That's another thing." Cocky smiled. "When the dope is *good*, dope fiends travel from as far as Philadelphia, New Jersey, Connecticut, and Boston to get it. So there's definitely enough bread coming through, for everyone to eat."

"I hear you." J.R. replied, then added, "Just be careful out here. The block can be sweet as candy, but trust me, *majority* of these niggas out here are sour. Matter of fact," Said J.R. "Blue just hit me off with this," lifting the front of his shirt, exposing the .45 caliber automatic pistol. "The nigga *says* it's brand spanking new, but I seriously doubt that, because it looks exactly like the one I recalled him using to pistol whip those two niggas that time." J.R. laughed. "But yo, you can hold it down since you're out here like this." J.R. removed the huge pistol from his waist, and quickly handed it over to Cocky, then added, "If I ever need it I know where you're at."

"For sure." Cocky nervously smiled, as he stuffed the gun into his waist, at the same time looking around to see if anyone had peeped the move. Satisfied that no one had, the two of them began rapping about other things.

Unbeknownst to the two of them, the two men who had previously pulled up in the Con Edison van, and were now repairing a blown out street light, were actually *undercover detectives*! Nor did the two young boys know that the black van, parked a hundred feet away, which appeared unoccupied, was indeed occupied by three other undercover detectives....one of whom was *Carmine*!

However, all was *revealed* when one of the men, dressed in the Con Edison uniform, radioed in that the two youngsters were in possession of a *firearm*!

"Well boys, today is y'all *lucky* day!" Exclaimed a smiling

Carmine. "Do y'all know *why* it's y'all lucky day?" He asked.

J.R. nor Cocky had the slightest idea as to what the cop was talking about. However, since he'd used the term *lucky day*, Cocky was hoping that meant the two of them were being released!

"Apparently neither of you little *girls* have a clue, as to why today's y'all lucky day. So, I guess I'll have to spell it out for the two of you." The cop smiled, then began spelling, "R,I,K,E.R,S, I,S,L,A,N,D!" Once he'd spelled out the infamous jail, he went on to explain, "It has been brought to my attention that the *both* of you has recently turned sixteen, which qualifies the two of you for the *Rock*!" The *Rock* being Riker's Island. With that being said, he turned the two youngsters over to the custody of a, clearly busy, processing officer at Central Booking.

"Would it be to much to ask, that you place the two new detainees in which ever cell may have some elbow room." The processing officer asked the detective, at the same time handing Carmine a ring of keys.

"No problem at all." Carmine escorted his two young detainees to the holding cell that was clearly the most crowded of the three, and inserted the key. He shoved Cocky into the crowded cell, then got directly in J.R.'s face and said, "Then again, maybe today isn't your lucky day Joshua Reed *Junior*, being that you can't take the .45 automatic with you!" He laughed, causing spit to fly into J.R.'s face.

Not only was J.R. upset by the cop spitting in his face, but also for referring to him and Cocky as little *girls*! In spite of knowing that the cop had a reputation for beating a niggas ass, while in handcuffs, J.R. could care less, when he replied.

"It's no secret that y'all crooked, racist ass cops have a tendency to put the drugs, and guns back on the streets, in hopes that we blacks kill each other. So, hopefully the .45 automatic *will* find its way back to the streets, into the right nigga's hand, and he blows *your* fucking head off!" J.R. and the cop was still face to face, as he added, "In fact, your racist ass better hope I'm not *that* nigga!" J.R. laughed, pushing his way pass the cop, and into the holding cell.

Carmine's face was beet red, with anger! He knew had they still been at the station house, opposed to crowded ass Central Booking, he would've beat the hell out of the little smart mouthed nigga! With a menacing stare, he spoke to J.R. through the bars of the cell, "I'm really tempted to screw up some paperwork, and even lose some evidence, because I'm dying to see if you're *that* nigga!" With that said, the cop walked off.

Upon their arrival at the Adolescent Reception Detention Center, also known as C-74, J.R. could not believe that the inmates who were working the intake area were youths! Although there were only four inmate workers, at least three of them could easily have passed for adults.

"From this point on, there will not be *any* talking! Unless, you're asked a question by myself, or one of the other receiving room officers!" Instructed the heavy set, dark skinned, receiving room Sergeant.

The new arrivals were lined up in two single file lines, the two inmates at the front of each line was instructed to stand behind the freshly painted red line.

"Trust me, I want to run through this process as quickly as I'm sure most of you want a meal, telephone call, shower, bed, or see some of your friends whom you haven't seen in a while." Continued the Sergeant, whose name tag read Sgt. B. Williams.

Immediately J.R. thought of Steve O, wondering if, in fact, he'd get to see his homeboy whom he hadn't seen in months.

"As you can see," Continued Sgt. B. Williams. "The receiving room consist of four holding cells, and two *why me* pens." The *why me* cells were for the trouble makers, who were sent to the receiving room to sit in the holding pen, some for hours, others for *days* with no access to water, commissary, a mattress, blanket, or cigarettes. "Unfortunately, two of the holding cells, plus the two *why me* cells are being used, to separate a few knuckle heads from the rest of the general population." The Sergeant said, looking towards each of the cells, at the nine trouble makers who occupied them.

The nine trouble makers who had been previously screw facing one another, were now focusing their attention on the new arrivals. Each with the same thought in mind, even the three who'd looked as if they'd caught the bad end of a beat down, and that thought was that they hoped they wouldn't be going to the *bing*, aka *lock up*, because that would mean some other lucky niggas, in general population, would have the pleasure of relieving the new arrivals of their footwear, jackets, jewelry, or *anything* else they possessed worth taking!

"Those of you lined up to my right, I want you all to file into bull pen number one, and those of you lined up to my left, I want you all to file into bull pen number two. In the pens you'll find a few other new arrivals, who are also awaiting bed space. I advise you all to try and get along, because none of you need to be making enemies amongst yourselves, because I'm sure you all will encounter enough of *those* when y'all reach general population." With that said, Sgt. Williams walked off to review each of their paperwork, while the twenty seven new arrivals filed into the two holding cells.

J.R. and Cocky had stuck close by each other, therefore they ended up in the same holding cell. Upon entering, they noticed about eight other inmates. Four of whom were stretched out across the long bench, taking it up completely. The remaining four, were laying across the floor, or underneath the bench.

"Yo, pardon me duke!" J.R. tapped one of the dudes who was taking up a great deal of space on the bench. At first, the dude looked up at J.R. as if he'd lost his mind! But then, seeing how J.R. had held his stare, as if to say, he wasn't impressed. Dude simply sat up, making room for the new arrival.

Cocky and about two others did the same. The rest of the new arrivals found a spot on the floor, and got comfortable.

Seated about five feet away from where J.R. sat, was one of the ugliest, blackest, peasiest headed dudes he had ever seen! And, dude had to weigh at least two hundred pounds, J.R. assessed. Not to mention, he was mean mugging each of the inmates who had stepped into the bull pen.

"Yo shorty, what *size* do you wear?" The big black dude menacingly asked one of the new arrivals, who was obviously five times smaller than he was, in every aspect.

"Wha, wha. What size do I wear in *what*?" The smaller guy stuttered in response. "In *everything* nigga!" Barked the big black dude, quickly adding, "Boy, I know I can't fit my big ass into none of your shit! But, nonetheless, them sneakers *and* that jacket looks type new." He said, giving the smaller dudes attire the once over. "Hopefully I can get a nigga in *pop dog* to come up off a carton of new ports, and some food since those are Addidas and the jacket is leather." Seeing the smaller dude hadn't made any objection thus far to what he'd said, big Black went on laying the tim down, "I don't know yet what housing unit we're going to, but if they separate us, you *better* let any nigga who inquires about your gear know, that everything you're wearing is already mine! You hear me nigga?" He barked into the smaller kids face.

Cocky couldn't be sure if the tears welling up in the smaller dudes eyes, were a result of anger or fear? However, he got his answer when the kid responded.

"Yeah, I *hear* you." Almost at a whisper, yet loud enough to produce a smile on Black's face.

The big black dude then looked around the bull pen, to see if anyone had a problem with how he'd just handled the smaller boy? No one bothered to say anything, or even return his stare. Yet, one dude was staring back at him, more so in awe, opposed to any other reason.

"What the fuck *you* looking at punk!" Snapped the big black dude.

Instead of replying, the awestruck kid *quickly* turned his head!

Satisfied by how niggas were intimated by him, the big black dude continued to look around the small holding cell. Focusing on one dude in particular, he suddenly burst out laughing! Then pointing towards a light skinned fat kid, who was sitting on the bull pen's floor looking *shook*, he asked, "Fat boy, what the fuck is your *shook* looking ass locked up for? Please don't tell me you're charged with eating someone out of house & home!"

At that, majority of the new arrivals couldn't help laughing as well.

When the fat boy didn't reply, the big black dude got serious, "Mother fucker you can't talk? I *asked* you, what yo shook ass is doing in jail?"

Clearing his throat, the boy responded, "They say I robbed somebody."

"They *say* you robbed somebody? Either you did, or you didn't? Which is it?"

The young fat boy didn't bother to respond. Apparently he wasn't *that* afraid of the big black dude, where he was about to incriminate himself.

"Lord have mercy, on us all!" The big black dude said, shaking his head. "I swear this world has gotten out of control! I mean, who the fuck would even *allow* a fat punk like you to rob'em? And, the police to even suspect you? Your fat ass probably couldn't even run a City block, without catching a heart attack!"

Again, majority of the new arrivals laughed at the black dudes comment.

"I may not know what this world is coming to, but I do know at least two things for sure. One, this is C-74, so your fat ass better know how to fight! Or two, yo'ass better be one helluva comedian!" The big black dude informed the fat kid.

After a few moments of silence had passed, the young fat kid cleared his throat, and asked the bigger black boy, "I can understand why I'd need to know how to fight, especially in a place such as this. But, how would being a helluva *comedian* benefit me?" The big black dude couldn't contain his laugh. In fact, he was holding his stomach as he thought, "Fat boy may *already* be learning the trick of the trade!" Once his laughter had subsided he looked fat boy in the eyes and replied, "Because *fat boy*, if you succeed in keeping niggas laughing, it'll keep their minds off of your booty!"

At that, almost the entire holding cell burst out in laughter! Those who hadn't bothered to laugh, were those who knew they could not fight....or tell jokes!!!

Once they were done being processed, and issued an identification card, which they were instructed to wear clipped onto their upper left collar, Sergeant Williams escorted the 27 of them down to the messhall to eat.

Standing in front of J.R. on the serving line, was a kid who looked no more than 12 or 13 years old. Yet, J.R. knew that wasn't the case, being that you had to be 16 to 21 to be housed in C-74. As they made their way down the line, one of the inmate servers asked the young looking boy, "Yo little man, do that gold front come out?"

The kid didn't even bother to respond, instead he continued down the serving line.

"Yo little nigga! I *know* you heard me!" The dude behind the serving line shouted, causing others in the vicinity to become real quiet. "Do that muh'fucking gold tooth come out!" He angrily repeated himself, at the same time screwing up his face to enhance the intimidation tactic.

This time the young looking inmate turned towards the food server, stared at him a moment, then replied, "I heard you the first time, but, I've never been one to entertain dumb ass questions! Yours, is not only dumb, but also irrelevant, because whether my shit comes out or not, the fact is, it's not *coming* out!" He stated matter of factly.

His response caused the inmate behind the serving line to smile, before asking,

"Little man, where you from?" Impressed by the young boys heart.

"Queens." He replied, then suddenly realizing that not too many parts of Queens, if any, were as thorough as his section he added, "Southside Jamaica."

"There's only like a handful of your homies holding it down in here, but not many. However, I see you have a lot of heart for a little nigga. I guess it remains to be seen, what category you *fall* into." Dude smiled from behind the serving line, before he added, "Just *pray* you don't fall into 4-*Main*!"

Considering J.R. was standing directly behind the young looking kid, he'd overheard the entire exchange, and definitely liked how the kid had handled himself. Plus the fact that he was from Jamaica, J.R. told himself that he'd ride with the kid if, or when niggas tried him!

Fortunately for the new arrivals, those who were under eighteen without a high school diploma, the Administration had recently turned 4-Dorm into a school dorm. Meaning, most of them qualified for that dorm, opposed to being housed in some of the rougher dormitories or housing unit. Only two new arrivals didn't qualify for the school dorm, a twenty year old Spanish dude and the big black dude who, earlier, had been bullying the rest of the inmates in the holding cell.

J.R. couldn't help noticing that the Spanish dude *and* the big black dude appeared somewhat *shook*, when Sergeant Williams stopped the line in front of 4-Main, and called off the two of their names. As the two of them stepped out of the line, J.R. tapped the big black dude on the arm and said, "Knock'em dead champ!"

Looking J.R. up and down, he asked, "What the fuck you mean by that?"

"I'm saying." J.R. smiled, speaking loud enough for all to hear. "If your knuckle game isn't up to parr, I just *hope* your punch lines are!"

At that, the entire group burst out laughing....even *fat boy*!

"Please tell me what are we waiting for, to go get those boys out of jail?" Yolanda was furious, and not trying to hear or feel her son spending another minute locked up.

"You know what? I'd really appreciate it if you'd stop *nagging* me about those boys!" Joshua complained. "If *one* wants to sell drugs, and the *other* wants to carry guns, *they* sure as hell will need this experience."

Yolanda stared at her husband as if he'd completely lost his mind.

Joshua smiled, got up from the kitchen table, kissed Yolanda on the cheek, and said, "I'll go post their bails in a few weeks."

"A few *weeks*!" She repeated incredulously, hoping she hadn't heard him correctly. "I *know* you didn't just say that you're leaving my baby in jail, for a few weeks." "He's not a baby, and that's *exactly* what I said." Joshua held her stare, before adding, "And, I *mean* what I said."

"I can't *believe* you!" Yolanda said, with tears in her eyes. "Just because *you* were able to survive that hell hole, doesn't mean J.R. can or will."

"Trust me baby, he too will survive. It's in his blood." Joshua smiled. "I never said *not* to visit the boy, because a visit will definitely lift his spirits, and possibly even *yours* too!" With that said, he headed towards his bedroom, discussion over.........

Chapter Six.

"I thought *chow* was at 11:00 a.m.?" J.R. asked Cocky, as he climbed out of his bunk, seeing that his watch read 1:30 p.m.

"That's what I hear." Cocky replied, before informing him, "But I also hear that they're bringing food trays to each of the dorms, opposed to us going to the messhall. One of the C.O.'s told us that a nigga got murdered down in 4-Main last night."

With that said, Cocky looked up at J.R., gave a slight shrug, then resumed his game of crazy eight, against his new friend Jamel.

"Murdered?" J.R. couldn't help wondering if *big black*, from the holding cell, was the victim? In any event, he was certainly glad that Cocky, Jamel, and himself were placed in 4-Dorm, opposed to 4-Main which even the C.O.'s called *the house of pain*!

As the food trays arrived, J.R. proceeded to the rest room to wash his face and brush his teeth. Just as he bent forward to spit into the sink, someone grabbed him in a bear hug so tight he could hardly breath! All he could think was, "Whoever dude is, he's a dead man when he lets go of me! If, he doesn't squeeze the *life* out of me that is! And, Cocky's a dead nigga too, for letting a nigga roll on me in the blind!"

"This the *wrong* place to be having ya head in the sink."

The voice was much deeper, but J.R. recognized it immediately!

As Steve O loosened his vise-like grip, and put J.R. down, he just stood there smiling. Obviously happy to see his homeboy, even though he wish it was under different circumstances.

"Damn Steve O!" J.R. snapped, now back on his feet. "What the fuck is wrong with you, sneaking up on a nigga like that? You *lucky* I recognized your voice, when I did, because I was sho'nuff bout to kill yo ass!"

Both boys laughed, then gave each other a brotherly hug.

J.R. took a few steps backwards to get a good look at his homeboy.

"Man, these folks must be lacing these food trays with steroids! Yo ass done got big as a muh'fucker! No *wonder* I couldn't get out of that bear hug!" J.R. laughed.

"Steroids?" Steve O laughed. "Nah kid, it's a result of potatoes everyday, four slices of bread with every meal, plenty of rest, and five hundred push ups every night before I go to bed." He informed him, as he flexed his muscles with a smile on his face, before adding, "And don't think I'm just getting my weight up to impress them hoes, when I get out, because the main reason I stay on top of my shit is because a nigga gotta be right, up in *this* piece! Shit is always jumping off in C-74! Especially involving niggas from Brooklyn. In fact, 90 percent of the population is cats from Brooklyn." Steve informed him. "I'm good though, niggas don't fuck with me. Me and *Spoon* got the A-side of 2-Main on smash. That's a *real* nigga right there" He said, referring to Spoon. "So I've heard." J.R. said. "I've never met dude, but I can tell Pam really digs him."

"Digs him!" Steve O exclaimed, looking at J.R. as if he'd just made the understatement of the year. "Kid, Pam be trooping, like no other, for that nigga!" He laughed. "But her efforts are definitely paying off, because that nigga be talking marriage, baby carriage, and the whole nine!"

At that, they both laughed.

"For real though." Steve O became serious, at the same time looking around to make sure that he and J.R. were the only two in the small rest room area. "I brought you these." He handed J.R. two *extremely* sharp ice picks! "Give one to Cocky, I got plenty of them if you have to flush it, or whatever. By the way, who's the kid Jamel, Cocky introduced me to?"

"Oh, he's home team." J.R. replied. "He's actually from Rockaway Boulevard. Some nigga tried to play him fucked up yesterday, coming through the messhall, for his gold tooth, but he *checked* that shit real quick!" J.R. smiled proudly, obviously pleased by Jamal's thoroughness.

"Oh yeah." Steve O too was impressed, being that the kid Jamel looked so young, not to mention somewhat fragile. Nevertheless, he'd been detained in the 4-Building for nearly eight months now, and had seen first hand how niggas came through with the right intentions and plenty of heart, but unfortunately most, at least eight out of ten, seemed to have a complete *change of heart* once they found out how *real* shit was in C-74! Especially in 2 & 4 Main. "I know one thing. "Steve O said, looking J.R. in the eyes.

"If little man *isn't* built like that, and that gold front *does* come out, I strongly *suggest* he puts it in his pocket. If not, you can *believe* niggas are going up in shorty's grill for that cap." He seriously *hoped* that the kid Jamel was built like that, because Steve O knew J.R., therefore he knew that J.R. would *ride* for anyone he embraced, and apparently he'd already embraced the young looking kid from Rockaway Boulevard, Steve O assessed.

"I think you better give Jamel one of the ice picks I gave you." Steve O suggested. "I'll bring Cocky one at dinner time." Realizing Jamal needed it more than Cocky.

"Alright." J.R. agreed. "Yo, what the fuck happened down in 4-Main last night?"

Steve O laughed at the question, then said, "The question is, *what isn't happening down in 4-Main!*" He shook his head. "I hear this Chinese cat named Chin Fu was extorting most of them chinks, who own various stores and restaurants on Canal Street, from right over the telephone!" He gave J.R. a look as if asking, *"Can you believe that shit?"* Instead, Steve O went on to say, "That's how petrified he had them chinks, when he was on the street. Anyway, once the calls were made Chin Fu sent his folks over to the place of business, to collect. I hear his wife would bring a percentage, of his portion, *to him* through the visiting room." Steve O explained, clearly impressed. "Well, to make a long story short, some Brooklyn niggas, down in 4-Main, got wind of what the Chinese boy was doing, and that was all she wrote. I hear, the kid Chin Fu was laying on *fifty grand* stuffed in his mattress!" He shook his head, as if to say, "*Un-fucking-believable!*" Instead he said, "Spoon has most of the coke *and* weed floating through the facility, so I'm sure he'll end up with most of the fifty grand."

"Damn!" J.R. was clearly impressed by all that Steve O had said. "So, did they actually *murder* the chink?"

Steve O looked at him incredulously, then said, "Shit, if *I* knew the muh'fucker was laying on that kind of bread, *I* would've pushed my food cart up into 4-Main and murdered his ass, my damn self!" He said, quickly adding, "As bad as *I* need a good lawyer!"

J.R. knew Steve O was dead serious.

"When I heard about the killing, from Cocky, I just *knew* the victim was this big black ass dude, who came through with the rest of us yesterday." Said J.R.

"Yeah, I *heard* about that character as well." Steve O laughed. "Apparently he came up in the housing unit *mean mugging* niggas, as if shit was sweet up in that piece." He shook his head. "Anyway, after this Brooklyn cat name Darzell put that head to *bed*, niggas decided to let the nigga live. Mainly because, he did *attempt* to fight back, didn't *snitch*, and have a *cousin* down in 4-Lower who's God body. However, niggas *did* confiscate his gold chain, jacket, and sneakers." Steve O laughed.

J.R. just shook his head. Changing the subject, he asked, "So what's the deal with your case?"

"Unfortunately, the Legal Aide Lawyer, the courts appointed me, isn't really doing *or* saying much in my behalf." Steve O revealed with a shrug, considering *that* was pretty much the case with countless others, represented by Public Defenders. "But, this cat name *Ski*, who works in the Law Library, seems to confidently believe that there are loop holes in my case. Actually, what he said is that, there's a medical term for how I completely *lost it* when I ran into the guy, who savagely beat and raped my sister." Steve O smiled, knowing J.R. and most of the hood knew that he had hunted the dude down, then bodied him in broad day light. "I don't be trying to remember exactly what the medical terminology is, because Ski also said that *this* isn't the time for me to be displaying any good sense."

Although the situation was nothing but serious, J.R. couldn't help laughing.

"I *know* it sounds crazy, but it just might work." Said Steve O.

"Hopefully." J.R. nodded, trying to be confident.

"But, I'll definitely need a better lawyer, to pull it off. The mouth piece They appointed me, is a straight idiot! The last time I went to court, he asked *me* to refresh *him* as to *who* I was? And *what* was my case about?" Steve O shook his head. "I've been making a few dollars, fucking with Spoon, as well as saving the chips my mom has been sending, but I'm still a long way from *lawyer* money." He frowned.

"I don't understand why my parents haven't posted my bail yet," J.R. said in dismay. "But, as soon as I get out me, K Smooth, and the rest of the crew are going to come up with a plan, to work it out for you. You can *believe* that."

Without question, Steve O *knew* J.R. would make good on his promise. He'd known J.R. basically all of his life, and one thing was for sure, even as a youngster J.R. had *always* said what he meant....and meant *whatever* he'd said!

"Joshua Reed *Jr*! You have a *visit*!" The dorm officer yelled out.

Immediately, J.R. knew the visitor was his mother. Regardless to whom or what, she never failed to add the "Jr." to his name. Upon his arrest, he'd never mentioned, to the desk Sergeant, that he was a "Jr.' therefore, in the paperwork, it was not included to his name. The detective, Carmine, had referred to him as *Jr*, simply because he'd long since done his homework on the *Reed*, and *Shannon*, family. Unfortunately, he was still making his way through the ranks, when Joshua and Eugene had their strong hold on the streets. Those who didn't know the two men, had undoubtedly heard the legend and stories of their endeavors. Through hearsay, J.R. had come to realize that his father had once been a *major* player in the game. Yet, what he couldn't understand was *why* his old man had never attempted, nor bothered to discuss the street life....with him? It wasn't like he was a youngster anymore, J.R. had told himself.

Once he'd reached the visitation area the officer, behind the counter, realizing J.R. had to be a new inmate being that he'd never seen his face before, handed him a gray jumpsuit and said,

"Strip down to your underwear, then put on the jumpsuit. Your clothes you can place into this basket." He handed J.R. a small wire rimmed basket. "The basket will be placed into one of the small lockers you see behind me, but it's up to *you* to remember your locker number. And trust me, this area *will* be crowded after visitation is over, so I will not entertain *any* guessing games, as far as locker numbers are concerned."

With that said, the officer moved further down the counter, and J.R. could hear him giving a similar speech to the next inmate who had entered the area.

As he entered the visiting room, J.R.'s smile broadened, seeing that his mother was not alone. Seated beside her was Pam, *and* a smiling Regina! He couldn't help feeling a little uneasy, noticing, as he made his way to the table, that just about every inmate in the visiting room was sweating *his* table!

"There goes *my* baby!" Yolanda screamed, as she rose from her chair to give her son a tight hug

"Mom, you can't *do* that! This is *jail*!" J.R. said under his breath, but loud enough for her to hear him.

"Boy please!" Yolanda laughed, at the same time taking a step back to get a better look at her baby. "I hope they're treating you okay in here?"

"I'm good." J.R. replied, before stepping around the table to give Pam a hug, followed by a kiss on the cheek.

"What's going on Regina?" J.R. asked, also giving her a quick hug, minus the kiss on the cheek.

"Oh know he *didn't* play you like that!" Pam shouted, then laughed, before adding, "Boy, you might as well stop acting stupid, because your cover has already been blown! So, you might as well go ahead and give your *girl* some tongue!"

J.R. just stood there looking as if he'd been caught, with his pants down around his ankles! Looking from Pam, to Regina, then to his mother.

"Have a seat baby." Yolanda smiled. "Regina told us, on the way here, about the two of you."

"I guess after all the years of lusting after her, you *finally* wore that ass down!" Pam burst out laughing. "Truthfully, I think it's a match made in Heaven, because I haven't seen Regina with a man in *ages*, and I've *never* seen J.R. with a female!"

"Pam, mind your business please." Yolanda interjected.

"There goes *my* business right there!" Pam smiled, seeing Spoon entering the visiting room. "I'ma head over to my table, but I'll bring Spoon over and introduce him to you all, before visiting hours are over." She got up and walked over to the table that was designated for her and Spoon.

About a half hour into their visit, Yolanda looked down at her wrist watch, then at her son and said, "I'm going to let you and Regina enjoy the last thirty minutes, in private. If *that's* even possible!" She said, looking around the now crowded room.

"Baby, *please* promise me you'll stay out of trouble. Your father is really acting beside himself thesedays, but he promised that we'd be here, to post you and Cocky's bail before the week is out." Unbeknownst to J.R., Yolanda was *still* fuming mad with his father for allowing their son to go through such an unnecessary experience. "Regina, before I head out I think I'll make my way over to Pam's table, so I can meet this *Spoon* fella who my daughter's so madly in love with. But, I'll meet the two of you down in the waiting area."

Both, mother and son, stood up at the same time, and J.R. spotted the tears welling up in her eyes. Giving his mom a tight hug, he whispered into her ear, "Momma please don't cry. The situation isn't nearly as bad as you probably *think* it is." Knowing she, like countless others, had indeed heard the horrific tales surrounding Rikers Island. "Besides, didn't you say, I'll be out of here shortly?" He backed up somewhat, to look her in the eyes.

Yolanda nodded her head, *Yes*, then used her right hand to wipe at her eyes, being that the tears had already began to fall. Taking J.R. back into her arms, Yolanda gave her son a tight hug, kissed him, then turned and walked out of the visitation room. Obviously forgetting her previous intentions, of going over to Pam's table to meet Spoon. But then, maybe she hadn't forgotten, thought J.R.

Seeing and feeling his mother's pain.

"So, how is my *other* favorite lady doing?" J.R. turned his attention to Regina.

"I'm good, but I'd be doing a whole lot better if you were home." Regina confessed, then quickly added, "Until you get there, I'll be strong for *both* of us." She smiled, squeezed his hand then remembered, "Oh, by the way, I put three hundred dollars on your card, as well as brought you three nice outfits to wear. Also, I put a hundred dollars on Cocky's card, so he too can buy some commissary. However, he can forget about an outfit, because I only shop for my *man*!" She smiled.

"I doubt he'll be mad at you." J.R. replied, returning her smile. "We've been seated across from each other over forty minutes now, and I haven't even told you *once* how much I've missed you, or how crazy I am about you."

"Yeah nigga, I was wondering how long it would be, before you realized how badly you're slipping." She smiled, exposing her deep dimples and perfect white teeth.

J.R. didn't need anyone to tell him that his girl was *eye candy*, even though every nigga seated in the visiting room confirmed it, by the way they were sweating his table. He didn't feel disrespected by their stares, as long as none of them became bold enough to *voice* their interest.

"Got damn!" Regina snapped, shacking J.R. from his train of thoughts. "Please tell me *why* this nigga keep staring in my face, flashing them crooked ass gold teeth, and licking them chapped ashy lips of his!" She was speaking loud enough for damn near *everyone* in the visiting room to hear.

By the time J.R. could turn around to see *who* the person was, she was referring to, Regina had already made it her business to *check* dude.

"Please tell me why the fuck you all up in my grill? Don't you see I'm sitting with the *only* nigga I'm trying to be with! I guess it's fair to assume that *some* of y'all mother fuckers are locked up, for a lack of mother fucking *respect!*" She went off on the inmate seated behind J.R., then suggested, "Baby, switch seats with me please, so I can enjoy the last few minutes of our visit, without this lizard face mother fucker sticking his tongue out at me,"

Switching seats enabled J.R. to get a *good* look at the inmate she was talking about. He noticed that the dude wasn't much bigger than he, nor did he appear as *tough* looking as some of the other inmates he'd encountered in the corridors. Despite those two facts, J.R. immediately realized that dude had to be *somebody*, because the contents, jewelry that is, that were glistening from his mouth, neck, ear, wrist, and fingers spoke loudly.

Niggas in C-74 weren't even wearing *wedding bands*, unless they were *somebody!* And here it was, J.R. found himself facing an inmate with a mouth full of gold teeth, a gold Movado watch, three *thick* gold chains, and at least *seven* gold and diamond rings on his fingers! "Damn!" J.R. mumbled to himself. "I know this girl has just succeeded, in getting my ass in some real *deep* shit!" As he thought about it, the inmate draped in jewelry pretty much *confirmed* it, as he sat across from J.R. nodding his head in an up , and down motion, as if to say, *"Yeah nigga, you better believe....it's on!"*

After the visit was over J.R. and Spoon stood in line talking, as they awaited their clothes baskets, when a voice from behind spoke, "Damn playboy, that pretty bitch of yours got a *vicious* mouth! In fact, it'll be wise, on your part, to put a muzzle on it.

Because I'd hate to see *you* get yourself murdered back here, on account of a *bitch* out there." As he spoke, the inmate draped in jewelry, locked eyes with J.R.

Holding dude's stare, and not at all appreciating dude calling Regina a bitch, J.R. replied, "Nah nigga, I think *you're* the bitch who needs a muzzle! Standing here talking about a nigga getting murdered, loud enough for the police to hear!"

The C.O. had worked the visiting room long enough, to recognize when a potentially dangerous situation was about to take place. Just as he knew it wasn't always good to intervene, especially when his back up squad had a tendency to move a bit slow sometime. So, if he had in fact heard the inmate, he certainly appeared not to had.

Spoon decided to step in between the two, before the situation got out of hand.

"Yo Dollar Bill, be easy parr, this here is my family." Spoon informed him, now locking eyes with the kid whose name was Dollar Bill. "So lets not take it there!"

While Spoon and the dude Dollar Bill were engaging in a heated exchange of words, J.R. had snatched his clothes basket, got dressed quickly, and slid his *ice pick* up his sleeve. It was just his luck when the *shake down* officer called out to the officer who was handing out clothes baskets, informing him that he had a call on line one.

All was silent, as Dollar Bill and Spoon went for their baskets as well.

When Dollar Bill bent forward to untie his sneaker laces, to enable him to step out of the gray jumpsuit…..J.R. *rushed* him!

Before Dollar Bill could stand upright, or even *try* to defend himself, J.R. had already stabbed him at least 12 times!

Before the riot squad were even alerted, that they were needed in the visitation area, J.R. had already passed the shank off to Spoon, whom he *knew* would know what to do with it, and the two of them slid off in different directions.

As soon as Spoon arrived back at his housing unit, he dialed Pam. Unfortunately, she hadn't made it home yet! Getting her answering machine, he left a message.

"I understand your Pops wanting to teach your little brother a lesson, by making him stay put for a minute, but love, shit *just* got ugly!!!!

And when I say *ugly*, I mean *real* ugly up in this piece. I can handle me, but J.R.'s not in my dorm, so it'll be damn near possible for me to hold him down. So please tell your Pops that bailing his son out, asap, may very boil down to a matter of life or death, right about now."

With that said, Spoon left the telephone area in search of Steve O, because they *all* needed to be on point.

Approximately two hours later, the same dorm officer yelled out J.R.'s name!

But this time it wasn't for a visit, because he added, "And bring *all* of your belongings with you, to the officers station!"

"Damn! Somebody must've *snitched* on me!" J.R. told

himself, assuming that he was heading to the *bing*, being that he'd been instructed to bring all of his belongings. Suddenly he realized *that* couldn't be the case, when the officer called out *Cornell Jackson,* Cocky's name, instructing him to do likewise. *Cocky wasn't even in the visiting area.* He told himself.

"This is the *last* time I'm going to call for the two of you!" The C.O. shouted, clearly upset by the two youngsters lack of promptness. "And y'all *better* bring all of y'all shit!" Using a cuss word this time, before adding, "The two of you are on the *bail out*!"

Chapter Seven.

After retrieving their property, which consisted of house keys and school identification, J.R. and Cocky awaited the bus that would take them over to the registration building. Upon arriving at the registration building, the two of them were surprised to find that *no one* was there to greet them, or take the two of them home. "Our bails were probably posted down at the Queens House of Detention, being that no one is here to pick us up." Cocky told J.R., as they awaited the second bus that would take them over the bridge, and off of thc island.

"I guess," J.R. replied, knowing his parents wouldn't bail him out, leaving him to find a way home. "Maybe they're waiting for us on the other side of the bridge."

As the bus was about to come to a stop, J.R. peered out of the window to see if he'd spot either of his parents, or maybe even Pam and Regina. If not, he and Cocky would just remain on the bus, which would take them to Queens Plaza, where they'd catch the **E,** or the **F** train to Supthin Boulevard. From there, they could walk home.

The two boys almost knocked over a couple of passengers, who were standing by the bus's rear door, when they spotted the brand new Oldsmobile 98, sitting on chrome spoke wheels, in the parking lot! As they hopped off the bus, and proceeded towards the vehicle, both driver and passenger doors swung open.

"Man, am I *glad* to see the two of you!" J.R. exclaimed, giving K Smooth some dap, then going around the car to give his father a hug.

"Me too!" Smiled Cocky, also giving K Smooth some dap, and a *thank you* hand shake to J.R.'s old man.

"I *bet* you are!" K Smooth laughed, looking at J.R. "From what I heard, *every* Brooklyn dude in the building had intentions of bum rushing *your* dorm, come breakfast time, to get at *you*! Spoon said, the *only* reason they even decided to wait until breakfast, was because it would've been the perfect time to *off* yo'ass and get away with it. Being that the officer who came on shortly before breakfast, to work your dorm, happens to be one of their homeboys from Brooklyn," K Smooth informed him, then added, "Why you think *no one* ratted on you?"

"It's all good." J.R.replied, with a shrug. "Just know that, if or when it went down me, Cocky, and Jamal would've had blood on *our* ice picks as well." Changing the subject, he asked, "And what have *you* been up to? I mean, you *could've* at least come through with Mom, Pam and Regina to check a nigga!"

"Kid, I had bigger *and* better things to attend to, opposed to sitting up in some jailhouse." K Smooth laughed. "How do you *think* y'all boys made bail?"

Dismayed by the question, J.R. looked from K Smooth to his father.

"I only gave him a thousand dollars, the other four thousand he came up with on his own." Joshua informed his son. In fact, he too, was impressed. Not so much by the fact that K Smooth had come up with the money, but more so by the show of loyalty amongst them at such a young age.

Opposed to going straight home, Joshua drove the three boys to a small diner, called *Buckineers,* located on Astoria Boulevard. As the four of them exited the vehicle, Joshua informed them, "It isn't your mother's cooking, but the food here is pretty decent." He said, looking at J.R. "You all can order whatever you like, because I can only imagine how hungry you boys must be." This time he looked from J.R. to Cocky.

Once their orders had arrived, the boys couldn't help laughing, seeing how the medium sized table resembled a Thanksgiving feast!

"I already know I'm gonna sleep *good* tonight." Cocky said, digging into his plate.

"I know that's right!" J.R. agreed, digging into his food as well.

"Y'all niggas act like y'all fresh off a *bid*, or something!" K Smooth laughed, before digging into his plate of spaghetti and meat sauce.

"I see you got jokes." J.R. looked over at K Smooth. "Then again, being a helluva comedian may very well have its benefits, if you ever landed in C-74." He laughed.

Cocky laughed as well, being that he'd caught on.

Joshua simply shook his head, obviously familiar with the

joke.

"A *smooth* cat like myself, doesn't have to worry about going to jail. But, if I ever found myself on rikers I'm sure I'll handle the situation smoothly, opposed to trying to get all of *Brooklyn* off my ass!" K Smooth laughed.

J.R. didn't bother to respond, instead, he visualized a nigga like *big black* taking all of K Smooth's belongings, and handing him some State issued shit to put on! His thoughts were interrupted when his father cleared his throat, and said, "Right now it's time to eat. We'll have plenty of time to rap, when we get to White Plains." Without bothering to look up from his plate.

The mention of *rapping*, and taking a trip to White Plains, New York, suddenly *superseded* their thoughts of a good night's rest,,,,,and their appetites!

Neither of the three boys had ever been to White Plains. In fact, they couldn't recall ever leaving outside of Queens, except on those occasions when their families went on outings to places such as Six Flags Great Adventures, Rye Playland, Bear Mountain, Hersey State Park, or when they were younger Far Rockaway Playland. They'd visited Coney Island so many times, it wasn't even considered an outing.

The only reason J.R. was familiar with the *name* White Plains, was he recalled his mother taking Pam and Regina to a big shopping mall located in that part of New York. Although each boy was itching to ask questions, they'd remained silent, knowing their questions would be answered soon enough. Therefore, they sat back taking in the change of scenery. As they neared their destination, the boys noticed how well kept the streets, landscape, and houses were. There wasn't a dilapidated building in sight!

"I hope we don't get stopped by the cops! Four Blacks riding through the suburbs, three of whom having *no* knowledge of their destination!" J.R. couldn't help thinking. Despite it being night time, the three boys were still able to see that the house, in which Joshua pulled into its driveway then the garage, was even *more* beautiful and spacious then majority of those they'd observed along the way!

Joshua pressed a button, in the Oldsmobile, and the garage quietly began to ascend at the same time deactivating the security alarm system. They entered the housc through the single door, located in the garage, which lead to the *biggest* kitchen either of the boys had ever seen! Around the kitchen table sat twelve chairs, K Smooth counted as Joshua took his seat at the head, motioning for the three of them to be seated as well.

"I realize the three of you are probably filled with questions, but my purpose for bringing you here is *not* to answer your questions." Joshua began, looking from one boy to the next, then went on, "I brought the three of you out here for *two* reasons. One, is to express some of my concerns, regarding you all. And two, enlighten you all to some of the *facts* of reality. Because it's inevitable that you all are *clueless* regarding some of the most pertinent facts of life. I see the three of you being drawn to a game, that's not even a *game* anymore. In any game, you have winners and losers. Thesedays, all you see is losers. That old philosophy, *Get Rich Or Die Trying!,* is already dead. Nowaday, the way the streets and the system is set up, any *Man* with potential and a plan, will only be afforded *one* chance. Only a *fool*, does the system enable to *die trying.* Because a fool does, what a fool do. Not only will *he* continuously take falls, but he'll also bring down those around him." Joshua explained, looking from one boy to the next. "Keep in mind that, nowadays, your *first* mistake can be your *worst* mistake." Looking from Cocky to J.R. he added, "The crimes the two of you allegedly committed, are of a petty nature. But please do not pat yourselves on the back when, or if the punishment is minimal. Remember, the *fool* is always afforded the pleasure of *die trying*! So in essence, the plan is actually to see if the two of you will fall into the *fool's* category, opposed to being viewed as a threat. The *threat*, of course, is the Man with potential and a plan." He let his words sink in, as he looked into the eyes of each of the three boys. "Do *I* think it's unfortunate, that the two of you found yourselves spending a few days, and a few nights in jail?" He asked, looking from J.R. to Cocky., before answering his own question. "Of course not. Because, what the two of you *must* learn is that, for every choice we make or action we take, there is *always* going to be a re-action. Too many young people, thesedays, make the choice of taking to the street life. Yet, so many do not have so much as a clue, as to the ways of the streets. Which is why *so many* end up falling victim *to* the streets. When the *fact* is, the *streets* protect only those who know and understand how to protect themselves! So in other words, the street in, and of, itself *doesn't* protect no one!"

With that said, Joshua sat back in his chair for like a minute or so, allowing the boys to take in all in which he'd said. Now it was time to really bring his point home, by having the three boys mirror themselves and their actions.

"In order to be successful in your endeavors, whatever they may be, you must first have a *plan*. But, even before the plan take effect, you must get in *tune* with your individual self. Your comrades, as a team. Your surroundings. As well as your *adversaries*. I've noticed how you all walk around with *The South Road Boyz* pressed onto your shirts, yet, I can not understand, for the life of me, how *you*," He said, looking at J.R. "Have a tendency to walk around toting guns, *unbeknownst* to the rest of your team." Looking at Cocky he said, "Cocky, you out there on the block, slinging your little dope packages *unbeknownst* to the rest of your team." Looking at K Smooth he said, "And here we have Kenny, who comes up with four thousand dollars, basically over night! How you've managed to accomplish such a feat, I'm sure, is also *unbeknownst* to the rest of the team. As for Reese, who I rarely even *see* thesedays, I'm willing to bet this lovely house we're sitting in, that his whereabouts, majority of the time, is also *unbeknownst* to this so-called team!" Joshua shook his head, then continued by asking, "And what about Steve O? How does the *team* intend to help *him* in his situation?"

Although their intentions were good, neither of the three boys had an answer to the question.

"I guess the *answer* to my question, is also *unbeknownst* to the team." Joshua laughed, not caring one bit that his *laugh* could be taken as adding insult, to injury.

"So, I guess it's safe to assume that there is not a *plan* any where in sight, because I, for one, certainly does not see one. Which brings me back to what I said earlier, if you all are not the ones with the potential, or the plan, then that undoubtedly makes you *all* a team of *fools*, huh?" Instead of laughing, Joshua simply shook his head, as if to say; *Now that's a damn shame!*

A gesture in which made all three boys realize that, their ways and actions had indeed been....*foolish*.

"Listen," Joshua began, "The reason I'm emphasizing the relevance of *choices* and *repercussions* is because, once you've acquired a clear understanding of the two, it'll enable you all to plan in terms of *long* range. Meaning, how to, and why you must precautiously chose the people, places, and things you deal with. A man who properly plans, in terms of long range, already knows what to expect in the *end*. Therefore, his *means* are justifiable. However, today it's common to see or hear, how so many of these so called *Ballers,* who have gotten *paid* in this so called game, get locked up and turn *snitch* as soon as they're threatened with a lengthy prison sentence. *They* are the characters who has never known, or understood the laws of actions and re-actions. Because had they, they'd know and understand, that choices are basically synonymous to rewards *and* penalties. A man who possesses such knowledge will *never* relish the rewards, gained as a result of his street endeavors, yet not be willing to accept the penalties!" Joshua explained. "Sort of like winning and losing. Just because a man finds himself in the penitentiary, with a lengthy prison sentence, does *not* mean he played the game….and didn't win. Especially if his ultimate goal was simply to change the condition, and position of his family. Countless white children, are born with silver spoons in their mouths, not because *they* are the chosen race, or even the fortunate ones. But, because of the actions, and capital in which, was more than likely unlawfully gained, by their so called *great* grandfathers, playing and planning in terms of *long* range. Even some of *them* landed in the penitentiary, or cemetery, but all you have to do is your homework, or just look around you to see that current conditions and positions of their seeds, born with the silver spoons in their mouths, further exemplifies that in the *end*, they played, planned….and *won.*"

The three boys sat there nodding their heads, with a smile on their faces, obviously grasping Joshua's point.

"Truthfully, nothing would make me more happier, then to see you all stay in school, and strive to get out of life *that* in which makes you happy. Yet, if it's the street life that entices either of you more, I suggest you get in it to *win* it. Just remember, to *win* also means you must be willing to sacrifice. That sacrifice can ultimately be your life *or* your freedom." Joshua looked each one of them in their eyes, then revealed, "I was once a *major* player, in the so called game, but I retired before prison or death fell upon me. Some consider me a legend, others consider me fortunate. But am *I* happy or content by how the *end* unfolded, for me?" Joshua had their full attention, being that it was the first time he'd ever confirmed, what the boys had only heard through hearsay. "My answer is *no*. Because, although I *am* sitting on some money, it is not even a *fraction* of enough to change the condition, or position of even my immediate family, let alone generations to come. Whereas, I *played* hard, I failed to *plan* in terms of *long* range."

The three boys sat there silently, just staring at Joshua.

"It is not my intentions, nor will I, sit here tonight and give you all the 101 of the so called game, as I know it. Because first, and foremost, you all have some *serious* choices to make. But, I *will* tell you this," Said Joshua, looking each boy in his eyes, before continuing, "If it's the street life that appeals to you all the most, *winning* will be virtually impossible, unless, at least *one* of you embark on an entirely different, and unassociated path. Yet, the *cause* will ultimately lead to one *end*."

The three boys continued to sit there silently, taking in every single word Joshua spoke.

"And please, Do not come running up to me tomorrow, or the day after, *or* the day after that! Telling me that you've made your decision." He stared at each boy. "Remember, I *did* play the game, therefore, my observations will tell me whatever I need to know. If you're feeling school, it's not long before you all graduate, so it's time that you get *all* that you can out of it. If you're feeling that street shit," He said, looking from Cocky to

J.R. "My best and only advice is, get out there. Not to commit a crime, but, to get in tune *with* the streets. See what's going on, in this day and time. Next time we come together like this, *if* there's even a next time, I'll pretty much know who's who and what's what. In the meantime," He said, giving the three of them a menacing stare, "Do not, and I *repeat*, do not bring any illegal substances in my house!" He then looked over at K Smooth and said, "That includes *Eugene's* house as well!" With that said, Joshua got up from the table, headed back out to the garage, and got into his Oldsmobile.

Chapter Eight.

J.R. looked down at his math paper, and was definitely pleased to see the *A*-, which was a step up from the *B*+ he'd consistently scored in the past. He had always been good in mathematics, whether it be adding, subtracting, multiplying, dividing, fractions, algebra, geometry, etc. Since elementary school his teachers had been impressed, by how quickly he'd cap the various divisions of mathematics.

Now, in high school, they were *still* impressed by J.R. So much so, majority of his teachers, especially his math teacher Mrs. Scott, often wondered why such a bright and articulate young man would even be attending Jamaica high, opposed to one of the *many* better schools throughout New York City? The fact that he had maintained a *B* average, in basically all of his subjects, opposed to an *A*, or better, was simply because English literature, Science, Social Studies, Foreign languages, or even Physical education didn't interest J.R. in the least. Not to mention, his mind was so preoccupied with *other* things.

A fact that, had him *surprised* to receive the *A*-.

No matter how hard he tried, J.R. couldn't get his mind off of all that his father had told him, K Smooth, and Cocky out in White Plains that day!

"Well, *last night* was an exception!" He smilingly told himself. Considering Regina had spent the night in his bed, and had succeeded in taking his mind off of any, and everything else! Smiling? The *recollection* had him outright grinning!

"Mr. Reed, an *A-* is certainly cause enough to bring a *smile* to anyone's face. However, in your case, it should have been an *A+*." Mrs. Scott commented, as she walked pass his desk.

Until recently, K Smooth had never really paid much attention to the number of white students in most of his classes. As he surveyed his History class, which was predominantly white, K Smooth couldn't help asking himself, "I wonder how many of my classmates were born with *silver spoons* in their mouths?" He still couldn't get over all that his Uncle Josh had said to him, J.R., and Cocky at the house out in White Plains. He had been calling J.R.'s father *Uncle Josh*, since he was eight years old.

Truthfully, Uncle Josh's speech had not only opened his eyes, but also his *mind* to a lot of things, in which K Smooth couldn't quite get *off* his mind. For one, he had made more than a few *choices*, in his sixteen years, that he now realized that he certainly was not ready, or prepared for the *repercussions!* Especially knowing that the *repercussions* would have only been *penalties*....opposed to *rewards*!

Like for instance, all the girls he'd already had *unprotected* sex with! Or, the fact that, he'd held illegal drugs in his mother's house, for Cocky, just so Cocky's mother wouldn't get a hold of them. In light of his many mistakes, K Smooth was just glad that none of his decisions had effected his grades! He'd been an *A+* student since elementary school, as well as gotten *skipped* a grade when he was a student at Shimar.

Never did it require long hours of study, for K Smooth to Ace a test. He also possessed the ability to see, or hear something *once* and memorize it.

Nonetheless, he often wished that he'd attended a school such as Andrew Jackson, Springfield Garden, or Jamaica high because none of his homeboys, who'd attended those schools, ever seemed to have as much school work, homework, or as many test as he received at Benjamin Cardoza.

K Smooth couldn't get out of his head, what Uncle Josh had pulled him to the side and said, when they'd returned from White Plains that night.

"I know I've emphasized that you all get in tune with yourselves, and surroundings. However, I do not want you to misconstrue *surroundings* to mean the *streets.* Nor do I want you to allow someone else's interest, to become yours. In a lot of ways, *your* thinking and surroundings already differ from that of J.R.'s, Cocky's, Reese's, and Steve O's. You just have to start paying more attention to the ways of people, places, and things within your daily circumference." Joshua explained, before inquiring, "The Caucasions have created a history, present, and an undeniable future using the *LLC* method. Do you know what that means?"

K Smooth smiled, considering it was an easy enough question.

"I know all about a Limited Liability Company." K Smooth answered.

At that, Joshua smiled as well, then said, "That's something in which every young Black male, and female should familiarize themselves with. However, the *LLC* method in question, is to Look, Learn, *and* Capitalize."

As K Smooth sat in his, predominantly white, History class *that* was exactly what he intended to do

"What's the deal stranger?" J.R. asked, as he approached Reese in front of Eddie's game room. "I thought maybe you *moved* out of the neighborhood."

"Nah, I'm still around." Reese laughed. "Me and my mom just been going through some shit, at the crib lately. So she decided it would probably be best if she and I stayed with some family, out in Red Hook for a little while." He explained, leaving out the part about his father becoming a heavy alcohol drinker, as a result of getting laid off of his job, and thus becoming physically abusive towards he and his mother. The last beating prompted his mother to pack up all her and Reese's belongings, and move in with her sister out in Red Hook, Brooklyn. After several *pleading* telephone calls, unexpected visits, flowers, tearful *promises* to seek professional help, and ultimately raising his right hand to God that he'd never lay another finger on her, or their son ever again....she and Reese returned home.

"I came by your crib a *few* times, over the past few weeks, and each time I stopped by your old man would yell *Reese doesn't live here anymore!* And slam the door in my face." J.R. said. "The first couple of times, I could tell he was drunk as a skunk!" He laughed. "But, he also had this crazy ass look in his eyes! And all I kept thinking to myself was, I hope his ass ain't go *Postal*, or have you and your moms *hostage* up in that piece!"

At that, Reese couldn't help laughing. "Nah, I wouldn't say it was *that* serious!" Changing the subject, he asked, "Man, is it true that you and Cocky caught a case?"

J.R. nodded his head, yes. Then said, "It's a long story, which I'll fill you in on later. Right now, I see Blue coming up the block." He said, spotting Blue's 79 Seville making its approach. "I talked him into taking me on a joy ride through Jamaica. You rolling or what?" He half *asked*, half *suggested.*

"I'm with you kid," Reese replied with a smile on his face, hearing Blue's sound system *thump*. Yet, the Caddy hadn't even made it half way up the block!

When Blue pulled up to the curb, the two boys were clearly in awe of the spanky clean black Cadillac! The vehicle was already approaching five years old, however, Blue had it shining as if he'd just driven it off the showroom floor! The interior was charcoal gray, charcoal gray carpeting, custom floor mats that had *Blue* engraved, wood grain on the dash board *and* doors, thin striped white walls, with an even thinner strip of gold running through them, and the shiniest chrome *spike* rims either boy had ever seen!

In the tape deck was, *Before I Let Go,* by Frankie Beverly and Maze, which Blue called, "Jamaica's anthem!"

Stepping out of the car, Blue was damn near shouting when he asked, "What's up little homies? Y'all ready to be out, or what?"

"Yeah, we ready!" Exclaimed Cocky, still eyeing the Caddy.

"For sure." J.R. added. "So, what's our first stop?" He asked.

"Well, Jamaica's pretty big, but I was thinking we'd swing through Rockaway Boulevard first. After we leave there we can ride through Baisley Projects, then stroll down the Boulevard." He said, referring to New York Boulevard. "See some of my people, then check out Forty Projects." As an after thought he added, "Oh yeah, if it's not too late, we can also swing through Rochdale Village, where *all* the honeys are at!" He laughed.

When they'd reached there first destination J.R. encountered more than a few cats, whom he'd went to *Shimar* with, and was surprised by how many of them were hustling!

"Nigga, we been clocking dollars before graduating *to* Shimar!" A few of them had revealed to him. Which, now, explained how and why so many of his school mates, from Rockaway Boulevard, stayed on top of their *wear* game! Back then, they used the term *freshly dipped!*

They didn't stick around too long, being that they had other stops to make, but J.R. did promise a few of his old school mates that they'd be seeing him again.

J.R. had heard *a lot* about Baisley Projects, yet, he couldn't help thinking that maybe some of what he'd heard was exaggeration, seeing how the project looked relatively small, quiet, and clean compared to some of the other housing developments he'd seen throughout Queens. Although he'd never been *inside* the project, he, his sister Pam, and their parents had eaten at Carmichael's Diner, which was located in the vicinity, on at least two occasions.

Once he, Reese, and Blue entered the projects J.R.could immediately tell that the inner walls, told an entirely different story from the outer bricks! Also, he couldn't help noticing that majority of the cats whom Blue introduced him and Cocky to, had names like Prince, Justice, Born, Supreme, Wise, Black, Cee Just, God Be, Education, and so on!

Getting back into the Caddy, Blue commented, "These niggas are getting so much bread around here, I wouldn't be surprised if they had money counting machines in *every* building!"

Driving down New York Boulevard was a scene unmatched by any of the previous stops! Niggas were making sells out in the open on 109th Avenue, while right up the street on 108th the cops had a group of young hustlers faced down on the ground!

"I guess we'll have to visit the Boulevard *another* time!" Blue laughed, as he made a left turn onto South Road, heading towards Forty Projects.

J.R. noticed that the scene around Forty, wasn't too much different from what he'd observed on the Boulevard. Young cats were selling various drugs right out in the open. In fact, it kind of reminded him of 150th Street, where drugs were bought, sold, and *used* as if it was legal. Yet, the difference was, on 150th street you didn't have so many children playing right there in the vicinity, young mothers strutting their stuff trying to attract the young dealers, and countless elderly people sitting in the windows taking it *all* in

Another obvious difference was, whereas cats from *Baisley* had showed love, or at least respect, cats from *Forty* gave off an entirely different vibe! A vibe that unmistakingly said, "If you ain't *copping*, you ain't got no fucking business around here!" Even the cats who knew Blue, and supposedly had respect for him, J.R. couldn't help feeling a vibe that said, "So what you're with Blue….*his* ass can get it too!"

J.R., K Smooth, Cocky, Steve O, and Reese had walked pass Forty Project on a number of occasions, en route to go swimming at Liberty pool, but never once did they enter into the belly of the project, until today! And from the vibe in which he received, J.R. *knew* that if, or when he did get into the game Forty Projects would undoubtedly be his most troublesome endeavor….that was for *sure*!

Nothing could've prepared them for Rochdale Village. The vibe, well maintained surroundings, and most notably the *girls* stood out from the rest!

"Are we still *in* Jamaica?" Reese asked Blue, smiling from ear to ear.

Blue was too preoccupied with the two red bones he

summoned over, to answer Reese's question.

"Ladies, what's good?" Blue asked the two females.

"We're just out here enjoying this beautiful day." One of the girls replied, with a smile.

"I know that's right." Blue smiled as well, then said, "Tonya and Cheryl, I want y'all to meet my two little homies." Instead of making the introduction, he looked the girl named Tonya up and down, licked his lips, then said, "Matter of fact, y'all two can introduce yourselves."

He didn't have to tell Reese twice. "Hey, how y'all doing? My name is Maurice, but everybody calls me Reese." He smiled.

"Hi Reese!" Both girls said in unison.

J.R.'s expression was more of a smirk, opposed to a smile, being that he didn't dig how Blue had referred to him and Reese as his *little* homies! "It's definitely a pleasure to meet two, such attractive, young ladies." J.R. smiled, extending his right hand to the female named Tonya, who happened to be standing directly in front of Blue.

Quickly stepping pass Blue, she took J.R.'s hand into hers, and the two of them exchanged handshakes.

"What does *J.R.* stand for?" She asked.

"Actually my name is Joshua Reed, but I'm also a *Junior*, so take your pick."

"I *like* him!" Tonya looked back at her home girl, and they *both* giggled.

Meanwhile, Blue stood there *heated!* Being that the attraction, on the girl Tonya's part, for J.R. was obvious.

"Now that y'all made y'all little introductions, lets be out!" Blue said, trying to camouflage his attitude.

Just as they were about to walk off the girl Tonya reached into her purse, pulled out a writing pen, scribbled something onto a small piece of paper, handed it to J.R. and said,

"Blue is hardly in the neighborhood, but that doesn't mean *you* have to be a stranger." Smiling flirtatiously, as she gave him her address and telephone number.

"If all goes well, I definitely do not plan on being a stranger to Rochdale Village."

Tonya was somewhat dismayed by his reply, however, she too hoped that all went well, *whatever that meant*, so she'd see the handsome guy again.

As they made their way through the tall buildings, J.R. was *feeling* how the young hustlers, in the building's lobbies, hustled. They were more discreet with it in Rochdale Village, yet a trained eye could see that they were making drug transactions, nonetheless.

He, and Reese, also noticed that a lot of the young hustlers were intimidated, or outright *afraid* of Blue! Nor could they believe, how Blue was able to get fist fulls of money out of the dealers. All he had to do was walk up to most of them, playfully pat their pockets, and say, "Let a nigga hold something!"

Once they were seated in the Caddy, J.R. handed Reese the piece of paper with the girl Tonya's address and telephone number written on it.

Reese stared at the small piece paper with wide eyes, and asked, "You mean to tell me you're going to let *me* have her?"

"Nah," J.R. laughed. "Regina basically *lives* at my crib thesedays, so I trust you not to lose the information. Tonya may very well prove to be an asset someday." He smiled. Blue was busy fumbling through his collection of cassette tapes, acting as if he wasn't paying any attention to the two boys conversation. Once he located the *Jamaica's Anthem*, he popped it into the cassette deck, looked over at J.R. and asked, "So, little homie, what do you think of the hood, being that you've never been off your front porch?" He laughed, giving the music *some* volume as he pulled away from the curb.

J.R. knew that Blue was still upset, by how he had scored points with the girl Tonya, in spite of Blue's *little* homies remark. Yet, he too, couldn't help feeling somewhat *heated* by how Blue had capped off his question. And, in front of Reese, who J.R. knew looked up to him, sort of, like a big brother even though they were the same age.

"Aside from the bad vibe I felt, while in Forty, I'm definitely *feeling* other parts of Jamaica." J.R. replied, then decided to respond to the slick remark Blue had made. "And by the way, *you*, if anybody, should know that I've *been* off of the front porch! I mean, had I not *been* at 48 Park, that night, *you* probably wouldn't even be around, to show Reese and myself around *today*."

Blue shot him a quick sideways glance, then shook his head

up and down, as if to say, *you got that one!*

About a minute or two, away from reaching the block, Blue turned the music all the way down and inquired, “So, what’s the deal with your sister?”

“She’s good.” Was J.R.’s reply.

“That’s not what the fuck I asked.” Blue said, not actually raising his voice. “I mean, what’s *up* with her?” He repeated himself.

“To be frank with you, I’m not the one to keep *up* with Pam, or her affairs.” J.R. deliberately added the word *affairs* knowing it would strike a nerve.

Blue, however, let out a slight laugh, before asking, “Is she still taking trips to rikers island, to visit that *fake* ass drug dealer, she calls a boyfriend?”

“Last I heard, everything was everything with her and Spoon.” J.R. replied, not at all digging him referring to Spoon as being fake, he added, “In fact, I believe they’re about to tie the knot, before Spoon goes up North. That way they can qualify for *conjugal* visits.”

“Oh yeah!” Blue replied with a raised eyebrow. “Damn, I guess that fake ass clown *really* does have it down on Sis, huh?” He shook his head.

“Apparently so,” J.R. answered, then with a smile on his face he added, “For Spoon to be such a fake ass clown, I guess he’s realer than some, considering he *took* Pam from a so called *real* nigga, huh?”

Blue didn’t respond, instead he pulled the Seville along

side the curb, in front of Eddie's, bobbed his head to Frankie B & Maze, then hit the door's unlock switch. Again, he turned the music completely down, and said, "You know what little homie?" Not bothering to look at J.R., before adding, "If you intend to live *long* in these streets, there's at least one thing I suggest you remember!"

"And *what's* that?" J.R. was not sure if he even wanted to know the answer.

""How you *talk* to me!" Blue replied, now making eye contact with J.R., before adding, "Now get the fuck *out* of my shit!"

Chapter Nine.

As a result of his *many* talks with Uncle Josh, K Smooth began to notice the difference in how he socialized, learned from, and interacted with others. Most of his teachers and classmates, thought of K Smooth as being very inquisitive. However, he on the other hand, knew that one must ascertain, *learn by inquiring*, opposed to taking things on face value!

In class, he relished constructive debates, which he would usually dominate. A fact that impressed most of his teachers, especially in History and Science. Yet, as intelligent as he was, people couldn't help liking K Smooth, because not only was he *not* arrogant, he also never projected himself as the *know it all* type. Therefore, only *he* was surprised, when his schoolmates voted him **most well known** *and* **well liked** student at Benjamin Cardoza.

In spite of all the wisdom Uncle Josh was instilling in him, as well as the achievements he'd made in school, K Smooth continued to be sexually active. However, thesedays, he made sure to use *protection*. Being that his school was made up of a mixture of nationalities, he'd slept with Black, Hispanic, Asian, and White females! As far as K Smooth was concerned, the

Hispanics and Asians had indeed lived up to their reputations, as far as being submissive bed partners. Whereas, the Black females had a tendency to teach him something *new*, each and every time. "Being the Mothers of Civilization, I guess it's in their *nature* to teach their men a thing, or two!" Yet, what he noticed about the White females was that, although the one's he'd been with were *freaky* as hell, something was missing. Maybe it was the *rythym,* maybe it was the *soul,* he couldn't be sure. Nevertheless, most of them were born with the silver, gold, or even *platinum* spoons in their mouths, so even though something was obviously missing….it worked out!

Actually, he'd only slept with maybe three White girls, which K Smooth kept on the hush hush, being that it was no secret that the *sisters* despised *brothers* who got down like that! On the same token, that suited the White girls just fine, considering *they* didn't want it out there, that they were into Black guys! So in essence, all those *climbing the fence*….were happy!

One White girl in particular, named Rebecca, who lived out in Rosedale with her father, who was a surgeon at Long Island Jewish hospital, went out of her way to let K Smooth know that there wasn't *anything* she wouldn't do for him! The first time he'd been to her house, he *knew* her old man was sitting on some *major* paper! The size of the house, the furniture, and the paintings said so! An observation in which made him wonder, "Why would such an obviously *privileged* girl, want to attend a *public* school such as Benjamin Cardoza?" It was actually a question K Smooth wanted to ask a number of the privileged

White students, he'd befriended.

Getting the best of his naturally inquisitive mind, K Smooth, one day decided to ask Rebecca, "Why would you attend Cardoza, opposed to one of the many better *private* schools, Queens has to offer? I mean, it's obvious that your Pops can afford to send you to the school of your choice."

"I've already *tried* the private thing, but I happen to like the public thing better." She replied.

"And why is that?" He inquired.

"For one," Began Rebecca, "The whole *private* school curriculum seems so far off base, from what's really going on. And two, there weren't many African American students at the school I attended."

By that, he was certainly dismayed. "And why was *that* a concern of yours?" He asked with a raised eyebrow.

"Well," Began Rebecca, this time reaching down, gently squeezing his genitalia, before continuing, "Because I tried the White *thing*, but I happen to like the Black *thing* better!" She smiled, then licked her lips.

Never mind the fact, that Rebecca too, was missing *something*! K Smooth decided that she was a keeper! One, because her father was *never* home, in fact she'd given him a key to the crib! Two, she had a tendency to spoil him with gifts *and* money, in fact it was Rebecca who had given him the *four thousand dollars* in which he used towards J.R. and Cocky's bail!

But, above all, Rebecca Schalwalski was a stone cold….

freak!!!

"Man are you *sure* this is a good idea?" K Smooth questioned J.R.

"Didn't you say Shorty *invited* you over to the crib?" J.R. answered his question *with* a question, before adding, "Besides, if niggas get stupid, I got this!" Reaching down, exposing the small .380 automatic handgun stuffed in his boot.

"That little ass gun!" Exclaimed K Smooth, looking from the gun to J.R., in disbelief. "You might as well have left that shit home! From what I've heard, about them niggas from Baisley projects, I wouldn't be surprised if they didn't have *Cannons* positioned at, more than a few apartment windows!"

"Whatever kid!" J.R. laughed, shaking his head. "She *did* give you the building, and apartment number, I hope?"

"Yeah, I have it right here." K Smooth replied, retrieving the small piece of paper from his pocket.

"Ai'ight then," J.R. smiled, marching ahead. He could care less about seeing the girl who'd invited K Smooth over to her crib, J.R.'s main concern was getting a more in depth look and the project, and it's surrounding areas, being that it had been a while ago since that time Blue had brought him, and Cocky, through.

"We got like four blocks, or so, before we reach the projects. So, how about you entertain me with one of your White girl stories, whom you happen to be so *fond* of thesedays." J.R.

looked over at K Smooth and laughed.

"Newsflash nigga," K Smooth interjected, although not really offended, "If it wasn't for me *fondling* at least one of those White girls, your ass would *still* be on rikers island! Matter of fact, let me rephrase that, them Brooklyn niggas would've undoubtedly murdered your behind!"

"Yeah, yeah, yeah," J.R. laughed. "Spare me the would've, could've, should've and just tell me one of your *cracker* stories!"

"Man, if I didn't know any better, I'd swear *you* had a thing for them so called crackers!" K Smooth looked at J.R. suspiciously, before adding, "Because you sure as hell like *hearing* about'em!"

With that said, J.R. left the subject alone.

However, once they were within a two block radius, of their destination, K Smooth thought about it, then said, "Man, tha first time I was with Rebecca,,,,,"

"Who the *fuck* is Rebecca?" J.R. cut him off.

"The girl who *bailed* your ass out!" K Smooth replied, not appreciating being interrupted. "Now, let me finish my story!" He added, then said, "We was at her crib, when she got down on her knees and began to un-do my pants, because you *know* how them snow bunnies go,,,,"

"Nah Bro, I *don't* know." Again, J.R. interrupted him. "But go on, I'm listening." "Well," K Smooth continued, more then ready to give J.R. the 101 on White chicks. "For some reason, they seem to love *giving* blow jobs, almost as much as a nigga loves *receiving* them!" He revealed with a smile. "So, when she finally got my zipper to act right, and succeeded in whipping my shit out, man you should've *seen* her eyes!" "Nigga, I didn't ask you to *make up* some shit!" J.R Laughed, then said, "If you ain't gonna tell me a *real* story,,,,"

This time it was K Smooth who interrupted him. "Man, I bullshit you *not*!" He exclaimed. "The damn girl's eyes were the size of golf balls!" He laughed. "So a nigga definitely proud and shit, seeing her reaction to what the kid be working with! But then, I look down, because the broad got me somewhat dismayed as she held my Johnson in one hand, yet she had her head bowed towards the floor! Shrugging her odd behavior off, I smiled, and asked, "So, would you say I'm *blessed*?"

Opposed to an immediate response, she continued to look down at whatever had her attention, on the floor. Then suddenly, she looked up into my eyes, with a huge smile on her face, and replied, "Of course you're *blessed*! Why else would you think I had my head bowed?" She asked, still smiling, before adding, "I was actually giving *thanks!"*

"With *that* said," Continued K Smooth. "She *swallowed* it!" He laughed.

J.R. knew the nigga was lying! Nevertheless, the two of them laughed all the way to the projects!

Upon locating the building in which they were looking for, they also spotted a crowd of at least fifteen dudes, standing in front of the building. As they got closer to the entrance, they observed at least another *fifteen* stationed in the building's lobby.

As the two of them entered the building, they could feel that all eyes were on them! Yet, J.R. and K Smooth avoided returning any eye contact, as they proceeded towards the elevator. Making matters worst, the elevator seemly took forever!

"Y'all niggas looking for someone specific, in *my* building?" Asked one of the dudes, who couldn't have been much older than they.

Looking in his direction, J.R. just shook his head, seeing how dude was putting on the mad screw face.

"Actually we are." K Smooth answered, before adding. "But considering *you're* obviously not *her*, we'll just try her apartment."

Even *J.R.* was caught off guard by K Smooth's reply!

Dude continued to stare at K Smooth, his expression clearly asking, "*Is this nigga for real? Or, is he just plain fucking crazy?"*

Unbeknownst to dude, J.R. was asking himself the *same* thing!

It wasn't long, at all, before the small lobby got *real* crowded, and *real* quiet! Being that the cats who were previously standing out front, were also now inside.

Seeing how potentially dangerous the situation had become, J.R. knew it was up to him to *try* to defuse it! Stepping directly beneath the lobby's dim florescent light, J.R. lifted his shirt, at the same time turning around slowly, enabling *all* to see that he wasn't strapped!

"Look man," J.R. began, looking into the eyes of the dude

who had initially questioned them. "We ain't *packing*, we ain't the *police*, and we certainly ain't come around here looking for *trouble*! Unfortunately, but *apparently* my younger brother here," He said, motioning towards K Smooth. "Has heard too many stories, and rumors, about how ruthless you niggas on this side are. Ironically, but again *apparently,* he has this misconstrued notion that it's in our best interest, if we displayed sort of a hardcore disposition, opposed to any signs of fear *or* weakness." J.R. explained. "Again, we're not here looking for trouble, or to bring any. Our purpose for coming through, is to visit a female named Nicole, who lives in this building, and happens to be a classmate of my brother here." He informed them, at the same time touching K Smooth on the shoulder.

The dude, who moments ago was wearing a *screw* face, was now standing there with a *smile* on his face! Not because he was impressed by J.R.'s humbleness, but, because he felt that it was his presence, alone, in which had the *stranger* explaining his position and reason for coming through.

However, a few of the older cats standing around, were indeed impressed by how the young stranger had handled the potentially deadly situation. Which prompted one of them to inquire, "Shorty, where y'all from?"

"South Road and Liverpool Street." J.R. answered.

The older cat nodded his head up and down, at the same time observing the young stranger more closely, before commenting, "I *knew* your face looked familiar. Blue brought you through here once." He recalled.

"Yeah, but that was a while back. So I seriously doubted that any if you cats would've remembered a nigga." J.R. replied, glad that at least one of them remembered his face.

"Matter of fact, if my memory serves me correctly, you're the *same* kid who, about a year ago, *hit up* that kid Dollar Bill from Brooklyn, in C-74." The older dude also recalled, then added, "All I can say, is that you're type lucky you got *bailed* that same day, because that cat was one of the strongest niggas *in* C-74. Even now, months later *and* out here on the bricks, you gotta be careful who you reveal that to, because dude's a ring leader of a *serious* crew. And as badly as you stabbed him up, I'm certain y'all two niggas got beef for life!" He said, before adding. "I was in C-74 when that shit happened. In fact, I was down in 2-Main with my nigga Spoon, and *your* partner Steve O, when you and your other partner came through. Anyway, my name is Born."

"I'm J.R., and this is my brother K Smooth."

Born nodded, then inquired, "Which one of y'all trying to holla at my *little* sister Nicole?"

Both boys were caught off guard, by the mention of the words, *little sister*!

K Smooth smiled, and said, "It ain't like that."

"It can *only* be like that, considering y'all walked all the way over here, from South Road. Not to mention, you being her schoolmate, means you *already* see each other at least five times out of the week." Born replied, letting the kid know that there wasn't anything *slow* about him.

J.R. cleared his throat, and spoke up, "Actually, my brother declined your sister's offer to come through. It was *my* idea that we take her up on her offer."

Born studied J.R. for a good minute, then said, "I like you kid. You're obviously a sharp young dude. In fact, some of these other young niggas can learn a lot from you." He said, looking into a number of faces about the lobby.

"Although my brother didn't want to come through, I do believe he's feeling your sister. I, on the other hand, insisted that we come through, because I'm *feeling* the environment." J.R. informed him.

"My sister's a very pretty girl, so I'm not surprised that your brother may be feeling her. But, I'm a little confused, as to *why* you'd be feeling this here environment?"

"Because, for years, I've been hearing how much money tends to flow through here." J.R. answered.

"And?" Born wanted to know what the kid was getting at.

"And," J.R. began. "I'm seriously thinking about taking over the drug game, in New York City." J.R. informed him, and all those stationed in the lobby, in a *matter of fact* tone of voice.

Whatever *cool* points J.R. had previously won with the dude Born, he'd certainly *lost* them, by making such a bold and crazy statement! A *statement* that caused laughter to erupt in the small, crowded lobby.

Born, however, wasn't laughing or even smiling. Yet, he couldn't help being intrigued by the young boy's confidence, and matter of fact tone. Which caused him to asked, “And how do you *suppose* to accomplish such a feat?”

J.R. looked around the crowded lobby, into the faces of all those who had laughed, and were now awaiting his response, returning his attention to *Born*, he replied,

“By *starting* with South Side Jamaica!”

Chapter Ten.

"Reese, what's good?

"Ain't to much J.R." Reese replied, giving him some dap.

"Isn't it kind of early in the day, to be hanging out on the corner?" J.R. asked, then said, "Don't tell me your Pops showing out again?"

"Nah." Reese laughed. "It's all gravy at the crib. I'm just waiting for Celeste's mom to leave for work." He informed J.R. with a smile on his face.

Celeste Carter was the neighborhood *freak*, who happened to live a few doors down from Eddie's.

"I hope you're *strapped*!" J.R. laughed.

"My nigga, I'm *always* strapped!" Reese replied, pulling out a three pack of Trojan condoms.

Changing the subject, J.R. informed him, "I stopped by you crib yesterday, but your moms said you weren't home, nor did she have any idea *where* you were."

"I got up early yesterday morning, hopped on the train, and headed out to Brooklyn to see my cousin Rock. He's the one who I was telling you, recently came home from Green Haven prison." Reese reminded him.

"Yeah, I recall you talking about him." J.R. replied, then asked, "What's up with him?"

"He's just laying." Reese answered. "And I mean that literally, seeing how so many niggas fear him, and has been breaking him off with money since day one of his release."

"Must be nice!" J.R. laughed.

"You should roll out there with me, next time, so you can meet him." Reese suggested.

"Ai'ight." J.R. agreed. "But on the real, I've been wanting to rap with you about something, for a minute now, but your ass is always on the move!"

"What about?" Reese gave him his full attention, as a result, failed to see Celeste's mom as she passed them by.

"I realize your cousin probably know everybody there is to, out in Red Hook. But, I want *you* to start establishing your own relationships, and ties with niggas while you're out there. As in who is really *who*, and what is actually *what*. Because if things go right, I need you to have already positioned yourself in Brooklyn." J.R. explained, yet not going too in depth.

"As terrified as niggas are of my cousin, I can pretty much do whatever I want. Especially in Red Hook." Reese smiled, honestly believing so.

"Listen Reese," J.R. began. "I've yet to meet your cousin Rock, therefore I do not know what kind of nigga he is. However, I just hope he's a *careful* nigga, because fear alone doesn't make niggas respect you. Some of those cats may be breaking him off, with money, out of fear. Whereas, others may be breaking him off, simply to lock him in. But, you can believe, *none* of them are breaking him off without a motive. Shit, is rough out here, so trust me, ain't nothing *free* thesedays." He explained. "Nevertheless, I need you to establish your *own* ties, because I wouldn't be surprised if you were able to get close to certain niggas, whom your cousin can not."

"I see your point." Reese smiled, then said, "I have a lot of family in the Bronx as well."

"That's good to know." J.R. was also smiling, "But right now, we'll just focus on Brooklyn, being that you're always out there anyway. Plus, I'm not trying to spread myself too thin, if I do decide to become a player in the game, or do some *things*!"

Reese wanted to ask, *what type of things?* But instead, he kept his curiosity to himself, because know matter what those *things* consisted of….he'd ride with J.R.!

"In other words, it's time I start making my trips to Red Hook *count*!" Reese said, with a smile.

"Til death do us part, remember that?" J.R. asked, yet, not looking for a response….because there was no more to be said. Changing the subject, he said,

"By the way, you don't need the whole three pack of Trojans nigga! Let me get one of them, so we can *tag team* Celeste!" He laughed.

J.R. felt like he could sleep for at least twelve hours, after his, and Reese's session with Celeste! Yet, he knew the only way that would happen, was if he turned the telephone's ringer *off*! Just as he got out of bed to do so, it rang.

"Hello?" He groggily answered.

"What's up kid!?!" It was K Smooth, sounding *full* of energy.

"Trying to get some rest." J.R. was hoping he'd gotten the

hint, *not now*!

"Rest? At *this* hour of the day?" K Smooth asked in disbelief, knowing it was out of character for J.R. "There's only two reasons why, I can see a nigga trying to get his rest on in the middle of the day. One, he'd been out *all* night, which I no isn't *your* case, because Aunt Yolanda would've skinned yo'ass alive! Or two, a nigga spent the morning at,,,,," Instead of completing the sentence, K Smooth burst out laughing.

"Yeah, me *and* Reese was over there this morning." J.R. tried to laugh.

"I *see* she's still a beast!" K Smooth shook his head, recalling the many times in which Celeste had worn *him* completely out!

"Anyway, Is there a specific reason for this call, because if not,,,,"

K Smooth cut him off, "I'm not trying to stop you from getting your sleep on, but check it, I just got off the phone with Nicole, and she said that her brother Born wants *us* to come through, tomorrow afternoon, because there's a basketball tournament going down in Baisley Park." K Smooth informed him, then said, "I told her to tell him we'll be there. But, you know me, I ain't try'na watch no damn basketball game! I'm try'na work up my own *sweat*, in apartment #3F!" He laughed, #3F was Nicole's apartment.

"If you told her to tell him we'd be there, *why* call me?" J.R. asked, more than ready to hang up. "I'll rap with you later."

Just as he was about to hang up, K Smooth suddenly

remembered that there was something else, he'd called to tell J.R.

"There's something else I meant to tell you," K Smooth said. "I heard *Blue* shot some nigga in the pool room, on Supthin, last night."

""What else is new? His ass is *always* doing some dumb shit!" J.R. was tired, unimpressed, and certainly ready to hang up. "Call me when you hear his name associated with getting some money!"

"I'm glad *you* know that, because *broke* niggas don't ride around on chrome wheels, and a booming system. Therefore, I wouldn't be the least bit surprised, if the nigga had you and Reese, joy riding through Jamaica in some stolen shit!" K Smooth laughed, even though he was serious.

After they'd hung up, J.R. gave some thought to what K Smooth had said, and told *himself*, "I wouldn't be surprised either."

"Do these tournaments always attract such large crowds?" J.R. inquired.

"Sometimes the crowd is *twice* this size." Born informed him.

"Damn! I never knew so many females were even into basketball." J.R. exclaimed, looking around the park, at all the fine girls, dressed in the skimpiest outfits.

"Trust me, majority of them could care less about basketball. Most of them are out here, for no other reason than to *catch*."

Born laughed, "It's no secret that some of New York City's biggest *Ballers* are out here! And I don't mean *basket ballers* either."

"So what brings *them* out here?" J.R. asked.

"They're the ones sponsoring the teams.Well, each *Baller* assembles a team, to represent their Borough. Infact, they bet *big* money on their team as well. However, not all of the Ballers you see out here have a team, some of them come out to side bet." Born explained, "My crew, sponsers two teams. One of our teams are playing a team from Harlem today, and our other team is playing some cats from the Bronx. Actually, my man Justice, is the one who sponsers both of the Jamaica teams."

Coming into the Park, J.R. had spotted just about *every* luxury car he could name! All of which, looked as if they'd just been professionally waxed, with the *Sun* beaming from their chrome rims!

Although J.R. wasn't much of a basketball fan, he *had* to admit, "These neighborhood ball players, are *definitely* NBA material!" In fact, their game, how they *handled* the ball, was much more fancier than what he'd seen on television.

He also couldn't help noticing, that *K Smooth* was no where in sight!

"His ass is probably up in Born's crib, knocking Nicole's boots off!" J.R. told himself, not at all understanding K Smooth. Realizing that he had a lot to learn. Especially, being that K Smooth was a dude who'd let a female lead him *wherever* she wanted to take him, simply by promising him some ass. Yet, he

knocks *me* for rolling with a *piece*! Thought J.R. A *gun* is what he'd meant by *piece*.

His thoughts were interrupted upon hearing Born shout," Damn, that was an ugly foul!"

J.R. looked down court to see what Born was talking about, but all he caught was a cat, on the sidelines, draped in diamonds and gold, shouting at one of the players!

"Motherfucker, how the hell you letting these soft ass niggas handle yo'ass like that? Nigga you from the *B.X.*! If you gonna play like a bitch, I suggest you put on one of *their* uniforms, and take *my* shit off!" Dude was clearly heated." As a matter of fact, if we *lose* yo'ass better hope one of these Queens niggas drive you home! I can't *believe* we're down 12 points, because of your dumb ass!"

J.R, shook his head, then looked over at Born and said, "I don't know how *cool* your crew is with dude, but it sure as hell sound like he's saying fuck Baisley, and fuck y'all too!"

"Yeah, it does sound like that, doesn't it?" Born laughed. "It's all good kid. In fact, it's home team knowledge, that Justice recently hit dude off with 50 of them things!" Born revealed. Them *things* being kilos of cocaine. "Since the dope is in his possession, it's sort of like a badge of protection, so I'm not surprised that dude feels as though he can say what he want." Born explained, before adding. "However, the fact is, we could care less what he *says*, in the heat of the moment, as long as that *seven hundred and fifty thousand dollars* comes back correct…. that's all that counts!" He revealed, not taking his eyes off the game in progress.

J.R. nodded his head, then said, "So I guess *that* explains the cat from Harlem attitude, last game?"

At that, Born took his eyes away from the court, looked J.R. in the eyes, and with a smile on his face he replied, "*Now* you're getting the picture!"

Chapter Eleven.

A full year had passed, since that night in which Joshua had taken the three boys to the house, out in White Plains.

"A *long* year!" Thought J.R., as his father whipped the Oldsmobile down the Major Deacon Expressway, en route to White Plains.

K Smooth sat silently, in the back seat, waiting to hear what Uncle Josh's plan, for the two of them consisted of. Without any doubt, or question, he was more than ready to play his position, he'd told himself.

Shortly after exiting the expressway, the two boys were both awestruck by the beauty and size of majority of the homes in which they passed! Joshua had taken the same route, their previous trip, however it had been dark outside.

Reaching their destination, both boys followed Joshua into the house, using the same garage entrance they'd used the first time.

Taking his seat at the head of the kitchen table, Joshua spoke, "I do not intend on being here all day, because we have another stop to make before it gets too late." He said, looking across the table at J.R. "Also, it's Sunday, and I promised your mother that we'd be home for dinner. Which I seriously doubt we'll make." He added, looking down at his Sub Marina Rolex watch.

"Anyway, I know quite some time has elapsed since our last visit to White Plains, but it's all good, because patience is indeed a virtue." Joshua looked from one boy to the other, then continued. "Since that time, I *have* noticed somewhat of a change in the both of you. A change that tells me that the two of you may indeed be ready, willing, and able to accomplish something major. That is, with the proper guidance, ability to make effective decisions, and being in tune with yourselves and surroundings. As I stated, I have noticed the changes in the two of you, and your potential is obvious." He smiled, looking each boy in his eyes, before continuing. "However, it is unfortunate that in order for us to be successful in our endeavors, I'll have to deal with the two of you on an individual basis. Mainly because the two of you are about to embark on completely different paths, unassociated paths at that, but they'll be for *one* cause. That one cause will ultimately lead to *one* end. Therefore, today I'll be speaking to each one of you *individually*, opposed to collectively, as I'd done last time we were here. But first, do I need to ask whether or not, the two of you are ready, willing, and able for the three of us to play and *win*?" Joshua asked the two boys.

Both of their response came out in unison, "We're *listening*?"

"All right then." Joshua smiled, then went on. "As you've noticed, I decided not to bring Cocky along for this trip. Although he's one of your comrades, the decision will be left in each of your hands, as to *who* you have on your team. Which is more so directed at you J.R., due to the path in which you'll be traveling down. But I do think it'll be in your best interest that you keep each of your childhood comrades beside you. In fact, I've already taken it upon myself to retain one of New York's best law firms, to represent Steve O on his case. I seriously doubt he'll walk away with time served, but the lawyers feel confident they can work out a decent plea bargain. Especially since the case has gotten quite old, and there isn't anymore Media hype surrounding it. Anyway," He said, looking towards J.R. "You can take a look around, since you didn't get to do so last time we came out here. While I rap with Kenny. The door behind me will lead you into the living room."

With that said, J.R. exited the kitchen, closing the door behind him.

Looking K Smooth directly in his eyes, Joshua began to speak, "Although you've referred to me as *Uncle* Josh for many years, I'm aware that you also view me as a *father* figure as well. Just as, I too, view you as my *son*. For quite some time now, I've emphasized the importance of *choices*, but in actuality every man's destiny is predetermined, because we are *all* born with greatness. Most of us, unfortunately, go through *life* not knowing, or getting in tune with who we really are. Making it impossible for us to tap into, and take advantage of our true potential." Joshua explained. "

"I told the two of you, that I've noticed some changes in

you all. But the fact is, it is inevitable that *you* are the one who must take an isolated route. In order for us to achieve our desired outcome, you must separate yourself from your friends, and your current environment." Joshua explained, then added. "I'm sure you already know, that it is *you* who will take the legitimate path, in all of this. Do I *wish* it was my biological son, J.R., who was taking the less dangerous path? Of course I do. But, our desired outcome is *winning*, and no team has ever *won* when, or if their strategy is infected with favoritism." K Smooth knew that Uncle Josh realized that it was *he*, who had the intellect, charisma, socializing skills, and patience to play his part.

"In time, I'll teach you *all* that I know, regarding banking, the stock market, investments, real estate, the importance of association, and the effectiveness of being politically connected. You're about to enter College, which is one of, if not *the*, most imperative phases of your life. So now, is when you *must* chose wisely. I'm aware that a number of excellent schools have accepted you, but it would undoubtedly benefit you to attend a College, or University right here in the tri-state area." Joshua suggested, meaning New York, New Jersey, or Connecticut.

"I say that, because *my* associates, connections, and overall influence are mainly in these regions. I'm not sure if you're familiar with, or even heard of Councilwoman Nadine Shepard?" Joshua asked.

K Smooth was very familiar with the name, and face, being that she was the City Councilwoman for the District of Queens, and her beautiful face seemed to always be on the television news, or in the news papers!

"In any event," Joshua continued. "I've prearranged for you to take a job, interning for her. It's not a paid position, but you'll be working closely with her, at her office in Kew Gardens. You can start whenever *you* feel you're ready. In the meantime, focus on the school you wish to attend, so we'll know what area to secure you an apartment. Also, I request that you start familiarizing yourself with current political events, and even attending some of those Community meetings which are open to the public. I'm sure it will all help to *wow* Ms. Shepard." Joshua laughed, before asking. "Are there any comments, or complaints regarding anything I've suggested thus far?"

"I'm cool with everything you've suggested, but I *do* have one question." K Smooth replied.

"And that is?"

"Would *tomorrow* be too soon to make my acquaintance with the Councilwoman?" K Smooth asked, with a smile on his face.

At that, Joshua too, couldn't help smiling. "That could certainly be arranged. Now, if you will, please go and find J.R. so I can have a few words with him."

Looking J.R. in the eyes, from across the table, Joshua smiled and posed his first question to his first and *only* born son.

"What is it that has you so drawn to the streets? It is

imperative that I hear you out, before we proceed with any further conversation, or planning."

Returning his father's stare, J.R. replied, "Although I've done some foolish things, in the past, which I'm sure has offended you and mom. I assure you, my actions weren't results of rebellion or any of that nonsense. Nor, did I set out to deliberately offend either of you, just as I hope my *response* doesn't offend you now. But, prior to our previous visit here, to White Plains, you've never revealed to *me* that you've played the game. Yet, I've found myself attracted to the streets, long *before* that visit even occurred. Be it as it may, although you didn't play the game as *long* as you've initially set out to, you admitted to playing it *hard*. Whereas, *hard* could only mean, that you *did* whatever you had to *do* in that course of time. Some say that nothing happens by coincidence, others say that we are the sole controllers of our destiny. But, I'm inclined to believe that sometimes, and it can very well be *unfortunate*, the father's sins are inevitably passed on to the son." Meaning it was more than likely in his....blood!

As Joshua continued to stare into the eyes of his teenage son, he didn't even bother to wipe away the tear, as it rolled down his left cheek.

"You know, it's funny how we, as parents, sometime have a tendency to underestimate our children's intelligence, because I've always felt that it would be an offense to *you*, for me to reveal that I was once a major player in the game. But I knew, even before we had our sit down last year, that it would be *you*, opposed to Kenny, whose path would involve the streets. Eugene was the businessman, who happened to venture into the streets. Whereas, I was the street soldier, who happened to venture into business. We were who *we* were, and I guess you're right, our sons are also who *we* are." Joshua shook his head.

"With all of my street knowledge, I know it sounds ironic for me to say this, but *your* path will be the more difficult of the two for me to give direction on. I say this because, the streets are forever changing, and so are the rules to the game. Which makes it unpredictable. So my most pertinent advice would be, to *not* let the streets predict you. Your ways, your actions, or your moves." Joshua explained. "Meaning, you'll have to set your own rules, and live by them. However, you can count on me to enlighten you to the most essential elements, as I know them, to survive this so called game, and how I see us winning in the end. Money, power, and respect has always, and always will be, pertinent elements of the game. But keep in mind, *they* are but three. There are *many* more elements required, and to learn in order to be successful in this endeavor of ours. Which we'll touch on as time passes. Right now, we have to work on setting you and Kenny up, into key player positions. Nothing falls into place over night, but I see you've taken my advice, which was getting in tune with the streets. And just because you possess this desire to obtain money, power, and respect you can *never* allow another man's definition of the three, become yours. The *money* you generate, I'll show you how to clean and invest it. Well, you *personally*, will not be a part of the cleaning and investing process, but it'll all be yours in the end. So it's important that you not get caught up into the cars, jewelry, clothes, and all that flashy material stuff. It'll only defeat our purpose if you do." Joshua explained, before continuing. "As for *power*, it's a combination of many things. Such as respect, fear, love, influence, manipulation, and so on. But truthfully, the most powerful and effective asset to our team, is going to be Kenneth Shannon." Joshua smiled proudly.

"As for *respect*," He continued. "You've already familiarized yourself with the streets, so I'm confident you have at least an idea of what must be done to *earn* yours. But I will tell you this, once you've made your mark, it'll be to your advantage that you become somewhat invisible. Because being *seen* goes back to being *predictable*. Yet, being seen and being *felt* are entirely different, because a man can definitely make his presence felt without constantly being seen." Joshua informed J.R. before also letting him know, "I've already reached out to some Italians, who I use to put in work for, and placed an order for 200 kilos of cocaine. They fronted me the weight, and they're asking for ten thousand dollars a brick. So, it is your responsibility to bring in two million dollars. But, being that this is your first flip, and a heavy one I might add," Joshua laughed. "I decided to hit the Italians off with half the paper up front, which I'll give them tomorrow, and tell them that you'll have the remaining one million in 60 days. I picked up the weight a few days ago, it's stashed at a place Eugene and I use to use for a stash house, out in Forest Hills. I'll take you by there tonight, after we drop Kenny off home. Under no circumstances is *he*, or *anyone* else, to know about your stash spot." Joshua instructed J.R. in a very serious tone of voice, before adding. "The Italians have also provided me with two vehicles, both equipped with hidden stash compartments. I'll provide you with the keys to the house and the cars, when we get to Forest Hills. In closing, just remember what I've previously told you." Joshua was staring J.R. directly in his eyes.

"For *every* choice we make, there's undoubtedly a reward or penalty. So, I suggest you choose your people wisely, because in this game a man is only as *strong* as his *weakest* link!" Pushing his chair back, and getting up from the table, Joshua asked the same question in which he'd previously asked K Smooth.

"Are there any comments or complaints, about anything I've said or suggested thus far?"

"Just one." J.R. replied.

"And that is?"

"After I flip the first couple of bricks, can I go and get my little homeboy Jamel out of jail?" J.R. asked.

All Joshua could do was smile, realizing that J.R. would do just fine in the game….

J.R. couldn't believe his eyes, as he looked around the spacious condo, his father referred to as the stash house.

"If *this* is what a stash house looks like, I guess *we* live in a shack!" J.R. commented, before letting out a laugh.

"I've been *trying* to get your mother, and KeKe, to move off of South Road for quite some time now, but apparently the two of them feel as though they'd be betraying the neighborhood by moving out. I swear, I just can't understand it! I told the two of them that it wasn't my desire to take the ghetto out of them, but at least they could let me take them out of the ghetto!" Joshua laughed, at the same time shaking his head.

"I guess they've put so much into each of their homes, they've become attached to them." J.R. replied, in his mom and KeKe's defense.

"I guess." Joshua said, shrugged his shoulders, then changed the subject. "As of right now, the condo and the two vehicles belongs to you. You *do* know how the stash compartments work?"

"Yeah, I was watching you very closing as you gave your demonstration." J.R. was clearly impressed by how the stash spots were set up, especially in the condo, where in its master bedroom closet a round PVC pipe was camouflaged by the thick carpet, and ran directly down to the condo beneath it. *Both* condos now belonged to J.R.

"Also, I want you to have Regina rent an apartment somewhere close by. It doesn't necessarily have to be in Forrest Hills, but, close enough to enable you to keep check on the condos." Joshua suggested.

"She'll be on it tomorrow." J.R. replied.

"From here on out, it's pretty much your show." Joshua smiled, even though he'd never been as serious, about a mission, as he was at that moment. "I know you have some big plans for South Jamaica, but don't try to accomplish them over night. I can take care of and protect your mom and I, you just protect yourself at all cost. Most people's motto is; keep your friends close, and your enemies even closer." Joshua shrugged, then added, "But *my* motto has always been; if he or she is a known enemy, get *rid* of them! And, if you feel you need to keep a so called friend *close*, get rid of him or her too! Always remember though, those you *do* trust, keep at a minimum." Joshua explained to J.R. what *his* philosophy had always been.

"I got you dad." J.R. nodded his understanding.

"No." Joshua laughed. "I was just saying *that* was *my* motto, when I was running the streets."

"I understand that." J.R. replied in a very serious tone, before adding, "But, if it worked for *you*, I'll make it work for *me*!"

Chapter Twelve.

"This really isn't a good time to be hanging out in the projects." Born informed J.R. "But you sounded kind of urgent, over the phone, this morning. What's the deal?"

"Actually, my intentions were to wait about a week, or two, before I sat down to rap with you about some things. But then, I heard your man Justice got picked up by them folks, so I decided to expedite things." J.R. explained.

"What does the Feds snatching my man have to do with anything you'd want to rap with me about?" Born was clearly dismayed.

"I realize Justice played a major role on your team, but what I really need to know is, does his arrest place the rest of y'all in a slump? Or, are y'all looking decent on the money and the work?" J.R .inquired, hoping Born would be truthful in his answer.

Before responding, Born asked himself if he should even be having such a conversation with the kid J.R? Considering it was no secret that, the Feds had intentions of bringing down the entire team, J.R. was an outsider, and they'd never rapped on that level before. Yet, he couldn't help feeling that the kid J.R. was a stand up dude, therefore he replied, "I'm sure you know, or at least *heard*, how big the family is. Which means, there are a lot of mouths to feed. Earlier today, I went and dropped two hundred thousand on Justice's people, so they can deal with the lawyers. Than I got with the Columbians, and paid off most of Justice's tab, or rather *our* tab. Now, after all is said and done, I'm sitting on a little over eighty grand." Born explained, then revealed, "I'm thinking about giving eight of my niggas, ten grand apiece, which they can use to grind with for a minute. Hopefully, in a few months, when we all meet at the table again, we'll be in a much better position. Financially that is." He smiled, showing optimism.

"Wouldn't it have been simpler to explain your position to the Columbians, when you went and broke bread with them today?" J.R. asked.

Born smiled, nodded his head, remembering why he liked the kid J.R. from jump. "I started to. But, it was Justice who had always dealt with them." Born revealed, before adding, "All I can do is *hope* that they recognize, and admire my thoroughness, and eventually holla back."

J.R. knew Born was referring to the fact that, he'd saw to it *immediately* that the connect had gotten their money. Or at least majority of it.

"Besides," Born continued. "I need for them to see, and realize what a thorough nigga *Justice* is as well. That niggas such as he do not fold under pressure. Once they see what time it is, I'm confident the Columbians will reach out to me." He produced a smile, which was followed by a wink. "In the meantime, I just gotta figure out which way I wanna proceed with the eighty cent we have left."

"How much were the Columbians giving y'all the bricks for?" J.R. inquired.

"Twelve thousand five hundred." Born replied.

J.R. nodded his head, then looked off, as he made a mental calculation. Looking back at Born, he said, "Check it, there's no way I can match, or beat, the Columbians price right now. But, give me a minute to prove my potential, and I'm confident I'll eventually be able to do twelve five as well."

"I'm not following you." Born was obviously confused by what J.R. was getting at.

"Listen," J.R. said with a smile. "I'm going to keep you, and your team in motion. In fact, I'm going to send my partner Reese through here later, to scoop up that eighty grand, which I'll deduct from the twenty five kilos I'll be hitting you off with today." Born too, was now smiling!

"Kid, I *know* you bullshitting?" He asked, hoping J.R. hadn't been.

"Did you *honestly* believe that I was bullshitting, when I said that I was thinking about taking over the game? And that, I would start with South Jamaica?" Before Born could reply, J.R. added, "I'm not out here trying to live off my father's reputation, but I assure you, *bullshitting* is definitely not in my blood."

All Born could do was stand there with a smile on his face.

"Let me get the keys to your jeep, and you can take this."

J.R. instructed, handing Born a single key.

Born accepted the key, then handed his over to J.R. "What am I suppose to do with this?" He asked, looking down at the mysterious key.

"*That* my man, will open the door to the empire we're about to build." J.R. laughed, even though he was serious as cancer. "Parked up the block, at the bus terminal on Linden & New York Boulevard, you'll find a black Mazda 626. I'll hit you on your cell phone, after Reese comes through and snatch that bread, and explain how the stash compartment works."

"So this here," Born repeated, looking at the lone key. "Is to the Mazda parked at the bus terminal?"

"To the Mazda, *and* the twenty *keys* in the stash compartment." J.R. turned, and proceeded towards Born's money green Cherokee.

As he drove down 150th street, J.R. couldn't help feeling more than a bit uneasy, being that it was where he'd already made his first mistake, getting arrested with Cocky. Therefore, he was certainly relieved to see that Cocky was already in front of his building, awaiting his arrival, when J.R. pulled alongside the curb.

"What's good homie?" J.R. asked smiling, once the passenger's window had completely descended.

"Ain't too much." Cocky replied, eyeing the spanking clean Cherokee, before asking, "What *you* know good?" With a smile on his face.

"Actually homie, it's *all* good." J.R. laughed, then added, "But I'm sure you don't expect me to elaborate, parked on *this* hot ass block?!?" With that said, he hit the unlock switch, and Cocky hopped in.

As J.R. pulled away from the curb, Cocky asked, "Where we heading?"

"I think I wanna stop by the Fish House, on Rockaway Boulevard, to see what I can catch." J.R. replied, giving no further detail.

"Nor did Cocky inquire further, being that he was down with J.R. for whatever.

Instead he asked, "Who's shit is this?" Checking out the jeep's interior.

"That's really not important at the moment. The relevant question is, *who's* holding down 150th street?"

"Who's holding it down?" Cocky was clearly dismayed by the question. Mainly because, it wasn't like J.R. to have been concerned with such a thing. Yet, seeing J.R. was serious, he answered, "Nobody really, considering everybody's locked the fuck up these days. You have various stragglers coming through with their packages from time to time, but nobody's doing anything major on the block."

"As of tomorrow, shop is officially closed to *any* and *all* stragglers, because 150th street is now yours." J.R. informed him, in a matter of fact tone.

"How you *figure* that?" Cocky wasn't quite getting what J.R. was implying.

"I like your attitude already." J.R. laughed, then said, "Seeing how you're already allowing *me* to do the figuring."

"I'm still listening." Cocky cut him off.

"Before the block officially becomes yours, there are a few loose ends that needs tying up. Such as, we need to get you an apartment not far from the area, because we damn sure can't have you *controlling* the block, and at the same time, resting your head *on* the block. Which Regina is already looking into, as we speak. It'll more than likely be in one of her girlfriend's name, being that she just copped a crib for she and I to lay our heads. Also, I'm sure you already know the importance of choosing your people wisely, to hold down their positions." J.R. looked Cocky in the eyes, then continued, "Lastly, you'll need to find a junkie, who will allow you to use his or her crib, for a few hours each day for the purpose of a stash location. Tell the junkie we'll hit'em off with five hundred dollars a day." J.R. explained in detail.

"Shit, for five hundred a day, my *moms* will let us use her crib!" Cocky laughed, even though he was serious.

"I'm sure she would, but I'd prefer not to use your old lady's spot." J.R. replied, before adding, "Truthfully, you're about to touch so much money, your moms may even sell us her dope habit."

"What's *that* suppose to mean?" Cocky was more dismayed, than offended by the comment.

"I didn't really mean to much by it, but when your paper *does* get straight, how about working on getting your moms straight as well?" J.R. suggested.

"All I can do is try." Cocky replied, yet sounding as if his mother was a hopeless case, opposed to being optimistic about her potential to become clean.

"Damn! Can you believe how openly these dudes are making sells out here?" Cocky noticed, as they turned onto Rockaway Boulevard.

Instead of responding, J.R. pulled the jeep alongside the curb, hopped out, and started up a conversation with a cat who'd obviously just made a sell, right in front of the small church located near the Van Wyck Expressway.

"What's the deal partner?" J.R. extended his right hand to the dude.

""What you *want* the deal to be?" Dude asked, displaying somewhat of an attitude, before adding, "The only *deal* going down is these." He said, brandishing a fist full of crack filled vials. "And if you and your man ain't copping, y'all need to keep it moving!"

"Nah, we definitely ain't out here to cop. My question was actually a form of greeting, nothing more, nothing less. Considering, we did meet a while back through my nigga Blue, from South Road."

Looking at J.R., and Cocky, more closely, dude smiled and said, "Yeah, your face does look familiar, now that you mention it. But, your man here, doesn't look like the cat who came through with you and Blue that time." Referring to Cocky.

"Damn kid! I bet you never forget a cop's face, as vivid

as your recollection is."

Dude smiled at the compliment.

J.R. went on, "That was actually my other partner Reese, who came through with me and Blue that day. This here is my man Cocky." He said, making the introduction.

"By the way, I doubt you remember the name. I'm J.R." He added.

"I'm Troy." Dude replied, now giving J.R., and Cocky some dap.

J.R. decided to throw a line out there to see Troy's reaction, or better yet response, when he said, "Troy? I don't know, but I'm almost certain that my nigga Jamel use to always talk about his nigga Troy, from Rockaway Boulevard, when he and I was running together in C-74."

"Yo!" The kid Troy exclaimed. "You know Jamel? That's my nigga right there! For real, for real!" He shouted.

"Yeah, he told me that." J.R. lied, with a smile on his face.

"I love that nigga! But, he was just too wild for these streets." Troy said, before adding, "His thing was, if you wasn't off of the *Boulevard*, you wasn't coming around here to eat. Plain and simple. That's how he caught that attempted murder beef, for shooting a nigga who apparently thought shit was candy over on this end."

"I heard." J.R. replied. "So, who got all these niggas out here hustling?" Looking up the block, he couldn't even count all the niggas who were out there getting money.

"It's funny you should ask that question, because it's actually Jamel's older brother C.L., who has the Boulevard on lock these days. But, from what I hear, the nigga's only copping like a half a bird." Troy informed them shaking his head. "That gold digging hooker, he calls a wife, be counting up all the money that comes in, gives him what he needs to re-up, and pocket the rest." Troy laughed, again shaking his head.

"If that's the case, his bitch ass is getting exactly what his hand calls for!" J.R. thought to himself, considering Jamel had informed him how his brother C.L. hadn't made any attempt to hold him down since he'd gotten arrested. *"I know one thing, his bitch ass even think about getting in Jamel's way, when I post his bail and he takes over the Boulevard, I'll personally blow his top off! Brother or not!"* J.R. also told himself. "Why are you way down here, by the expressway and in front of the church making sells, opposed to the heart of the Boulevard?" Cocky asked the kid Troy.

"Shit, you don't *see* the number of niggas down by the Fish House alone! Besides, from where I'm standing, I get to catch all the heads coming off the expressway, and those coming from across the Van Wyck." Troy smiled.

"Makes sense. But damn, in front of the Church?" J.R. thought. Just then, his pager began to vibrate. Thinking it was Born, calling to find out what time he'd be returning the Cherokee, J.R. looked down and was surprised to see that it was Regina paging him. What made him take off running towards the pay phone, directly across the street from the church, was the

fact that she'd put *911* behind her number!

"Regina, what's up?" He asked, once she was on the line.

"Baby," She began, sounding somewhat hysterical. "You need to get down to Jamaica Hospital as soon as possible!"

"Jamaica Hospital?" J.R. asked, completely dismayed, and caught off guard by her instruction. "For what?" He was almost too afraid of her answer.

"It's Pam!" Regina sobbed into the phone. "Blue beat her up *real* bad!!!"

Chapter Thirteen.

"So Kenneth," Councilwoman Nadine Shepard began, "What school will you be attending come Fall?" She asked.

"I've enrolled at Long Island University, and I'll also be taking a few bonus courses at York Community College."

"What subject will you be majoring in?" She further inquired.

"Business Administration. But, allowing me this opportunity to intern for you, will also benefit me tremendously, being that I'm also studying Political Science." K Smooth answered.

Councilwoman Shepard nodded her head, clearly impressed, before responding.

"A businessman well versed in Politics, I *like* that." She smiled.

"Who knows, I may end up a Politician well versed in Business." K Smooth laughed.

"Either, or, you'll be all right." She smiled confidently, yet made herself clear as she added, "As long as you remain focused, because College has just as many distractions as any High School. In fact, you may even find that the older females can be much more aggressive in their approach."

"Thank you Ma'am, for your concern, and your advice. I'll

certainly keep it in mind." K Smooth replied, before producing his perfect white teeth smile, then added,

"However, you can rest assure that no one, or no thing will distract me from the goals I've already set out to attain."

Again, Councilwoman Shepard nodded her head, obviously impressed by the young man who'd only recently come to work for her. "It pleases me to encounter young Black, confident men. Even though, such encounters these days are too few, and far in between." She sighed, then changing the subject she said, "By the way, I realize it's a show of respect, on your part, but Kenneth, I'd greatly appreciate it if you wouldn't address me as *Ma'am.* It makes me feel old!" She laughed, then added, "Besides, I'm really not much older than you are." She smiled, already having knowledge that there was a nine year age gap, between the two of them.

"Yes Ma'am. I mean *Ms. Shepard.*" He corrected himself. "I guess once I get to know you better, or rather working so closely by you, I'll be alright." K Smooth smiled, then revealed, "This being my first job, and working in such close proximity of a mature woman, I'm actually practicing getting use to the whole *Ma'am* thing." He laughed.

Appreciating his honesty, Councilwoman Shepard laughed as well.

"But seriously though," K Smooth became serious. "I've always prided myself for maintaining such a high level of respect for others, especially women."

"I wish *all* men carried themselves in such a manner,

maybe I'd have a husband already." She replied, half joking, half serious.

"Not to be all up in your business," K Smooth smiled. "But I couldn't help noticing, the absence of a wedding ring, on your finger. I guess you weren't just talking about *younger* men, when you said your encounter with Black, confident men were too few and far in between." He shook his head, as if saying, "*What a shame!*"

Looking into her eyes, he added, "It's truly a travesty to find that, such a beautiful, intelligent, and obviously successful lady such as yourself, is unattached. I've often heard how a lot of men have a tendency to be intimidated by strong, intelligent, independent, successful women. Upon hearing such, I couldn't help finding myself baffled. I mean, how can *I*, or *any man,* hope, wish, or expect for their *children* to be strong, intelligent, independent, and successful if we don't look for, appreciate, or respect those traits and qualities in our *women*? In fact, any woman who capitalizes from her God given potential, can only contribute to her man being all that *he* can be."

As Nadine Shepard sat behind her desk, she was indeed speechless! She couldn't believe the mind set, and apparent wisdom Kenneth Shannon obviously possessed.

"And he's still at least eighteen months shy of his 20th birthday!" She reminded herself, incredulously.

"Well, I guess I better get a move on." K Smooth stood up, interrupting her thoughts, as he made his way towards her office's door. "I'm sure there's a stack of paperwork, in the outer office, waiting to be filed, stapled, or mailed out."

"Luckily it doesn't get *too* backed up around here." The Councilwoman smiled, before adding, "*You* just keep in mind that, interning also includes *verbal* training from your boss lady, from time to time. Alright?"

"Whatever you say!" K Smooth laughed. "You *are* the boss."

With that said, he cuffed the small stack of paperwork she'd previously handed him, and made his way out of the office.

As he exited, Nadine watched him closely, realizing that she'd undoubtedly have to be *extra* careful training the 18 year old intern. If not, it would certainly be a devastating blow to her reputation, and future political endeavors if word got out that she had an affair, or seduced a young intern at her office. The public would care less about his physical, or mental level of maturity.

As K Smooth stood over the copy machine, he knew he'd have to be careful working in such close proximity of Councilwoman Nadine Shepard. Not so much because of her obvious inner, and outer beauty. Or, that Uncle Josh had made it a point to instill in him the importance of *not* falling victim to lust, or any and every women whom he'd find attractive. "*Countless men have spent their entire lives striving to attain what they deem success, only to end up losing everything, as a result of falling victim to lust!*" Uncle Josh had told him. However, *neither* were actually K Smooth's reasons, for feeling that he'd need to be extra careful working with Nadine Shepard. It was actually what he'd read in her eyes. Eyes that plainly revealed, "*I, and all of this, can all be yours....if you play your hand right!"*

"What time are you heading out to rikers, to post Jamel's bail?" Joshua asked his son.

"Steve O said he'd be calling me around 3:00 p.m., right after the count clears, so I have to await his call. Once he and are finish rapping, I'm out. Besides, they can snatch him any day, for up North." J.R. replied.

"I think he did the right thing, copping out to the five to fifteen years." Joshua said, referring to the plea Steve O accepted. "I believe he'll go to Elmira for reception, opposed to Downstate."

"He's cool with that. In fact, he hopes they sends him next door, to Elmira population, being that Spoon is there."

Joshua nodded in agreement, hoping that Steve O didn't land in Attica, Clinton, Comstock, or Green Haven considering he was still quite young. Yet, he felt Steve O would be all right regardless! Not to mention, Joshua had already sent word to a number of his incarcerated comrades, to be on the look out for Steven Hughes.

"Speaking of *Spoon*," Joshua said, "Does he know what Blue did to Pam?"

"Nah, by the time he finds out though, the situation will already be dealt with. Besides, on that three to life bid he received, Spoon already qualifies for one of those Shock Incarceration Programs, being that his charge is a non violent offense."

J.R. relayed information he'd previously gotten from Pam. "Therefore, I'm not trying to be the bearer of such bad news, that'll certainly cause him to spazz out up in there, and hinder him from coming home."

"I can't lie, it's certainly been a while, but the ole man definitely have the tools and the experience to deal with a fool like Blue." Joshua smiled. "Besides, I'd much rather you focus on getting that other *million* squared away, because although I told the Italians we'd need 60 days, it's a much better showing to come clean in like 30. A quick flip is always better than a huge profit, especially when you're trying to make an impression." "I feel you Pop." J.R. agreed, and understood. "But, as for Blue, he's been sticking his chest out at me for a minute now, so I think it's time *I* let some of that air out. Besides, it's time I bring the pistols *out*, so every nigga in every money spot in Jamaica, know that I'm coming *in*!"

"I take it you're stopping by the hospital to see your sister today?" Joshua asked. "Actually, it'll be tomorrow when I pay her a visit."

"Why tomorrow, opposed to some time today?" Joshua inquired.

"Because Blue will be *dead* by then." J.R. informed his old man, before adding, "Seeing Pam all scarred up will undoubtedly have its effect, but at least I'll know the nigga who did it....*paid with his life*!!!"

As soon as J.R. exited his crib, he hit Born on his cellular phone.

"I realize you have your hands full," J.R. stated, referring to the 25 kilos, he'd recently hit Born off with, when he came on the line. "But do you think it's possible you'd be able persuade *Blue* to come down to the projects, around 10:00p.m. tonight?" Born's reply brought a huge smile to J.R.'s face...........

Before heading to rikers island, J.R. swung through 150th street to holla at Cocky right quick. Upon spotting him, J.R. blew his car's horn then signaled for Cocky to come over, and get in.

"Listen," J.R. began, as soon as Cocky hopped in, closing the vehicle's door. "The *take over* is set for tomorrow. So I suggest you have your crew ready, and on point. Also, make sure everything is properly set up with the junkie, whose crib we'll be using as our stash spot. And lastly, the niggas you have a rapport with out here, need to see *you* as of tomorrow, because anyone who is not down with our team better find a new block to hustle on. Any questions?" J.R. asked.

"Did Regina set you out with the keys to my new apartment? Because I can see that shit is about to get real ugly around here!" Cocky shook his head.

"Damn kid!" Jamel exclaimed, smiling from ear to ear, upon seeing J.R. awaiting him at the registration building, on rikers island. "When that bitch ass C.O. called my name '*on the bail out'* I was under the impression, that maybe my bitch ass brother *finally* had a change of priority! And decided to come get a nigga." Jamel shook his head, seeing that was not the case, yet he was still smiling....happy to see J.R.

"Actually, I'm much happier to see *you* my nigga, because now I'll feel no remorse when I run C.L. and his lieutenants off the Boulevard." Jamel laughed, then gave J.R. a brotherly hug.

"Yeah, we need to talk about *that*." J.R. informed him. "But it'll have to wait, because right now I have to meet with some people my ole man plugged me into."

"We picking up some weight?" Jamel smiled, already *ready* to get his hands dirty. "Nah homie, we already have plenty of that." J.R. smiled, then revealed, "We have some serious business to attend to, so I'm actually picking up the *tools* we'll need."

Jamel knew that *tools* meant *guns*, and again, he was smiling from ear to ear, before responding, "Say no more!"

Once they'd crossed the bridge, and was now headed towards the Grand Central Parkway, J.R. looked over at his little partner and said, "I'll drop you off at your folks cribs, because I know they'll be happy to know you're home. Also, there's a little something in the glove compartment, for you to get yourself situated. On the gear, that is."

Jamel reached into the glove box, and came out with a thick yellow envelope. Looking at J.R. with a dismayed expression on his face.

J.R. laughed, then informed him, "In that envelope is *ten grand*, take it and do whatever you choose. I'll swing back through, later tonight and pick you up."

Jamel continued to look down at the envelope in hand, yet he didn't bother opening it. Instead he spoke, "Listen big homie, if the *business* you've mentioned involve gunplay, there's no telling how it will ultimately unfold. Therefore, if I end up taking a ride to the cemetery, *or* back to the penitentiary I'd prefer my folks not know about my release."

J.R. nodded his head, not at all surprised by Jamel's thoroughness. Focusing his attention on the road ahead, he replied, "In *that* case, lets go pick us out an arsenal!"

"You mean to tell me *you* don't know the cats name?" Blue asked, in total disbelief!

"I already told you that." Born repeated himself, feigning frustration. "But, you and I both know how niggas talk, so I sent one of my niggas down to Forty projects, to find out all that he can."

"I still can't *believe* that bitch made nigga Spoon, even has the audacity to send a nigga at *me*! Blue!" Blue emphasized by beating his chest. "Isn't his ass in one of those bullshit Shock Programs? I *knew* his ass was a fake wanna be drug dealer. Since when do *kingpins* qualify for Shook Programs?" Blue shook his head laughing.

"I don't believe they moved him to the program yet, but I hear he definitely have a good chance of getting it." Born informed him, then added, "As for a kingpin qualifying for such a program, I *hope* I can qualify my damn self, if I ever get bagged!" He laughed, even though he was dead serious.

"That's because yo'ass is a *wanna be* too! Nigga!" Blue thought to himself, before actually replying, "Anyway, that faggot nigga can send 20 of his people *my* way, watch me send 20 obituaries *his* way! Shit, his lame ass better be easy, if he know what I know." Blue screwed up his face, adding, "Fuck around, I'll catch a bullshit case and be waiting on his ass at Shock!"

Born laughed at that, then inflated Blue's ego by co signing, "I hear you kid! Niggas *know* how you get down for yours." Giving Blue some dap on it, he added,

"But on the same token, you can't sleep on, or underestimate no one. That's why I took it upon myself to see if I could come up with that *name* for you."

"True that, true that." Blue was obviously appreciative. "As soon as you get that niggas handle, get at me with it, so I can show that bitch nigga Spoon that he might have the *right* plan, but, I'm the *wrong* man for him to be sending his toy soldiers at! In fact, I'm done talking. Just holla back with that info."

"True." Born agreed. "What I'll do, if I come up with something, is page you. In your pager, I'll put an appropriate *time* for you to come through and snatch the info. If I don't get at you, that means I haven't found out anything on dude."

"Niggas as strong as *you* are, out here in these streets, don't come up with blanks! I wouldn't be surprised if you *already* knew who this nigga was." Blue looked at Born suspiciously. "It's all good though. I realize that there's a meter attached to favors, so I don't mine owing a real nigga, when all is said and done." Blue smirked, then added, "Just don't hold out on the name for too long! Otherwise, I'll have to come on the set, and start *picking* niggas out!"

"You safe baby!" Born replied, with a reassuring laugh. "Just don't have me waiting too long, for you to come back through, when I hit you on the pager."

The time was 8:30p.m., and Blue's '*Jamaica's Anthem*' was at mid volume, as he sat reclined in the passenger's seat of his Cadillac Seville, while the 19 year old, neighborhood whore, by the name of Yvette, better known as *Easy* licked, sucked, and deep throated his dick! Confirming her reputation, in the hood, as *head specialist*!

Actually, at that very moment, Blue was undecided as to which of the two aroused him more? The superb blow job? Or, seeing his *pager*, clamped onto the sunvisor, indicating Born's number.....followed by 10:00p.m.!

Blue couldn't *stop* talking about the young girl *Easy* Yvette!

"Man, I'm telling you, this chick had me thinking to myself '*fuck coming back over this way' or even worrying about niggas wanting to kill me!*" Blue laughed.

"Oh yeah? Why was that?" Born asked, not really caring either way.

"Because the little nympho fucked *and* sucked me so righteously, I thought I already died and was *in* fucking Heaven!" Again, Blue laughed.

"Damn, like that!?" Born asked wide eyed, seeming impressed.

"Man, I bullshit you *not*!" Blue emphasized *not*. "Had the little hooker been from St. Albans, I'd swear she had to be the same *Yvette* that nigga LL Cool J made that song about!"

"If she like that, you *definitely* gotta bring shorty through one of these days.You no it ain't no fun, if the *team* doesn't get none!" Born laughed.

Blue laughed as well, then replied, "I might just do that, considering it'll be an *easy* payment, on the favor!"

At that, they both laughed.

"Seriously though." Born said, changing the subject, at the same time looking at his gold & stainless steal date-just Rolex, which he wore as an everyday timepiece. Realizing it was *that* time, he continued, "My sources tell me that, the cat who took the hit on you, name is Love. However, you and I both know that there are at least four *Loves* from Forty projects. So, my little man decided to parlay a bit longer, down on that side, until he can narrow it down to the exact nigga you want."

Just then, Born's cellular phone began ringing, which was actually his cue.

"Yeah," Born spoke into the phone. "Damn nigga, how the fuck you gonna call me with all that fucking noise in the backround?" He barked at the caller. "*Of course*, I want you to move to a more quieter spot, stupid!" He shook his head, at the same time placing his hand over the mouth piece, telling Blue, "This my little man calling with that info, but I'ma step out side of the car, so I can hear him better. Matter of fact, Give me something to write with, so I can jot down the nigga Love's address." With that said, Born exited the Cadillac, and shut the door behind him.

"That's what I'm talking bout!" Blue playfully jabbed at the steering wheel. *"If this info pans out, I might just pay yo'ass afterall!"* Blue laughed, with Born in mind. Talking to himself, he added, *"Yeah, I'ma teach that bitch nigga Spoon a lesson about comig at real killers! His so called brother in law, J.R., even knew not to come at me fucked up! And I know for a fact that J.R. has much more heart than his fake drug dealing ass! I swear, the nerve of these characters these days!"* Blue thought to himself incredulously!

Reaching under his seat for his case, which held his cassette collection, he searched until he found his Frankie Beverly & Maze. Smiling, he kissed the cassette, then leaned in to insert it into the tape deck. Adjusting the treble, then the bass, Blue couldn't quite get the girl *Easy* off of his mind!

A distant shadow caught his attention, and Blue looked up to see a young boy, who couldn't have been no more than 13 years old, walking towards his car. In fact, the kid was approaching the car *head on*! An observation that made Blue shake his head , and mumble to himself, *"His little ass better be thankful I don't have the ignition on, because I'd certainly run his young dumb ass over!"* He laughed, then went back to adjusting the sound system to his liking.

The hard tap, on his driver's side window *startled* Blue! However, what *scared* him was seeing the young looking kid standing directly in front of his windshield, pointing what could've only been a .44 magnum, directly at him! Not to mention, J.R. was standing approximately two feet from the drivers side window, yet Blue couldn't assess the huge pistol he was holding, being that it was too close up on the glass! Before he could even flinch, never mind reach for the .9mm Blue kept in his glove compartment....*both* J.R. and Jamel emptied their guns into the car!

J.R. knew that Blue was dead instantly, when his first shell struck him in his left temple! Nonetheless, he inserted another *full* clip into the 18 shot .380, opened the Cadillac's door, leaned directly over Blue's lifeless body, and emptied the *second* clip! Jamel was already behind the wheel of the stolen Volkswagon Jetta when J.R. hopped in, and instructed him, "Lets be out!"

Once they'd gotten about a quarter mile from the crime scene, neither of them saying a word, J.R. smiled and thought to himself, "*Damn, I should've took the Jamaica's Anthem!"*

Chapter Fourteen

When J.R. walked into hospital room 33, all he could do was shake his head, seeing Pam *and* Regina glued to the small television screen, watching *The Young And The Restless*! The two of them were so into their favorite daytime television show, neither of them noticed J.R. enter the room.

Clearing his throat, J.R. spoke, "What's up sis?" With a huge smile on his face.

Simultaneously, the two girls looked in his direction.

Regina returned his smile.

Pam simply rolled her bloodshot eyes, looked him up and down, then as she returned her attention to the soap opera she replied, "Don't come up in here try'na butter me up now!" With an attitude, before adding, "I'm going on my second day in the hospital, and you're just *now* getting here?"

J.R. walked up to her bed, kissed his older sister on her cheek, and replied, "As your brother, who happens to love very much, I know I had a responsibility to see to it that something like this," He said, gently running a finger across her bruised forehead, "*never* happens again. Besides, had I came yesterday, or the day before, I would not have been able to comfort you, because *I* was too filled with rage. But all is well now, *you* just need to get better."

"Ummm humm," Pam half smiled, half smirked.

"By the way, I spoke to your fiancée this morning." J.R. informed her.

Although her eyes were still terribly bloodshot red, they clearly lit up at the mention of Spoon. "What did he say? I hope you assured him that I wasn't hanging out with Blue? Did you tell him how much I love him?" Pam bombarded him with questions. J.R. shook his head, laughed, then said, "Spoon said to tell you he loves you, he knows you weren't with Blue. And no, I did not tell him how *much* you love him."

At that, all three of them laughed.

"What *else* did he have to say?" Pam inquired.

"And I was under the impression *you* were glad to see *me* today!" J.R. shook his head.

"Come here boy!" Pam exclaimed with open arms, giving her brother a tight hug, before adding, "You *know* I love you, and you've certainly made my day, by coming to check on me."

"Yeah, I love you too." J.R. looked at her suspiciously.

Releasing one another from the embrace, Pam looked down at her hands, then looked up into J.R.'s eyes, with an embarrassed smile on her face she asked, "So, what *else* did my baby have to say?"

Regina burst out laughing.

J.R. simply looked up at the ceiling, thinking to himself, "*I guess this is what they mean by hopelessly in love!*"

Returning his attention to Pam, J.R. responded, "He just wants you to hurry up and get well, so he can see you. Also, he asked me to pick up a gift for you, which I did. However, you can't get it until you're released from this place." He said, looking around the pale hospital room.

"Okay." Pam smiled, then asked, "Is *Blue* as badly bruised as I am?" Somewhat understanding what J.R. had implied earlier.

"I'd have to say his condition is much worst than yours, because unlike you, Morphine, Demoral, or no other pain medicine can help him."

It was common for many young, and old hustlers to take trips to areas such as, Baisley projects, Forty projects, and 225th Street & Merrick Boulevard to spend approximately six hundred dollars, for a thousand dollar package of crack cocaine.

The thousand dollar packages consisted of 100 ten dollar vials, or capsules, which most of the hustlers would tap into, turning the 100 into as many as 140! Meaning, the hustlers stood to make at least eight hundred dollars in profit.

Cocky, using the junkie's apartment, recruited six neighborhood females for the purpose of packaging the thousand dollar packages. Unlike the others, Cocky gave the packages to his workers for *five* hundred dollars! He started out with ten workers, each of whom, *easily* moved over ten packages a day! His capsules were sealed with green tops, a nigga coming on the block with any *other* color….got shot!

Cocky also had other workers, who sold powder cocaine as well. The coke was sold in various size capsules, also sealed with green tops, ranging from nickels, dimes, twenties, half grams, and grams.

Everything was moving along like clock work, yet, Cocky did however have one complaint, which he decided to express to J.R., whom he spotted coming up the block.

Pulling along side the curb, J.R. let the pasenger's side window down, and inquired, "Is everything good?"

Before answering, Cocky opened the passenger's door, and climbed inside the Mazda. "Everything is everything out here. But, things could *certainly* be better."

"Oh yeah, how so?" J.R. asked, at the same time pulling the vehicle away from the curb.

"Right now, we're doing phenomenal numbers on the block, but the only reason the cocaine is selling so well is because, majority of the dope fiends like to speed ball. So, if you *truly* want to lock down 150th street, we need to find us a heroin connect." Cocky explained. "Because truth be told, the heroin pushers are the ones who *really* have the block on lock. And we definitely can't run them off, because our coke sells rely heavily on their presence."

Although he understood, J.R. certainly did not like the fact that, someone else had a stronger hold on the block than he! Nor was he trying to accept it.

"In that case, I guess it's time we give the heroin pushers their eviction notices, because I'm sure my people can get us some of that China white. We'll just need for someone to show us how to cut and bag it." J.R. informed him.

"That shouldn't be a problem." Cocky replied.

"Who's moving most of the Harry O on the block these days?"

"An old school cat, name Red." Cocky answered.

J.R. nodded, then rubbed his chin, before instructing him, "Find out *all* you can on this Red character, and get back to me as soon as possible." With that said, J.R. pulled the Mazda along side the same curb, after circling the block. Before Cocky got out, he added, "Tell Red, *J.R.* said, he has twenty four hours." With that said, he pulled off.

He and Jamel had taken over Rockaway Boulevard, with ease! They didn't even have to put the pistol on C.L.'s bitch ass, or any of his crew. As it turned out, C.L. was actually relieved to *be* relieved, as head nigga in charge, of the Boulevard! Mainly because, he had long since grown tired of hugging the block, simply to satisfy a greedy, trifling, and ungrateful wife! And also because, he'd heard the *Feds* were investigating him! Unlike his younger brother Jamel, C.L. was scared to death of going to prison!

Jamel had basically implemented the same program on the Boulevard, as Cocky had on the block. The only difference was, whereas Cocky now had like 20 workers, Jamel had more like 50!!!

Now that everything was in its proper perspective, as far as J.R. was concerned, he couldn't help pulling Jamel aside one day, to inform him, “This is entirely *your* show out here, I’m just supplying the work. However, I would appreciate it if you’d grant me this one favor.” J.R. smiled

“You’ve been more like a big brother to me, than my *own* big brother. So, I’m sure you know that whatever you want goes without saying, or asking!” Jamel assured him, then added, “Til death do us part, remember that?”

“For sure.” J.R. nodded, realizing he’d made a good call, making Jamel a part of his team. “In that case, please inform your workers, from this day forth, nothing is to be sold….*in front of the Church.*”

“Check it,” J.R. was speaking to Reese. “Spoon and I had a conversation today, over the phone, and he informed me that Fat Boy is slowly, but surely, losing his grip on the Forty side. Apparently niggas are starting to feel that his ass ain’t coming home no time soon. But, there’s another cat, name Head, who I hear is filling his shoes, and quick!” J.R. filled him in, then added, “I also hear, this *Head* character has been making inquiries, as to *who* has 150th street. From what I hear, dude is suppose to be somewhat of a strategist of war.” J.R. laughed, even though he knew he couldn’t underestimate *no* nigga, in the streets. “Anyway, as I see it, we need to do something about this cat before he *really* starts feeling himself.” Unconsciously J.R. ran his hand across the handle of his .40 caliber, which was tucked beneath his shirt.

"I agree." Said Reese.

"Spoon suggests that I send *you* down to the projects, to get with one of his former lieutenants, a kid name Wop. He says, Wop has a great deal of respect on that side, not to mention, knows a lot about Head and his crew. You'll hang out with Wop for a few days., posing as a cousin or something, you should be good at that considering you have cousins in all five Boroughs!" J.R. joked, even though it wasn't far from the truth. "Find out all that you can. I want this nigga Head's *head*, and his *territory*. So, we might as well kill two birds with one stone."

"Say no more. I'm on it." Reese assured him.

"If *anything*, don't hesitate to get at me." J.R. said, meaning if the vibe wasn't *right* on the kid Wop's part, which Reese understood.

"Oh yeah," Reese suddenly remembered there was something he needed to bring to J.R.'s attention. "My folks out in Brooklyn, are ready when we are."

"Ai'ight." J.R. smiled. "That'll be our next priority."

Cocky knew he was *clean*, therefore, he didn't even attempt to run, as the gray van pulled to an abrupt stop beside him! Three white plain clothes Detective hopped out, and surrounded him.... Carmine remained seated inside of the van, with a smile on his face. The van's sliding door was wide open, enabling Cocky a clear view of the cop!

"There's no need to place the cuffs on him." Carmine

informed the other officers, before adding, "Truthfully, I was hoping he'd ran, so I could've gotten some target practice." He laughed, at the same time climbing out of the van, getting directly in Cocky's face. "I hear you're doing big things out here these days. I *like* that." He smiled, before continuing, "It means, I'll have a fresh breed of young niggas to haul off to prison. If I'm lucky, I'll get to shoot a few of you in the process."

The other three detectives laughed at that.

Seeing Cocky didn't appear the least bit intimidated, or afraid, the cop instructed him, "Get your black ass in the van!" He barked, as the other three officers proceeded to shove Cocky into the van.

Cocky was smart enough not to try and put up a fight, or resist. Plus, he was aware of the number of eye witnesses on the block, so he seriously doubted that the cops had intentions of doing him bodily harm. What dismayed him was the fact that, Carmine was the only detective to climb into the van behind him.

"It's unfortunate how so much time has elapsed, since I've run into you. But, it's your smart mouthed partner, I can't wait to see." Carmine was referring to J.R. "Lucky for him." The cop smirked, then said, "I was glad to hear that the two of you only received a year probation, on the gun charge. But, had either of your lawyers been half way competent, they would've submitted a motion for dismissal, or at least suppress the gun." The detective laughed, shaking his head, as a result of their lawyers not providing the two of them effective assistance of counsel. "I say that because, I made *sure* that the Prosecutor didn't have any physical evidence to secure a conviction. Do you want to know *why* I did such a thing?" He asked, then reached into his waist and pulled out the huge .45 automatic hand gun, which Cocky recognized immediately. Pointing the pistol directly at Cocky's forehead, he said, "I should shoot your sorry ass right here, right now! But lucky for you, you're not the bastard I want. But what I do want, is for you to make sure that Joshua Reed *Jr*. meets back up with this here *four-fifth*."

He dropped the heavy pistol into Cocky's lap. "Because I've been dying to find out, if *he's* that nigga!"

Chapter Fifteen.

Already College had proven to be an experience for K Smooth. He noticed that, whereas high school had been more of a supervised environment, college required that an individual be responsible or even independent to a degree. To say he enjoyed college would be an understatement, however, it didn't compare to how much he enjoyed working for Councilwoman Nadine Shepard.

In fact, K Smooth had already surpassed the status of *intern* at her office. Whereas, these days, he acted as her personal receptionist, schedule coordinator, file manager, as well as accompanied his boss to a number of speaking engagements. Not to mention, the functions he'd appeared at, in Councilwoman Shepard's behalf, when or if she was otherwise engaged.

K Smooth was certainly impressed, if not astounded by some of the well known, respected, and prominent people he'd met or even had dinner with since working for the Councilwoman. Among them were, Surgeon Generals, Attorney Generals, Governors, Mayors, Police Chiefs, Senators, House Representatives, Representatives from various Organizations such as; BLACK CAUCUS, NAACP, RAINBOW PUSH, ACLU, and countless others! It also surprised him how warmly he'd been embraced by just about all, and how he had fit in, amongst such high ranking/ status individuals, without effort. " *I guess it's destined for me to be among the rich & powerful.*" K Smooth often told himself, with a laugh.

Also, K Smooth was pleased, in that, he'd listened to his Uncle Josh who suggested that he start attending and establishing ties with the Church. As a result of accompanying Aunt Janice, J.R.'s mother's sister, to church on Sundays, he'd come to meet the Reverend Frank L. McCarthy.

Shortly after their acquaintance was made, K Smooth began to notice Reverend McCarthy at a number of the functions in which he and Councilwoman Shepard had also attended. During those functions, the Reverend made it a point to introduce K Smooth to other prominent folks in attendance, usually saying, "Since the day I've met this young man, it has been obvious that God has a divine plan in store for him. Not only am I proud to have him as a member of my church, but also to see how closely he has been working with Councilwomen Shepard, whose efforts in our community have been tremendous."

The day Councilwoman Shepard announced that she'd decided to run for Queens Borough President, K Smooth was not only her biggest supporter, he knew he'd do all within *his* power to insure her that seat.

K Smooth had maintained communication with a number of his former high school classmates, mainly because he recognized that the potential, *and money*, was there for many of them to do big things in their future. And Uncle Josh had long since taught him the importance of association, with the *right* people that is. One by one, K Smooth placed his calls, informing them of his work along side Nadine Shepard and why it was extremely important that she become the next Queens Borough President, considering they had *all* once, and most still did, reside in Queens! Each of his former classmates assured him that they would consider voting for Councilwoman Shepard, even those who hadn't been aware of her endeavors or accomplishments.

Next, K Smooth visited his former high school, and was pleased to see *how* pleased his former teachers, guidance counselors, dean, and some of the students who knew him, or *of* him, who were in lesser grades during his time at Benjamin Cardoza, were to see him! After explaining the reason for his visit, the teachers, guidance counselors, and the dean assured him that they'd take his wish, that they each vote for Nadine Shepard, into account. He was equally impressed when the school's dean allowed him the Auditorium, so that K Smooth could speak to a large group of students, explaining to them the *importance* of voting! At which time, he cleverly slipped in *all* that Councilwoman Shepard had done during her tenor in office, and how much she intended to do in the future, hoping it would influence the students to *influence* their parents and older siblings to consider giving her their vote, in the upcoming election.

Being that both his parents were raised in far Rockaway Queens, and it appeared as though he had countless relatives who resided in Redfern Houses, Ocean Village, Forty, Edgemere,

Hamils, Arvern, and Bay Towers, K Smooth knew a stop through Far Rockaway was without question! Also, he'd gotten Aunt Janice and Reverend McCarthy to use their clout, with various churches, to assist him in his efforts. He already knew that he could count on his mother, Aunt Yolanda, Pam, Regina, their friends, his friends, and his Uncle Joshua's vote. However, what he didn't know was that Joshua had *friends,* who pretty much out numbered, any and all, that K Smooth had reached out to thus far.

Lastly, he placed a call to Rebecca, who cheerfully informed him, "You're gonna live a *long* time, because I was just talking about you to some of my girlfriends!"

"Oh really?" K Smooth laughed, pretty much knowing the nature of their conversation, being that he and Rebecca hadn't been much more than fuck buddies. "I'm glad to hear that you be keeping the lines open with your girlfriends, because I'm campaigning for a friend of mine, who's currently running for Queens Borough President, and we can definitely use all the votes we can get." K Smooth informed her. Responding in a seductive tone of voice, Rebecca replied, "*Anything for you.*" Before adding, "Did I ever tell you how much clout my father has throughout Rosedale, Laurelton, Cambria Heights, Elmhurst, and most of Nassau County."

Even though he didn't need Nassau County, K Smooth was nonetheless impressed.

"I can't say I recall you telling as much, but I'd greatly appreciate having him on my team." He smiled, then asked, "Do you think the good Doctor can be swayed."

"Although I'm a grown woman now, I'll always be Daddy's little girl!" She laughed. "Need I say more?"

"I guess not." K Smooth was sold, yet had his fingers crossed nonetheless.

"My father will do *anything* for me. The question is, what is Kenneth Shannon ready, willing, and able to provide *daddy's little girl* for her assistance?" Rebecca asked.

K Smooth seriously doubted she was lying, or exaggerating the extent of her father's clout, therefore he replied, "I still have the set of keys to your place in Rosedale, so I guess the question is, what time shall I come over?"

Regina knew that it was irrelevant to add any make up to her beautiful flawless caramel skin, therefore all she applied was some raspberry lip gloss to her lips, which she checked in the rear view mirror of the brand new Honda Accord LX, as she drove down South Road. Before leaving her house, she pretty much knew that her Levi 501's were hugging her thighs, and perfectly rounded ass like a pair of stockings! Just as her sheer, almost see through, halter top barely covered her breast!

"*Perfect*!" Regina told herself with a satisfied smile.

As the stop light turned green, Regina made a right turn onto New York Boulevard, where she immediately spotted the guy from the photograph, in which J.R. and Reese had shown her, standing amongst a group of other guys in front of a grocery store. Reese had previously informed her that the grocery store was his main hang out location. Pulling alongside the curb, Regina took her time getting out of the Accord. Closing her door, she walked around to the passengers side, leaned into it's window to retrieve her handbag, at the same time giving the group of guys a clear view of her assets. "*Gotdamn!* Baby girl!" A male's voice loudly exclaimed, superseding the whistles and catcalls. " Something told me *today* was gonna be my lucky day!" He added. As Regina made her way towards the store's entrance she looked in the direction of the guy who'd made the comment, and produced a smile. Meanwhile, thinking to herself, *"I guess some niggas can't help viewing a pretty face and nice ass as a gift, opposed to a curse."* Seeing that the cat who'd made himself heard, was none other than the guy whom J.R. sent her at. Turning to face him, Regina couldn't help inquiring, "If you don't mind me asking, why is it that you feel *today* is your lucky day? Because I would hate to think that you're implying that a sister is *that* easy, or something." She said with just a *little* attitude.

"Nah love!" Dude laughed. "It's just that, we don't get too much *sunshine* around here. It's just sells, bullet shells, and *more* sells!"

Regina nodded her understanding, then turned and headed into the grocery store. She sensed that all eyes were glued to her shapely behind, therefore, she added some extra bounce.

Looking around the small store, Regina felt someone come up behind her.

"What would such a beautiful Queen such as yourself, be needing out of such a hole- in- the- wall store as this?" It was the same dude who had spoken to her outside.

Regina simply smiled, as she made her way towards the counter.

"Actually, all I need is a pack of chewing gum." She responded.

"I'll tell you what. I'ma wait outside, for you, while you get your Juicy Fruit. That way, I can assess which of my hawking ass homeboys I may have to shoot." He laughed, before exiting the store. Holding the door, he turned and added, "When you become mine, I'ma definitely have to bar you from this block! Especially, in them 501's and that halter top!" He shook his head, then made his exodus.

"That boy is crazy!" Laughed the Arab, from behind the counter.

"For *his* sake, he better not be too crazy." Regina mumbled to herself, as she paid for her gum. Chewing gum in hand, she noticed the guy who'd been pursuing her, standing beside her vehicle as she emerged from the store.

"If you're not feeling a nigga, I'll accept that and be on my way, but I would very much appreciate it if you'd give a brother a *minute* of your time?" Dude smiled.

"I'm not into *minute* brothers, but speak your piece." Regina laughed, then took a seat on the hood of her car.

"Baby girl, you'd be surprised by what all I could do to you in sixty seconds!" He laughed, at the same time licking his lips, before adding, "With your sexy chocolate self." "Like I said, I'm not into minute men." Regina reiterated. "By the way, you've already *wasted* like thirty seconds of yours."

"Listen," Dude began, moving in a bit closer. "I honestly feel that today is my lucky day, because beautiful females such as yourself, rarely come through the Boulevard. However, this is definitely the *wrong* place for you and I to be trying to make each others acquaintance." He explained, looking around to make sure no cops were in the vicinity. "Therefore, how about you bless a nigga with a number, address, or some other means to contact you?" He smiled, then added, "And maybe we can put our heads together and come up with the *right* place, to get together."

"You are handsome." Regina replied with a smile, looking him up and down, before adding, "I say, why wait until later to engage in something that can potentially happen now?"

Instead of replying, he simply looked towards the sky and said, "Father, despite all the wrong I've committed, I obviously still have favor! So, You can trust that you'll see your boy, along with his new wifey, in Church come Sunday!" Returning his attention to Regina, he added, "That's a promise." With a wink of the eye.

"Don't make promises you can't,,,," Regina caught herself. "Won't keep."

"Well, if it's not *this* Sunday," He smiled reaching for her left hand, actually her ring finger, and added, "It'll definitely be *one day*."

"*This nigga swear he has game for a bitches ass!*" Regina thought to herself.

Summonsing one of his crew members over, Dude whispered something in his partner's ear. Still gently caressing Regina's finger, he then led her around to the driver's side of the Honda Accord, opened her door, closed it once she was seated behind the wheel, then walked around to the passenger's side and got in.

Seeing how Regina was eyeing him, he smiled, rubbed the crotch of his pants, and said, "Lets be out!"

"Cocky, what's the feed back on the dog food?" J.R. inquired about the heroin he'd copped from his connect.

"Man!" Smiled Cocky. "The fiends are loving it! Especially after word got out that three niggas done *oh deed* already!" He exclaimed excitedly.

"That's what's up." J.R. replied, visibly satisfied. "Here," He added, handing Cocky what looked like a stamp and ink pad.

"What's this for?" Asked a dismayed Cocky, seeing the word *Explosive* on the stamp. "We doing real good with the stamp we already have." He informed J.R.

"I see that." J.R. replied. "But what I want you to do is, keep that *Special Effect* stamp in circulation. Yet, we're also going to put out the *Explosive,* but in powder blue baggies."

"Two different stamps, yet the same product?" Cocky didn't understand the logic. "And I thought *you* were well versed in the heroin game!" J.R. laughed at his homie, then explained, "You and I know it's the same product, but the fiends will feel like they have an option. Some of them will even *rate* the dope differently." He shrugged, not quite believing it himself when his father had explained it that way to him. Getting the picture, Cocky smiled, then said, "It's all about variety!"

"Even with the junkies." J.R. nodded.

"I'll send one of my people to go cop those baggies, quick like." Said Cocky.

Turning to be out, J.R. looked back and said, "If *anything*, you know how to get at me." Tapping the pager attached to his belt.

"For sure." Cocky replied, then suddenly remembering that there was something important he needed to hip J.R. to, he added. "By the way, I did forget to pull your coat to something that took place earlier."

Stopping in his tracks, J.R. faced Cocky and asked, "What's that?"

"This," Cocky lifted the front of his sweat shirt, exposing the .45 automatic hand gun.

"Where'd you get that from?" J.R. admired the huge pistol.

"Actually, it's a gift intended for you." Cocky informed him, then added, "From none other than Carmine himself."

"Oh yeah?" J.R. couldn't help smiling.

"He instructed me to make sure you received it, because he's dying to see if you're *that* nigga."

Still smiling, J.R. reached for the pistol. "In *that* case, let me get it." Stuffing it into his waist, then jetting.

"Damn baby girl! You so fine, you got a nigga feeling other than himself right about now." The wavy haired light skinned dude, sitting in Regina's passenger's seat revealed, at the same time looking down at her pretty pedicured toes as she drove.

"You say that to say what?" Regina asked.

"I've been in your company for what? At least 45 minutes now, yet I've forgotten to ask you the most basic question, of all questions, when making someone's acquaintance." He shook his head, somewhat embarrassed.

"I assume that would be my name?" Regina laughed.

Dude nodded, then said, "You got that one." Eyeing her suspiciously, then laughing himself.

"It's Regina."

"Regina, humm," He nodded. "I like that." He smiled, as if the name wasn't common.

"And yours?"

"It's Maurice, but the streets call me Mousey." He smiled.

"Mousey?" Regina shot him a questionable look. "What kind of name is that? Especially for a man?"

"I know right!" Mousey couldn't help laughing.

"I mean, I *do* hope you're a man." Regina made fun of him. "Because anything less will *not* cut it."

"Baby girl, I'm *all* man! Believe that!" Mousey assured her.

"I guess that remains to be seen huh?" Regina smiled, meanwhile thinking to herself, "*Yes, we will see, and soon enough, Mr. Mousey!*"

J.R. couldn't help feeling the weight of the huge pistol, tucked in his waist, as he climbed into his father's black Ford Bronco. Suddenly, he remembered the envelope in which his father had handed him earlier that day. Inside, he found a key along with a brief note, which read;

Uncle Josh informed me that you were in need of a location, for the purpose of handling some most pertinent business. Enclosed, along with this note, you'll find a lone key and address, for which you'll find suitable to handle your handle. However, I trust you will not make, or better yet leave a mess behind.

Til Death Do Us Part, Remember That?

One Love, I Remain; K Smooth.

P.S.,

I'm not really certain what her Pop's schedule be like, these days, so I'd suggest you be out of there as quickly as possible!!!

Completing the note, J.R. tucked it, and it's other contents into his pocket, then headed out to *Rosedale*...........

Regina looked down at her wrist watch and was pleased by the time was making.

"*J.R. will undoubtedly be impressed by my potential!*" She excitedly told herself. "Before we left the Boulevard, I thought coming up with the *right* place was going to be a collaborated thing." Mousey broke the silence. "But apparently, you already have a destination in mind." He assumed, seeing how she maneuvered the Accord through the traffic on the Belt Parkway.

"Never mind what impression you were under. I've decided to give you the opportunity to *make* an impression." Regina looked over at him, winked, then seductively ran her tongue across her glossy red lips.

"How so?" Mousey weakly inquired, unable to take his eyes off such juicy red lips. "By bringing you to my house, because I'm quite curious to see if you're a man, or mouse." She laughed, as a result of the rhyme she'd come up with as a response.

"Say no more!" Mousey was excited, in fact, he couldn't believe his luck!

Seeing they'd passed the exit for Springfield Boulevard, and clearly out of his territory, Mousey couldn't help asking, "If you don't mine me asking, where the hell *do* you live?"

Without taking her eyes off the road, Regina smiled and answered, "*Rosedale.*"

Uncle Josh had informed K Smooth, early on, the *benefits* that came as a result of, assisting the right people in securing themselves a desired position, *especially those with Political aspirations,* achieve their goals.

Yet, it wasn't about what Nadine Shepard could, or would be able to do for him, somewhere down the line, thought K Smooth. His assistance and drive, regarding her campaign, was based on the fact that he genuinely liked the person whom she was. In fact, if there was ever a such thing of an honest politician, Nadine Shepard was it! As far as K Smooth was concerned anyway. Plus, she'd been true to her words since day one they'd met.

As the two of them, along with countless others from her party, awaited the verdict from the polls, announcing who'd be the next Queens Borough President, K Smooth looked over at Nadine and smiled as he thought about the promise she'd made to him earlier that evening.

"*If I win this election, I'm bringing you to my new office as my personal assistant.*" Nadine Shepard had informed him with a smile.

The entire room exploded with cheers, when it was announced that Councilwoman Shepard was now *officially* Queens Borough President!!!

Handing his boss a glass of champagne, then raising his for the purpose of a toast, K Smooth smiled and said, "Congratulations! Even though I *knew* you'd be victorious!"

With eyes sparkling more so, then even the champagne,

Nadine returned the smile and replied, "Word is, I won by far, considering the astonishing high percentage of young voters who came out to the polls and casted their votes." She looked into his eyes knowingly.

"I say, you chalk your victory up to, the *best* person for the job winning the seat." Nadine playfully tapped K Smooth on his arm, being that he refused to take any credit for her victory.

"Remember, you're still that strong, intelligent, successful Black female," K Smooth smiled, then continued. "Not to mention *beautiful* lady, who we both knew, early on, could achieve *whatever* she set out to."

Still eyeing him over the rim of her champagne glass, Nadine was more than just impressed by the young man who'd done so much for her campaign, as well as in her office. The fact was, she'd genuinely liked Kenneth Shannon.

"My God, it's so noisy in this place!" Nadine complained, doing a quick scan of the crowded hall. Seeing everyone was in a festive mood, and doing their own thing, she returned her attention to K Smooth and said, "You mind if I borrowed your *ear* for just a second?"

Leaning towards her so he could her what his boss wanted to tell him, K Smooth was careful not to get *too* close.

"Remember earlier, when I promised you I'd be bringing you to my new office, as my personal assistant?" Nadine asked.

K Smooth simply nodded his head, *"Yes."* Remembering clearly what she'd said.

"Well," Nadine continued, yet darted her tongue quickly and discreetly across his earlobe, "Tonight, I've decided to take you to my bed."

Regina was blown away by how huge, *and* beautiful, the house in Rosedale actually was! She'd only seen it from the outside, and it was dark the previous night when she and J.R. rode pass it, so they'd know it's exact location the following day.

"Damn baby girl!" Mousey looked around in disbelief. "Your folks *must* be rich!" Leading the way to the living room area, Regina prayed she wouldn't give herself away being that she was just as impressed as Mousey, if not more, by the expensively furnished house! And to think, they'd only seen the front area! She thought.

"You can have a seat." She offered, motioning towards the huge sofa. "I'll go and get us something to drink." Exiting the living room she made sure to add that extra bounce to her behind, as she had done earlier at the grocery store.

Mousey bit his lower lip admiring her assets, then looked up towards the high ceiling, and said, "*Look here Father, I realize I may not be among your list of favorites, but can you pleeeaasee not fail your boy now!!!*" He spoke almost at a whisper.

Not sure if he was more startled by the fact that someone had heard his brief prayer, or the male's voice that said, "That, depends on your ability to come up with an effective line to lure your boss man *Head* out here to Rosedale, within the next hour!" The hard, not to mention cold, piece of steel pressed against the back of Mousey's head *already* had him thinking of a line that wouldn't raise Head's suspicions!!!!

Chapter Sixteen.

Red wasn't one of those *out in the open* type cats, nor did he like putting the streets into his business. Never mind the fact that, his *business* was out in the streets! Instead, he prided himself on being from the so called *old school* of hustlers, even though he was only 31 years old, and valued the jewels he'd acquired along the way.

Therefore, he allowed the streets to assume that he had gracefully bowed out, of the game, as the young hustlers presence became so dominant on the block. Those young hustlers being J.R., Cocky, and their massive crew!

Yet, the streets were certainly not fooled by his sudden departure. Whereas *he* termed it bowing out gracefully, the streets called it....*getting ran off*!!!

Nonetheless, Red however, realized that he had to strategize and think like the general in which he was, and therefore allowed some time to pass before he brought any gunplay to J.R., Cocky, and their crew. He wasn't trying to murder anyone for the purpose of notoriety, because Dirty Red was certainly *not* trying to be Sing Sing's next top drug dealer! He simply wanted 150th street back under his control, as far as the heroin game was concerned.

He still found it hard to believe Cocky's young, wet behind the motherfucking ear ass, rolled on him *Dirty Red*, out the blue, one day and said, "*Be off the block by 8:0;clock....or get shot!!!"*

"The nerve of them young niggas!" Thought a furious Red, as he sat in the pool hall/ gambling joint, on 105th street & Northern Boulevard, sipping on his Rum & Coke. Suddenly, he thought his ears were playing tricks on him, as he caught bits and pieces of the two young boys conversation.

"I told you it would only be a matter of time, before I got a line on that nigga J.R. for you. I even got you the address to his stash crib." The boy who was the younger looking, of the two, smiled then added, "I know how badly you've been wanting, and waiting to get some *get back* for that shit he did to you on riker's island."

"Get back?" The older looking kid exclaimed, obviously furious. "I'm going to torture that nigga, before I blow his top off!" He barked, then stuffed the small piece of paper, containing J.R.'s address, into the pocket of his bright red Polo goose down jacket, before adding, "I owe you big time for this one, my nigga!"

"Don't thank me nigga, handle your business!" The smaller kid laughed. "I believe his girlfriend stays with him, at that same address."

"Then she's a dead bitch too!" The older kid spat. "I spotted his man Cocky on 150th street, a few days ago, but I couldn't lay'em down being that there was so many heads out on the block that day. But now that I have J.R.'s info, fuck the workers,

I can focus on them later."

"Whatever, whatever. You *no* I'm with you kid!" Smiled his younger comrade.

"Nigga you all right!" His partner nodded his head up & down, at the same time exchanging dap. "After I murder J.R. and those fake ass niggas he call a crew, I think I'ma look for a connect of my own and take over 150th street. And you, my nigga," He smiled at his younger comrade. "Will be my numero uno lieutenant!"

"Lets make it happen then." The younger boy was certainly *feeling* that thought! Red however, could not believe what he was hearing! Or his luck!

"*Talk about being in the right place at the right time!!*" He couldn't help thinking.

Before the two young boys could make their departure, Red got up from the bar stool in which he'd been sitting on, and calmly made his approach. Addressing the older looking kid, he said, "Not to be all up in y'alls conversation, but it appears youngblood, that you and I may share a common enemy."

The youngster looked Red up & down, screwed up his face, and asked, "Oh yeah? And *who* might that be?" Wondering how much the old head had actually heard.

"Listen you little piece of shit," Red had become agitated. "I don't have time to be up in here playing some *beat around the bush* bullshit with no young punks!" He snapped. "I'm a very busy, not to mention wealthy man, who happens to have a team of killers out on the streets, as we speak, trying to obtain that same information your little partner here just provided you with! Not only will I pay you handsomely for what's jotted down on that piece of paper, but I'll also guarantee you J.R.'s head by Sunrise tomorrow. The two of you can torture his man Cocky, and the rest of those wanna bees they call a crew. When the smoke clears, you won't have to look for a connect." Red smiled as he peered into the young boy's eyes, then informed him. "I *am* the connect."

The two boys looked at each other, before the one who was in possession of the piece of paper spoke, "We probably shouldn't be discussing this up in here. Just as, in the case with you, we never know *who* may be listening."

"*This kid just might have some potential after all.*" Red thought to himself with a nod, certainly agreeing with the kid. "I couldn't agree more. How about we take a walk outside to my BMW? Or better yet, take a ride out to City Island or somewhere nice so we can discuss this thing further?" Red suggested with a smile.

"Ai'ight." The boy agreed, then whispered something in his young partner's ear. Turning his attention back to Red, he said, "Lets be out!" A s the two of them approached the platinum gray BMW 535I, with its butter soft gray leather upholstery, the young boy was indeed impressed!

"I guess you *are* the connect! Riding around in this!" The kid smiled, eyeing the vehicle's interior.

"Youngblood, this here is nothing!" Red replied, with a wave of the hand. "Play your hand right, and you can have it. I damn sure won't miss it." He laughed, then added, "I have three others, plus two Benz's parked in my garage."

The youngster watched Red closely trying to assess whether or not he was exaggerating, and from Red's expression, he could tell that the old head wasn't lying! Mainly because of Red's matter of fact tone, and the seriousness of his stare.

"*Wow these seats are comfortable!*" The young dude told himself, as he reclined in the passenger's seat.

Just as Red proceeded to put the key into the ignition, the younger looking boy who had handed his friend the piece of paper with J.R.'s address on it, approached the BMW, and tapped on the driver's side window.

Once Red had let the window completely down, the kid informed him, "The bar tender said you left without getting your change."

"Change?" Red screwed up his face. "I don't *do* change. Whatever I put on the table is what they keep. Matter of fact, tell the bar tender I said *you* can have it."

"Thanks." The kid smiled, then before Red could hit the switch for the window to ascend, he added. "I know you may not want *this* either, but J.R. told me to give it to you anyway!" With that said, Jamel raised the .380 automatic hand gun, with the silencer attached, at the same time noticing Reese lean back in his seat, before he shot Red three times in his face!

The two boys jumped into their hooptie, a Mazda 626, and Jamel quickly pulled away from the curb.

Reese however, noticed a *hole* in the sleeve of his jacket. Immediately he realized that one of the bullets must've exited the back of Red's skull, and lodged into his jacket's sleeve.

"Thank God, my Polo is a Goose down!" Reese thought to himself with a smile, as they headed for the Grand Central parkway, en route to the Van Wyck Expressway, which would ultimately take them back to Southside Jamaica!!!

Nadine Shepard was quite overwhelmed with excitement, considering the wonderful course her life was taking these days. Her job was fulfilling, her health was excellent, and her personal life was nothing less than satisfactory. The latter, thanks to a handsome, intelligent, and young lover named Kenneth Shannon, she thought to herself with a smile plastered across her face.

She'd been completely surprised, yet thoroughly pleased, by how skillful a lover he'd proven to be. *"Especially at his age!"* Nadine had told herself, after their love making session that first night.

"When I become President of the United States, I think I'll pass a Bill with Kenneth Shannon's name on it, authorizing him the right to teach 'all' men how to make a lovely first impression!" Nadine jokingly told herself.

Besides being attentive to her physical needs, Kenneth also played a major role in her office. Just as he had, at her previous office, when she'd been City Councilwoman. He kept *everything* properly filed, arranged her entire schedule, saw to it that the rest of her staff was on point, as well as provided Nadine with advice and opinion regarding certain issues.

As far as down time was concerned, K Smooth took time to give her massages, ran warm fragrant baths, prepared candle light dinners, and made love to her at least four times a week. Most of the time, their love making was slow and passionate. However, there were days when Nadine preferred it rough and sweaty, and loved the fact that Kenneth, literally, *arose* to either occasion.

Words couldn't describe Nadine's love, and gratitude towards Joshua Reed, the man who had brought Kenneth Shannon into her life. The same man she had known, and appreciated most of her life. Whom she also knew was guiding and influencing most of Kenneth's decisions education wise, finance wise, and association wise.

"*Yes, Mr. Joshua Reed, you certainly are a good man!*" Nadine thought with a smile.

K Smooth couldn't believe that his credit score was already in the low *eights!* Especially in such a relatively short amount of time! Nor could he believe how well most of his investments were *already* beginning to pay off! Investments in which Uncle Josh had suggested he look more closely into.

"I see how closely you've been watching your investments,

but it's equally important that you keep a record of every dollar in which J.R. has been bringing in." Uncle Josh instructed him.

"Trust me Uncle Josh, I've been keeping a *mental* note of every penny you've put into my hands, thus far." K Smooth smiled, priding himself on his ability to store pertinent information inside his memory bank, opposed to jotting things down on paper.

"If you're confident with your method of keeping account, then I guess we can move right along with our other plans." Uncle Josh replied, then continued, "I have an associate name Nathan Hollingsworth who happens to be a well respected stock broker, on Wall Street, who has agreed to sit down with you at least three evenings out the week, to show you the ins and outs regarding the stock market. Buying, selling, trading, you name it." Joshua smiled, then went on, "So far, we've been receiving some profitable information from our *inside* traders. But, I want you to sit down with Nathan because he'll teach you how to recognize the investments that are potential filled. Next, we need to start capitalizing off the countless *properties* that have been, and are being seized on a daily basis by the Government, or foreclosed by numerous banking institutions. Properties in which we'll purchase for little to nothing, renovate, and re-sell. Some we may even rent out, depending on the property. Also, we'll set our sight on acquiring whatever *land* that's up for sale, especially in the Metropolitan regions of the city. A number of my Italian friends are actually licensed contractors, who happen to own cement companies as well. Since you work for the

Queens Borough President it will be easy, nor is it illegal, well not to my knowledge anyway," Joshua laughed. "For you to get a complete up to date listing, of all *properties* that are being sold, or auctioned. Your position at Nadine's office, enables us first dabs on *everything!* Nor will you and I have to worry about renovation cost, because, like I said, I have friends who are contractors. Who have agreed to put in whatever work we need done, in exchange for Nadine influencing the *biddings* to secure their companies some of the contracts, to build at least some of the sites the City has planned for the Borough of Queens. Namely, along Archer Avenue at the moment. It'll sweeten the pie if she'll assist them with some of their zoning issues with the City." Joshua smiled.

"Do you think she'll do either?" K Smooth was somewhat doubtful, seeing how Nadine did everything by the book.

"I'll discuss it with her." Joshua replied, then changing the subject he added, "I realize our plan will take some serious capital, but I think we're good."

K Smooth remained silent, simply listening to get a full understanding of all in which Uncle Josh would entail.

"Besides the two hundred and fifty thousand dollars we currently have, some saved, majority invested. We also have the 1.3 million dollars J.R. recently brought in. Which is all profit." Joshua smiled, appreciating how J.R. made a rule of getting the Italians their money as promptly as possible. "But, the good part is that, it's really not going to cost us nearly as much as we think, to make our plans work."

"I'm listening." K Smooth smiled, pretty much knowing Uncle Josh had things all figured out from the start.

"I'm banking on the *banks* working with you." Joshua informed him.

"Why would they?" K Smooth was dismayed. "I mean, it isn't like a quarter of a million dollars is a whole lot of money these days."

"True," Joshua agreed. "But, we'll set up some corporations, bankroll them, as well as establish a line of credit for each of them. Not to mention, your *personal* credit is superb."

"But is it enough?" K Smooth inquired.

"All that, combined with the two million dollars worth of investments, in which *Eugene* wisely made, will undoubtedly make the banks work with you. Especially considering all of those investments were done in *your* name."

"Head, I'm *telling* you fam!" Mousey exclaimed excitedly. "Yes, I'm sitting in the nigga's crib as we speak!" He spoke into his cellular phone.

"Exactly! The broad I just finished sexing is his girlfriend's sister, who happens to live with them. I know the bitch ain't lying either, because there are pictures of the nigga J.R. *all over* this joint!" Mousey lied. Hearing Head's reply, he added, "She said, her sister and dude usually get home around 3:00p.m., shortly before she leaves for evening school." Now bringing his voice to a whisper, Mousey added, "Little do the bitch know, evening school is over with! Because as soon as you get here, her ass is getting tied the fuck up, and when J.R. and big sis comes through the door the three of them can take an evening class together! Which will be *History*!" Mousey giggled into the phone.

"I have to admit though, the pussy is *blazing* fam! In fact, since your hour is more like *two hours*, I think I'll get another nut!" Mousey laughed, then after a brief pause, he said, "Ai'ight, ai'ight, ai'ight! But, if yo'ass ain't here in one hour you *will* be camping out on the front porch for a minute, because ya'boy will certainly be eight inches deep, probably even sleep!" He laughed, then said, "One hour!" Before hanging up.

"*Yeah, I'ma definitely have to murder this nigga! His deception skills is a mother!*" J.R. told himself, looking over at Regina, who was shaking her head, indicating that she too was impressed by the cat Mousey's deception skills.

"I hope your word is your *bond*, that a nigga's good when all this is over with?" Mousey eyed J.R. suspiciously as he handed him back the cellular phone.

"I thought I've already made myself clear on that? I told you, all I need is the nigga Head out of the way." J.R. replied. "You? You're an asset to me, and what I'm trying to do. Do you think it's a secret that it's *you* who's actually making shit happen in the project, and on the Boulevard? Head's nothing more then the connect. Trust me kid, I've done my homework." J.R. said with a smile.

Mousey couldn't help smiling also, before replying, "So I

see!"

"Right now though, what the three of us need to do is, cover up this couch and the carpet with some of this thick plastic I brought." J.R. instructed Mousey and Regina, as he made his way over to the thick roll of plastic, which Mousey hadn't noticed until then.

"I feel you." Mousey said with a nod, realizing that J.R. didn't want to get any of Head's blood on the expensive furniture and carpet. "How about you tell wifey here," He said, motioning towards Regina. "That it's cool to put the pistol down!" Not feeling comfortable what so ever, with the pistol being pointed at him.

"Head isn't dead yet." J.R. reminded him. "Therefore, it still remains to be seen where your loyalty lie. It's nothing personal though."

"I understand." Mousey shook his head. "But eventually you'll see, that I'm probably the loyalist nigga on your team!" He smiled.

J.R. just looked at the clown in disbelief, meanwhile thinking to himself, "*Yeah, I bet that's what you told 'Head' as well!*"

When the front doorbell rang, at ten minutes after 4:00p.m., Mousey took his seat on the plastic covered couch.

J.R. crouched down low behind the huge wet bar, with his two guns at the ready.

Regina tucked her pistol, fixed her clothes, then headed for the front door.

"Well, well. I presume you're the infamous Head, whom

I've heard so much about." Regina said with her beautiful deep dimpled smile, at the same time ushering him inside.

"The one *and* only!" Head replied with a smile of his own, at the same time looking Regina up and down, licking his full lips, obviously impressed by her looks. "But then again, you can't believe *everything* you hear."

"Even if it's a *turn on*?" Regina flirted.

"In that case, I'm everything they say I am!" Head joked. "But seriously, it's unfair that you know, or heard so much about me. Yet, I don't know a thing about you." He frowned, while looking at Regina as if she was a piece of candy in which he couldn't wait to bite into. "However, I must admit, my boy Mousey is doing *real well* for himself these days."

"I try to remind him of that fact, as often as I can." Regina smiled, then said, "You can follow me, he's in the living room relaxing." With that said, she turned and led the way towards the living room area of the house, and although her perfectly round butt had a natural *bounce* to it, Regina put some emphasis to her sway, knowing Head was watching! Or better yet, *staring*!

"*When the guns blast, I gotta make sure shorty catches it last, because I'll be damned if I'm not gonna get me some of that phat ass!*" Head promised himself, as he followed Regina's lead.

"Please excuse the mess in here." Regina apologized, referring to all the plastic coverings. "We're in the process of painting the ceiling." She explained.

"Don't sweat it love." Head replied, looking around the

spacious, expensively decorated living room. "The owner of this pad must *really* be doing some big things!" He remarked, while thinking to himself, "*The nigga J.R. will definitely be leading me to the safe, before I kill him!*" Looking over at Mousey, who was seated on the huge sofa with an '*I told you so*' expression on his face, Head inquired, "What's the deal?"

"Everything is everything." Mousey answered.

"So it's *all* good then?" Head inquired, looking Regina up and down.

"You can't tell?" Mousey laughed out loud, also looking in Regina's direction.

"If the two of you will excuse me for just a second, I'll be right back." Regina excused herself, quickly adding, "I have to use the ladies room." Again, making sure to add some extra bounce to her behind as she exited the room.

Head, who was momentarily distracted by Regina's departing assets, was completely caught off guard when he'd heard the plastic squeak, directly behind him!

"I want you to *reach* for your piece, so I can splatter your brains all over the sofa!" J.R. spoke, quickly coming from behind the bar and sofa, making direct eye contact with Head, who quickly moved his hand away from his waist, putting both hands in the air where J.R. could see them.

"Mousey, how about you relieve your former boss man of his gun?" J.R. half asked, more so instructed, letting Head know that he'd been set up. Nor did J.R. care that Mousey now had a pistol in his possession, being that he saw through his peripheral that *Regina* had her gun trained on Mousey!

None of them were surprised to see that Head's .32 automatic had a silencer attached, being that it was no secret he'd came for the purpose of assassination!

"All right Mousey! The time has arrived for you to prove your loyalty." J.R. informed him, with his gun still pointed at Head's head.

Mousey understood clearly that he'd just been given his first order, yet, he still hesitated in pulling the trigger. Mainly because he'd been under the impression that role was merely to set Head up. Making eye contact with J.R., he knew what he had to do. "Shoot him!" J.R. instructed him, in a calm voice.

Realizing he was now in a kill, or be killed situation, Mousey let off his first shot! The bullet caught Head in the right side of his chest. However, the wound was not that severe whereas it stopped him from rushing towards the already scared Mousey!

Unfortunately for Head, Mousey was too quick on his feet. He side stepped Head, then stood over him and shot him four more times!

Mousey had earned his respect on the streets of Southside Jamaica for two reasons, and two reasons only. One, he was a natural born hustler. And two, he ran with a crew that consisted of some of Queens most notorious murderers. However, he himself had never fired a pistol on anyone!

Unconsciously, Mousey dropped the smoking gun on the plastic covered floor, as he stood over Head's dead body, basically in shock, as he witnessed the clear plastic covering turn bloody red.

"All right Regina, the time has arrived for you too, to prove your loyalty." J.R. spoke.

Before Mousey could even look up, Regina placed the barrel of her .38 revolver to the back of his skull, and blew his brains out…………

Quickly, J.R. and Regina slipped their gloves on, and proceeded to roll the two bodies up into the thick plastic. Once done, they wiped down any and everything they may have touch in the house.

The Honda Accord was already parked in the driveway, directly beside the side door of the house, and one at a time they carried each body to the vehicle, where they placed it in the trunk. Being that it was winter, J.R. knew the sun would be going down by 5:30p.m. However, he decided to wait in the car until 6:15p.m., before he and Regina drove the short distance to Brookville Park, where he'd left his Ford Bronco parked, putting the car in Neutral, he and Regina watched as the stolen Honda Accord rolled into the pond!!!!!

Chapter Seventeen.

June, 10th 1990 - Roseland Ballroom...

Steve O was overwhelmed by the size of the crowd, and some of the faces that were present at his welcome home party! He mixed and mingled with Pepper, from Salt & Pepper, Mike Tyson, Teddy Riley, Bobby Brown, Charles Oakley, Kenny Anderson, Ice Cube, L.L. Cool J, Russell Simmons, Miss Jones, Jam Master Jay, and a number of other celebrities who were associates of K Smooth, or simply there to hang out.

Besides being overwhelmed by the party that was put together in his honor, Steve O was very much surprised by how much, in general, had changed since he'd been away! He noticed that, New York Boulevard was now named *Guy R. Brewer Boulevard.* His old junior high school *Shimar*, was now a school for special children. His right hand man, K Smooth, was not only politically connected, but was also a well known and respected businessman/ entrepreneur. Pam was not only the owner of a chain of Beauty Salons throughout New York, New Jersey, and Connecticut, she was *also* the proud mother of a two year old girl named Silver (who was conceived during one of her and Spoon's conjugal visits up North). Spoon, he'd already heard had failed to complete the Shock Program, and was turned down by the Parole Board at least twice already. Cocky, Reese, and Jamel were all ghetto famous, not to mention, *filthy* rich!

"*Last, but not least,*" Steve O couldn't help smiling with *J.R.* in mind. J.R., who was not only his beloved and most trusted comrade, but, was also the one person who, despite being labeled one of New York's *Kingpins*, made it his business to *personally* pay Steve O a visit at least once a month, the entire eighty four months he'd spent in prison! He'd also saw to it that, Steve O owned a house, two cars, and was also a *millionaire* upon stepping out of Eastern Correctional Facility!

Taking in, the famous faces, as well as the huge crowd of people who'd come out to party in *his* honor, all Steve O could say to himself was, "*Yes, shit has certainly changed!*"

Feeling a hand on his shoulder, Steve O spent around to find a smiling Reese.

"Ain't no need to be standing in the cut, like you're crowd fright. Nigga, this is *your* night!" Reese informed him, still with a smile on his face. Playfully throwing a jab at Steve O's mid section, he suggested, "Lets go mingle with some of the ladies. As long as your ass been *gone*, it'll probably take a whole year's worth of sex before your nuts finally feel like they're out of *pawn*!"

At that, they both laughed.

"Man I'm *good*!" Steve O replied between laughter. "I've only been home a week, yet, I've already hit more chicks than I can count!"

"I know that's right!" Reese smiled, turning his attention

towards a fine milk chocolate honey, walking by, in a cream colored mini dress that barely covered her ass cheeks. Once she'd disappeared into the crowd, he turned his attention back to Steve O and suggested, "In that case, follow me. I want to introduce you to some of *our* peoples." As they made their way through the VIP section, Reese led the way towards a table in which Steve O noticed sat at least 25 bottles of Moet champagne! Yet, there were *only* four cats sitting at the table!

"Fellas. I *hope* you all are enjoying yourselves?" Reese inquired with a smile, as he and Steve O stood over their table. Knowing they were, he added, "I'd like for y'all to meet my brother Steve O."

At the mention of Steve O's name, the four cats stood to there feet. One by one, they introduced themselves to *J.R.'s* comrade, whom they'd each heard so much about. It wasn't until later on that night, Reese explained to him *who* the four cats actually were.

"The dude Calvin is from Brooklyn. Rich, is from Harlem. Billy, is from the Bronx, and Divine, is from Staten Island. *All* of them are pretty much what I'd call, our extended family." Reese smiled.

Besides their attire, and the expensive jewelry Steve O noticed each of the four cats were wearing, he also noticed that, whereas majority of the cats partying in the VIP were obviously on the pussy prowl, it was also obvious that majority of the pussy was *prowling* around the table in which the four Ballers sat! "*These four niggas have to be some major players*!" Steve

O told himself, seeing how the four of them weren't even paying much attention to the ladies!

Excusing themselves, Reese and Steve O continued on, making their way around and about the club, meeting and greeting numerous people.

Reese could tell that there was something on Steve O's mind, being that he was obviously becoming uninterested in the people and excitement, which led him to ask, "What's on your mind big homie?"

"I was just wondering if Cocky and Jamel were coming through?" Steve O inquired.

"What kind of question is that?" Reese laughed, then said, "I wouldn't be surprised if they aren't already in here somewhere."

That definitely brought a smile to Steve O's face.

"What about J.R.?"

"It's a possibility, but you and I both know how unpredictable he can be." Reese laughed as he said it, yet they both knew it was the truth.

"And K Smooth?" Steve asked.

"I wouldn't count on *him* showing up!" Reese replied matter of factly.

"Why not?" Steve asked with a raised eyebrow.

"For the same reason *J.R.* more than likely will not be showing up."

Clearly confused, Steve O further inquired, "And what *reason* would that be?"

Realizing that Steve O had been away for quite some years, and couldn't possibility know to what magnitude and length his comrades had taken things, which ultimately enabled each of them to have and own *all* in which they did. As well as the enemies in which they'd incurred throughout the process. Looking Steve O in his eyes, Reese, who had a habit of smiling, responded, "Because, you best believe this Ballroom is *infested* with Federal Agents!"

"Have you seen your friend Steve O yet?" Nadine inquired, as she and K Smooth both lied nude beneath the red silk sheets.

"Actually, I haven't." K Smooth answered. "But I've been informed by my mother, that she's throwing him a welcome home dinner party, which is scheduled for tomorrow night. I'll see him then."

"I'm sure he'll be glad to see you." Nadine smiled, at the same time running her fingers up and down his chest. "How long has it been, since the two of you last seen one another?" She was certain he'd told her before, yet she couldn't quite remember.

"Seven *long* years!" K Smooth answered. Feeling bad that he hadn't seen his comrade in so many years, he added, "However, it seems as though it's been about *twenty!* Hopefully he'll understand my reasons for *not* keeping the lines, of direct communication open."

"Which kind of dismays *me* as well. I mean, you're this incredibly loyal guy, especially to those you care about. Yet, you haven't even attempted to reach out to a childhood friend, whom you obviously have a great deal of love for." Nadine just couldn't shake the feeling that there was more to it, because his actions, where Steve O had been concerned, was totally contradictory to the man's whom she'd come to know and love.

"It's kind of hard to explain right now." K Smooth replied. "Lets just hope he doesn't hold anything against me, and focus more on the fact that he and his family are *all* well off."

"Which I wouldn't be surprised if *you* had a hand, in seeing to it." Nadine looked at him suspiciously.

K Smooth's smile pretty much confirmed her suspicions.

"Okay, *Mr. Make It Happen*! I can appreciate a man who looks after his family and friends, but how about you attend to some *other* needs?" With that said, Nadine seductively traced his ear with her tongue, at the same time using her hand, to place *his* hand between her thighs, allowing him to feel how wet she was.

"Yes your Honor." K Smooth responded with a smile, before adding. "*Anything* for the first female Mayor, of New York City. Especially with a body like this." Lifting her atop of him.

Straddling him, Nadine asked, "How do you know *I* want to be in control tonight?"

"Probably because, being in control *fits* you." K Smooth laughed.

"No my dear Kenneth, it is *you* who fits *me*." Nadine corrected him, between her moans, as she gently sank down on his manhood. "It may even have something to do with why I've fallen in love with you." She added, increasing her tempo.

Letting out a moan, or two, of his own, K Smooth replied, "I love you too, *Governor.*"

Gyrating her body, in an effort to take him deeper, Nadine whispered in his ear, "I realize my stuff is good, but I'm the Mayor, *not* the Governor."

"I know." K Smooth half whispered, half moaned.

"So why did you refer to me as Governor?" She'd managed to ask.

"Because if I have anything to do with it, you *will* be."

Leaning forward, to enable him to suck on her breast, which she knew *he knew* she loved, whenever she was on top, she whispered. "I believe you."

After a few minutes of licking, sucking, and gently nibbling on both her breast, which were both fully erect, K Smooth looked into her eyes and said, "Thank you for *always* believing in me."

"You're welcome." Nadine moaned somewhat breathlessly, then managed to get out the words, "Now how about you be quiet, and make me cum?"

"I hear an old enemy of yours, and some of his people, had Steve O's party staked out last night, hoping you appeared." Reese informed J.R. over the telephone.

"Oh yeah?" J.R. laughed at that, pretty much knowing that Reese was referring to the kid Dollar Bill, who was now home, making a name for himself in the streets, especially throughout Brooklyn, and was also making it known that he and J.R. had some *unfinished* beef.

"*Nigga, you're the least of my worries!*" J.R. thought to himself with the cat Dollar Bill in mind. Whereas Dollar Bill was just getting his feet wet, in the game, J.R. had taken over entire neighborhoods, as well as brought the pistols to Blacks, Puerto Ricans, Dominicans, Cubans, Jamaicans, and Columbians over the years! So as far as Dollar Bill was concerned, *he'd have to get in line!*

On second thought, J.R. realized it would probably be best if he went ahead and took care of the dude Dollar Bill, before he accumulated any *real* strength.

"Reese, I want you to place a call to Calvin, to see if he can put you on to a weak link." J.R. instructed.

"Say no more." Reese replied, understanding his order. "I'll get on it *asap*."

Changing the conversation, J.R. asked, "What's the deal with Steve O? I know he's overwhelmed by the cars, women, and *money*." He laughed out loud.

"He's real good." Reese replied, recalling the amount of females Steve O had told him he'd bedded since his release. "I hear Mrs. KeKe is throwing him a surprise dinner party at her house tonight."

"Yeah, my old man told me about it." J.R. responded. "You stopping by?" He asked.

"I can't say for sure. That depends on how my conversation with Calvin, concerning them folks, turns out."

J.R. had always liked the fact that with Reese, it was always business before pleasure.

"What about you? Will you be there?" Reese inquired.

"Had I not been so far away, I'd definitely be there." J.R. answered, without mentioning that he and Regina were in Aruba. Not because he didn't trust Reese, but, because he didn't trust telling his whereabouts over the telephone. In fact, he didn't trust *telephones* period! That's why he made it a point to carry throwaway cellular phones, which were actually phones that couldn't be traced back to him. "I trust that K Smooth will explain the reason for my absence. Plus, I had Pam go out and purchase a gift, from Regina and I."

"An explanation and a gift," Reese laughed. "That's cool, but you know that nigga wants to *see* you!"

"I know." J.R. replied. "I'll surprise him shortly. But it just isn't a good time right now, for me to be visible. The way the streets have been calling my name, and that motherfucker Carmine, who happens to be out for my blood, all I can *do* is creep these days."

"The way the streets have been calling your name for a minute now, I'd say fuck Carmine! It's the Feds you need to be on the look out for." Reese said, telling him what he'd already knew.

J.R. didn't bother responding to the comment, instead he asked, "What's the deal with Cocky and Jamel?"

"They're both good. Cocky flew to Vegas with some chick he met at Steve O's party, and Jamel I'm sure isn't to far away from the Boulevard." Reese laughed.

All J.R. could do was shake his head! He knew what Cocky's tricking habits had become, but *damn*! Flying a chick, whom he'd only knew a few hours, out to Las Vegas? As for Jamel, it didn't matter his status, nor how rich he now was, he'd *forever* make his presence felt on Rockaway Boulevard!

"Anyway," Reese continued. "Give Regina my regards. Hopefully I'll be able to line dude up, and take care of the situation before you get back in town."

"Whatever the case, just hit me."

"I got you." Reese replied, then hung up.

Just when Steve O thought that nothing, or no one, could surprise him more than his comrades already had, all he could do was stand there *wide eyed* and *mouth agape*, seeing how huge KeKe's house, out in Jamaica Estates, was! Nor could he believe it, when the thirty plus, familiar faces, all yelled out, "*Surprise*!" in unison, as he walked through the front door!

The first face he noticed, was his mother's. Giving her a tight embrace, he smiled seeing his sister, brother, Mrs. KeKe, J.R.'s parents, Ms. Janice, Pam and a number of others he recognized from the old neighborhood. It wasn't until after he'd greeted each and every one of them, that he'd noticed K Smooth standing far off, by the dining room door, with a huge smile on his face.

After the two of them embraced each other, in a brotherly hug, Steve O stepped back to get a better look at his childhood comrade, before commenting, "I was wondering how long it would be, before you finally came through to check your boy out! Mr. Successful Businessman, and Politician!" He laughed, once again hugging K Smooth in a tight embrace.

"Man, if you don't let me out of this bear hug!" K Smooth laughed, yet, he couldn't believe how *huge* Steve O had gotten. "I knew I would be seeing you here today, so I was just giving you some space to get back into the groove of things. Because a lot has changed in the seven years in which you've been gone. If you haven't *already* noticed."

"Noticed? Man, I don't even know my way *around* this town anymore!" Steve O half joked. "Not to mention, damn near every chick that passes me by, looks like a beauty queen!"

"On that last note, I think you're exaggerating." K Smooth laughed.

Looking around, certain he'd missed a few people, Steve O returned his attention to K Smooth and asked, "Yo, where's J.R.? I *do* hope he's coming through?"

"I hear he's out of town. So I doubt he'll make it." K Smooth answered apologetically. "Don't feel bad though, he and I haven't seen each other in over five years." He revealed, then added, "At least the two of you got to sit down, throughout the years."

Blown away by what K Smooth had just revealed, Steve O asked, "You gotta be kidding me right?" In total disbelief.

"We've spoken a time, or two. So it's all good." K Smooth replied with a shrug. Still, not quite believing what he'd heard, Steve O just shook his head and asked,

"You're kidding me aren't you?" Waiting for K Smooth to say, he was only joking. When he didn't, Steve O asked, "What's *that* about?"

"All I can say is that, he's been doing *him*, while I've been busy doing *me*. You dig?" K Smooth smiled, trying to make light of the matter.

"Nah homie, I *don't* dig." Steve O gave him a questionable look, before adding, "But I *hear* you." None of what he was hearing was making any sense. "J.R. made it his business to come check me at least once a month, my entire bid! Now I'm home, free, and I've yet to see him!" Shaking his head, he went on, "He hasn't even allowed me the opportunity to *thank him* for all he's done for me, and my family, over the years."

"Although J.R. and I haven't seen each other in quite some time, I assure you that his and my endeavors have been one. Therefore, you're *welcome*." K Smooth smiled. "But there's really no need for *either*, being that you're family. I mean, *til death do us part,* remember that?" K Smooth asked, still smiling.

"Always, my nigga!" Steve O replied.

"Actually, J.R. did ask that I give you this." K Smooth informed him, handing Steve O what appeared to be a gift wrapped VCR tape. "We can go downstairs in the basement, so you can see what's on it." He suggested, then led the way.

"How come I have a feeling you already *know* what's on it?" Steve O laughed. K Smooth didn't reply. Instead, once they were in the basement, he pointed towards the entertainment system, which housed the VCR player.

"It's your tape." K Smooth said, motioning for Steve O to do the honors.

With that said, Steve O walked over to the video cassette recorder and inserted the tape. When the 57 inch screen came to life, all Steve O could do was smile, seeing J.R.'s smiling face come across the screen! Turning up the surround sound system, K Smooth stood back so Steve O could focus his attention on what J.R. had to say.

"*First, and foremost, I'd like to start off by saying; Welcome home!*" J.R. said with a smile, then went on. "*I'm sure you've gotten to see everyone 'but' me by now. And I do apologize for not being present for the welcome home party, but nonetheless, K Smooth and I put together your party at the Roseland Ballroom because it is imperative that you be recognized as the major figure in which you are, and 'by' the same media who'd once portrayed you as a worthless young Black male, when you went in. I've rode with you throughout your bid, so please do not misconstrue my absence, right now, to mean something in which it does not, and never will, because I love you my nigga! In fact, it was less than 60 days ago, that you and I sat across from one another, at which time we discussed some things, at length, regarding some of my plans. Well my nigga, this is actually the day and time, for which they are to be carried out. My enemies aren't as many as they appear to be, being that I made it a rule, along the way, to get rid of all those who I felt were against me. But unfortunately, my eyes have come to see that every enemy, is not always a known enemy 'but' the niggas who you've put food into their mouths, when it should've been the pistol! Therefore, my unfinished business is with all those who have revealed their true selves, as well as their intentions. Believe me, I know first hand how 'you' get down."* Again, J.R. produced a smile. "*But, what I want for you, is to relish your freedom, and new found wealth. Please, and I repeat 'please' do not be offended that I already have my soldiers picked out, to assist me in carrying out my endeavors. My father once told me, to make my own rules to play by, which I've done. But, I'm no longer in the drug game, nor do I want any of my people to partake in it, because in this day and time there are 'no rules'! No rules, no principles, and no codes! Therefore, with this new breed of hustlers any 'and' everything is fair, and embraced. Even snitching!"* J.R. explained, then went on. "*K Smooth and I have seen to it, that upon your release you'd be a rich man. So, on that note, I strongly suggest that you take your money and Capitalize! There's no one better qualified then K Smooth, to assist you in making your money grow. Again, welcome home my nigga! You've been through the struggle, now it's time to make it count...Til Death Do Us Part, Remember That?*

I'll see you shortly homie!" J.R. smiled before the huge television screen went blank......................

Chapter Eighteen.

"Come on Dollar," Calvin tried to convince him. "You and I both know that I'm the only nigga, in Brooklyn, who can get within a hundred yards of the nigga J.R."

"True." Dollar Bill agreed. "Even while I was up in the mountains, I heard how that Queens ass nigga was blessing your ass with work. Which leads me to wonder *two* things? One, why haven't you been set his bitch ass up? And two, how come all of a sudden you're ready, and willing to bite the hand that has been feeding you?" He eyed Calvin suspiciously.

Opposed to answering the questions, Calvin just shook his head, from where he sat across the table.

"Also," Dollar Bill added, "If I find out that your ass is really from Queens, running around B.K. on some imposter shit, yo'ass is getting it too!" He warned, face all screwed up.

"Dawg, I'm not here to entertain your concerns, nor listen to your disdain for niggas from Queens." Calvin replied, somewhat angrily. "I'm just here to deliver you *one* in particular."

Eyeing Calvin suspiciously, Dollar Bill responded, "I really hope you don't take the fact that I've been in prison, for nearly a decade, to mean that I'm ignorant or slow, because I assure you there's *nothing* slow about me! So, I'm still waiting for you to make me understand your readiness to betray the nigga whose been feeding you?" He repeated the question, then added, "I'm *listening*? To your motives, that is?"

"Listen man," Calvin was clearly agitated by the interrogation. "I didn't come here to politic with you about my business, intentions, motives, nor my reasoning. Therefore, I'm not about to put my business on the block. I came here because it's street knowledge what dude did to you back in the day, and how badly you want to touch him."

"Personally, I don't give a flying fuck about your business! Or your intentions!" Dollar Bill himself had clearly become angry. "In fact, never mind what you came here for, if your intentions are to *leave* here alive, I strongly suggest that you convince me, within the next 30 seconds, that you're not trying to set *me* up! Because apparently, you're having trouble answering my questions."

Not appreciating the threat, Calvin just stared across the table at Dollar Bill.

"One!" Dollar Bill began to count off the 30 seconds, at the same time reaching into his jacket, exposing the handle of what Calvin assessed to be a .357 Dessert Eagle.

"Listen man," Calvin began explaining. "I owe J.R. some money. Eighty thousand dollars to be exact. Instead of pressing me though, he recently fronted me an additional 50 kilos to enable me the means to pay off my debt, as well as accumulate some bread of my own, because he's made up his mind that he's finished with the drug game." He revealed, then continued, "The

50 keys is love, but I really don't want to pay him anything, because I feel it is he who's betraying me by shutting everything down once he's paid."

Dollar Bill just sat there observing Calvin, then producing a gold tooth smile, he spoke, "That's all you had to say from jump nigga! On *that* note, you go ahead and line him up. I'll do the rest." He instructed Calvin, then added, "Once he's dead, you can deliver *my* 25, out of that 50 he gave you."

"Twenty five out of *what* 50?" Calvin was dismayed.

"Out of the 50 kilos he fronted yo'ass! Is there *another* 50 I don't know about?" Dollar Bill shot him a menacing stare, again reaching into his jacket. "Don't allow *greed* to be the death of you."

Once he was out of the apartment, Calvin couldn't help thinking to himself, "*I see why J.R. stabbed his ass up! Dude is a real fucking character!*" Getting inside of his 300CE Benz, Calvin picked up his car phone and dialed Reese's cell phone number. Once he had Reese on the line, he informed him, "I've just concluded my sit down with a clown named Dollar Bill." He laughed.

"Hook, line, and sinker." Calvin replied to Reese's question. "Everything is set for Friday night, so that gives us three days to strategize the assassination."

"That nigga *Calvin* thinks he has all the sense!" Dollar Bill laughed out loud.

Meanwhile, his partner Jack, who was sitting across from

him, remained silent and expressionless. The streets use to refer to Jack as Kojack, due to his bald head, but being that his reputation for *jacking* niggas, by far, superceded his appearance, he'd become just….Jack!

"We're definitely going to take J.R.'s ass out, but Calvin will have to *get it* too." Dollar Bill continued. "Because I don't trust him for one minute! But, before I put one to his brain, I want *all* 50 of them thangs!" He laughed, even though he was dead serious. "Even if it means *confiscating* them from his workers, on the streets!"

"And I thought we were laying low for a minute!" Jack replied, being that not even a full week had passed, since they'd robbed some Cubans for 20 bricks.

"We'll lay low after this one." Dollar Bill informed him. "Right now, we only have three days to strategize our assassination. So, on that note, lets round up our folks."

Jack, however, was already on the phone letting his team of hit men know that *lay down* season had not officially began…. already, the time had arrived to bring the guns back out!!!

Recognizing Born's voice, as soon as he came on the line, J.R. greeted him.

"Peace, what's good with you?" He asked.

"Everything is good on this end." Born replied.

"That's what's up." J.R. was satisfied hearing that. "Listen, I need you to set up a meeting for me. I think it's time I had a sit down with the music man."

"The *music* man?" Born asked confused.

"The fat nigga from around the way, whose face happens to stay on Video Music Box these days!"

"Oh *him*!" Born laughed out loud. "I'll reach out to him today."

"Actually I won't be in town until tomorrow. You can set it up for the day after tomorrow."

"I got you." Born replied, before asking, "Am I correct to assume that *payback* time has arrived?"

"Something like that." J.R. answered. "I'll fill you in later though."

The day of the meeting, J.R. entered the lobby area of Street Life Records, and was glad to see that the label's CEO, Mark Anthony Wright, was awaiting him at the front desk. Glad, because he didn't feel like having to deal with some nosey receptionist.

Instead of exchanging a brotherly hug, J.R. simply extended his right hand for a handshake.

"To what do I owe the pleasure, of such an *out of the blue* meeting, with such an important man as yourself?" Mark Wright inquired, right there in the lobby area.

Walking pass the CEO, en route to the elevator, J.R. asked, "Is it *really* a pleasure, on your part, to see me Mark? If that's the case, why wasn't it a pleasure to see K Smooth, when he stopped by recently to see you? In fact, he tells me that you and his meeting was anything 'but' pleasurable. Which I found extremely hard to believe, being that he and I were the ones who fronted you the money to start this whole Street Life shit." The calmness, in which J.R. spoke, did not mask the fact that he was highly upset. Straightening his tie, which actually was already straight, the CEO cleared his throat, and replied, "I'm certainly disappointed, even surprised that K Smooth would bring to your attention, such an inaccurate description of our last meeting."

Not really listening to what Mark was saying, mainly because he knew K Smooth would never lie to him, J.R., instead, was very impressed when he stepped out of the elevator, which opened into Mark's spacious office. The elevator went directly to Mark's office, because his office took up the entire third floor!

Not only were the walls covered with Platinum & Gold plaques, there were also photographs of anyone who *was* someone, in the music industry. The shelves, held countless Awards, such as; Grammy's, American Music, Soul Train, BET, VH1, and MTV, among others.

As for the furnishings, J.R. assessed that Mark had to have spent *at least* a couple of hundreds of thousands of dollars, in decorating his office!

"*Yeah, Fat Markie from the block, was definitely doing some big things these days!*" J.R. told himself. He could remember, as if it were just yesterday, when Mark was in his backyard trying to scratch and backspin records, on a set of plastic & wood grain BCR turntables! Too poor to afford Techniques!

Back then, Mark couldn't so much as do a house party, let alone a block party, without the presence of the South Road Boyz, because niggas would have certainly *housed* his equipment! Not only did they hold him down back then, but, it was J.R.'s money, and K Smooth ability to recognize potential that led to Mark's establishing Street Life Records.

Approaching Mark's large wood polished desk, J.R. pulled out the leather reclining seat, and sat down. "I take it, you have some of those expensive Cuban cigars somewhere around here." J.R. shook his head, then continued. "K Smooth tells me that he, recently, came to you for assistance and you turned him away?" He questioned with a raised eyebrow. "*Please* tell me he misinterpreted your response?"

"J.R. listen," Mark began to plead his position, at the same time taking a seat in the chair that was designated for a visitor. "I'm in the music business, *not* politics!"

"I beg to differ," J.R. replied, leaning halfway over the desk top, so that he was now looking Mark directly in his eyes. "*You* listen. Until you pay me my ten million *plus,* your dancing ass is into *whatever* my comrade and I *say* you're into! Because right now, what your *in* is debt with me, and since I'm not K Smooth, I *strongly* suggest you not tell me what you're not into! Because then, what you'll also be *in* is trouble with me!" J.R. didn't so much as blink as he went on. "The choice is yours, you can take down what it is that K Smooth informs me he needs you to do. Or, you can stick to your position, and play Mr. Successful CEO, and turn *me* away as well. Choose the latter, and I assure you, matter of fact I *promise* you, at least two things. One, this entire fake ass Street Life shit will be *dead* before the week is out! And two, so will *you!*"

With that said, J.R. got up from the Executive's seat and headed towards the elevator.

From behind, he heard Mark Wright say, "K Smooth must've *misunderstood* me. Please sit back down, and explain to me what it is he needs me to do!"

"Guess who *that* was?" K Smooth smilingly asked Nadine.

"Who?"

"Mr. Mark Anthony Wright." K Smooth informed her, still smiling.

"Is he someone whom I should be familiar with?" Nadine asked, not placing the name, nor the face.

"Actually, I should be the *only man*, whom you're familiar with! But I won't hold any past encounters against you." K Smooth joked, causing her to playfully hit him on the arm, before further explaining, "Mark Wright is the CEO of a prominent, independent record label."

"Please don't tell me you're trying to get a record deal?" Nadine joked, yet, seriously hoping it *wasn't* the case, considering she'd heard him sing, more than once, in the shower and around the office.

"No!" He laughed out loud. "The call was actually in reference to you. Mr. Wright wants to meet with me, so we can discuss how he can use his influence in assisting you, in your up coming campaign for Governor of New York State."

"Why would such a man display such an act of generosity, when he and I have never even met?" Nadine was confused.

"Good question." K Smooth acted as if he was giving it some thought, then said,

"Maybe he's jumping on that whole *rock the vote* bandwagon, or something." He smiled.

"Yeah right!" Nadine shook her head, at the same time giving him a suspicious look, before adding, "Sometimes I can't help feeling as though you'd tell me anything, to quench my curiosity."

"Spoken like a true hypocrite." K Smooth laughed.

"No you did not say that!" Nadine looked at him in disbelief.

"Just last week, while we were making love, you told me that you *believed* whatever it is I speak." He reminded her.

At that, all she could do was laugh!!!

At first, Steve O wasn't feeling the club thing, being that he was now getting bored with the whole club scene. *" How ironic!"* He thought, when Born revealed that the club they were heading to was called, "The Scene!"

The club was located on Guy R. Brewer Boulevard, directly across the street from Rochdale Village.

As they made their way pass the front door, Steve O had to admit; *the small club was certainly packed wall to wall with females!*

Nor was it a secret, amongst any of the females, that Steve O, Born, and the rest of their crew, were the biggest $Ballers$ on 'the scene' that night! A fact, that made them the *main* attraction as well!

"Man, you might think I'm bullshitting. But I'm *still* trying to get use to having all this money, status, material shit, and the attention!" Steve O confessed to Born. "This shit seems almost unreal!"

"That's because it *is* unreal, for most cats fresh out of the penitentiary." Born laughed. "Seriously though, you're just a fortunate nigga, to be a part of a *family* that had your best interest at heart, while you were gone. It's all *real,* so you may as well get use to it."

"I'm trying!" Steve O laughed.

Lowering his voice a bit, Born said, "I just hope all goes well across town tonight."

"You say that to say what?" Steve O inquired.

"The plan J.R. and Reese put together, to body that nigga Dollar Bill from Brooklyn, who J.R. had that old beef with. One of our folks name Calvin lined dude up, by putting it out there that J.R. would be at the Q – Club tonight." Born filled him in. Steve O was on the island when that episode with J.R. and Dollar Bill popped off, yet he couldn't believe that the two of them were still beefing!

"That old beef?" Steve O asked in disbelief. "As major as J.R. is these days, why would he even entertain bringing it to dude?"

"Because, Dollar Bill too, is a major player these days. Who also, have been letting it be known that wherever he sees J.R., that's where he'll leave him laying. So, it's basically boiled down to, a kill, or *be* killed situation." Born explained.

"I see," Was all Steve O said, before asking, "Are you strapped?"

"I wouldn't be *in* this piece, if my *piece* couldn't get in with me!" Born smiled, lifting his shirt slightly, to expose his baby .9mm.

"So, I can assume that the rest of the crew is packing as well?" Steve O asked. "Without question kid! I mean, this is pretty much our turf." Born smiled.

"Good answer." Steve O smiled as well, then said, "In that case, I can borrow yours, and you'd still be good." With that said, he relieved Born of the .9mm glock, before fleeing *The Scene!!!*

Chapter Nineteen.

Dollar Bill couldn't be certain who the *third* man was, who'd emerged from the club, beside Calvin and the dude Reese. He hadn't seen J.R.'s face in years, plus, it didn't help that his Pathfinder was parked nearly half a block from the club!

Stepping out of the jeep, to get a closer look, Dollar Bill punched Calvin's number into his cell phone. "Is that Duke standing beside you?" He asked when Calvin came on the line.

Moving slightly away from Reese and the other cat, Calvin spoke low into the phone, "No, that's not J.R. I left him inside talking to shorty at the coat check, but he should be coming out in a second. He's dressed in all gray, but you'll know it's him when you see me whisper something in his ear. After that, I'll turn and walk back into the club as if I forgot something. Once I'm out of the way, do your thing playboy."

Dollar Bill wanted to ask him, *"Who the fuck was he calling 'playboy'?"* Which to him, sounded like some gay shit! Instead, he simply replied, "Say no more."

Before Dollar could hang up, Calvin asked, "Where you at anyway?"

"Nigga, didn't you just hear me say, *say no more*?" Dollar Bill snapped. "All your ass needs to know is, I'm close enough to handle my business! And when the smoke clears, you just have my 25 keys ready for pick up! How about that?" Hanging up before Calvin could respond.

All six of Dollar's hit men were laying low, in various locations outside of the club, locations that would enable them a clear and direct line of sight on any, and everyone exiting the club.

Reese, on the other hand, had the vicinity surrounded with at least 20 gunmen! He just hoped that he didn't catch a stray, when Dollar Bill realized that J.R. was a no show! Dollar Bill was confident that no one would detect him, since his jeep was parked in a dark, and somewhat secluded area. And he was right, up until then, no one did pin point his position. Well, no one, *except*....Steve O!!!

When the cat dressed in all gray exited the club, Reese did a quick scan of the area to see if any of Dollar Bill's people, or possibly be even him, would expose themselves. Sure enough, at least five or six gunmen suddenly emerged from behind parked vehicles! Quickly, he whispered something in Calvin's ear, however, Calvin was *already* on his cell phone giving the word!

Dollar Bill was bewildered by the fact that Calvin was obviously taking his time getting back inside of the club! "*You have exactly ten seconds to get out of the way! If not, fuck those 50 keys, you're catching it too!*" Dollar Bill whispered to himself, hoping for Calvin's sake, he would hear him. Or rather, for the sake of the 50 keys!

After quickly describing a few of the vehicles in which Dollar's people had taken up position behind, Calvin whispered something in the ear of the cat wearing all gray.

Suddenly, Calvin, Reese, the guy standing beside them, and the dude dressed in all gray, *all* rushed the entrance door of the club!

The first shot to erupt, was *extremely* loud! No one knew, or even saw, where it erupted from, but those that followed were rapid....and continuous!!!

The scene outside of the Q-Club was nothing less than a battlefield.

Yet, unbeknownst to anyone, that *first* shot that triggered it all, was actually the bullet in which Steve O put into the back of Dollar Bill's head!!!

Well no one, *except* Jack....who emptied his .10mm into Steve O's body!!!!

K Smooth knew that it was Nadine's overall performance, as Mayor of New York City, which earned her the victory as Gubernatorial elect!

"Congratulations! Although your opponent was a well liked, respected, and prominent candidate, I must say; the best person for the job, is the *lady* who won." K Smooth smiled, at the same time giving Nadine a hug. It was a very brief hug, being that they won at her victory party and *all* eyes were on the new Governor! The first *female* Governor of New York State!

"You and I both know that I couldn't have pulled this thing off without you." Nadine looked him in the eyes. "I'll congratulate *you* later!" She smiled, then walked off to take pictures, shake hands, and talk to those who were there in support of, media personalities, and fellow Democrats.

K Smooth however, fell back, and made a mental note of all those whom he'd send thank you gifts, for their support.

It was overwhelming to see the number of Black Churches, Organizations, and even the large percentage of Italians who came out to vote for Nadine Shepard, as Governor. As with her previous runs for office, the number of young voters who took to the polls, in her support, was nothing less than astounding!

K Smooth had no idea what J.R. had said to Mark Wright, but each of them certainly deserved a *thank you* gift! It was unbelievable seeing how zealously the CEO, of Street Life records, took to Nadine's cause! His efforts, and zeal, had K Smooth wondering if Mark Wright, himself, had political aspirations?

Mark Wright had organized a Summit/ Concert in Flushing Meadow Park, where he, his Artists, and a whole slew of industry folks took to the stage and emphasized, to the huge crowd, the importance of voting!

"It's a *Right,* we as young Black people, *must* learn to exercise!" Mark Wright had told the crowd, which consisted mostly of Black teenagers, young adults, and their parents. "It's coming together, for a common cause, that enables us to be heard!" He shouted.

After each of his Artist spoke their piece, in regards to voting, they each performed two songs. Following the performances, Nadine's campaign manager, none other than 'Kenneth Shannon', took to the stage and addressed the crowd. "First, and foremost, I'd like to thank you all for coming out here today. As well as thank, a man whom I've known nearly my entire life." K Smooth looked over at Mark Wright, and produced a smile, before he continued, "Mr. Mark Anthony Wright, for putting this Summit together, as well as for his *overall* support in this very important campaign. I don't know how many of you know Mayor Nadine Shepard, but I'm quite sure you all, especially those of you who are residents of New York City, have seen and felt the effects of her efforts, drive, capabilities, and accomplishments. As City Councilwoman, she made decisions and changes, which improved the majority of housing and schools throughout the Borough of Queens. As Queens Borough President, she obtained the necessary funding to clean up and renovate some of Queens most poverty stricken areas. As Mayor, in just four years we've witnessed Nadine Shepard repair the damages, to this City, which unfortunately were imposed by her predecessor. Unemployment is at a *record breaking* low, crime is at an *all time* low, and the economy *overall* is thriving!" K Smooth smiled for the crowd, then said, "So basically, the quality of life, in New York City, has undoubtedly been restored since Mayor Nadine Shepard had been in office. With that said, *imagine* the things she can and will accomplish for this State, as your next Governor!"

Mark Wright returned to the stage, taking hold of the microphone, he added, "The number of you who came out for this Summit, is indeed impressive," He told the crowd, producing a wide colgate smile, as if he, himself, was a true politician. "But, the turnout could, and should have been of greater proportion! So, what my organizers and I have decided to do is, in approximately 90 days from today, I'm going to put together a *Mega* Summer Jam! Which will be held in Central Park!" The applause from the crowd was thunderous. Raising his hand in the air, to quiet the crowd, he added, "The reason I'm calling it a *Mega* Summit is because, I'm going to arrange for 50 *plus*, of the biggest named Rap and R&B Artist to take to the stage! Children are welcomed. Teens are welcomed. But, all those of age, to vote, and can produce a voter's registration card, will receive free CDs, Cassette tapes, Autographed photos and posters, and free tickets to upcoming concerts in the New York City area. Not to mention, there will be free non alcoholic beverages provided the entire day!" Again, the crowd went crazy, and the applause was thunderous! Again, raising his hand to quiet the crowd, also letting them know he was not done speaking. In closing, he informed the crowd, "Her Honor, Mayor Nadine Shepard will give a speech, as well as take pictures with as many of those in attendance as possible, and sign autographs the entire day!"

What no one knew was that it was J.R., who had funded the Summit. Those Artists who had shows to perform, on the day of the Summit, J.R. not only paid them for their brief appearances, he also provided them with a private jet to enable them to make their other engagements. Also, he footed the bill for Mark

Wright to make television, radio, and magazine interviews and advertisements, in behalf of Nadine Shepard for Governor. A s a result, Mark Wright couldn't believe his new found level of fame, respect, business alliances and offers, supporters, as well as a whole new audience of fans!

"*And to think 'I' was under the impression that business and politics didn't mix! Boy was 'I' wrong!"* He'd told himself. However, what surprised Mark Wright *most of all*, was the day in which he'd approached J.R., and out of curiosity, asked, "If you don't mine me asking, when and where did you *meet* Mayor Nadine Shepard?"

"Actually, she and have *never* met." J.R. revealed.

"How the *fuck* did Steve O find out about what was going down?" J.R. angrily shouted into the telephone.

"I have the slightest idea!" Reese honestly replied, being that he hadn't seen or spoken to Steve O in three days, prior to the shoot out. "You know I was busy putting the plan together." He reminded J,R.

"This shit can't be happening! Shit, it doesn't even *sound* right!" J.R. responded, obviously broken up, and in disbelief.

"I did not know Steve O was on the scene, until I saw the News this morning, and they mentioned *his* name along with 19 others, all killed in the shootings." Reese said, obviously on the verge of breaking down.

Repeating himself, J.R. felt as though he was about to lose it! "*I can not believe this shit!*"Again, he shouted into the phone!

Gaining his composure, he asked, “Did you hear them mention Dollar Bill’s name?”

“I don’t even know his real name, but I’ll find out everything we need to know before the day is out.” Reese assured him. “But, I seriously doubt he could’ve escaped that war zone, in front of the Q Club last night. I don’t know how *anyone* could’ve.”

“Never mind your opinion. Just find out if he’s still breathing.” With that said, J.R. hung up the phone. He knew that if Dollar Bill was still alive, he’d have to kill him himself. Yet, he still couldn’t believe that Steve O was dead! “*Why were you even there? Didn’t you watch the VCR tape I sent to you?*” Those were just some of the questions running through J.R.’s mind, as the tears streamed down his face. “*I’m not going to rest until I find out who the fuck told you about what was going down, and where!*” He promised himself. The unanswered questions, in his mind, was definitely driving him crazy, but what had J.R.’s Spirits down the most, was knowing how badly Steve O had wanted to see *him*….prior to his death!

Born knew that he couldn’t let it get out that he provided Steve O with not only a pistol, but also the details regarding what was to transpire at the Q-Club, the night of the shooting. Because, he also knew that if those two facts were to ever get out, J.R. would *undoubtedly* kill him!!!

The crowd outside of Crowe’s Funeral Home was so thick, that traffic, between Lakewood & Supthin Boulevard, was at a complete standstill.

Although Steve O's family had long since moved out of South Jamaica, it was where he'd been born and raised, therefore, his mother consented to his funeral service being held at a location which would allow all those who knew her son, to pay their last respects.

Initially, J.R. decided to skip the funeral service at Crowe's, but attend the burial, which was to be held out in Hempstead, Long Island. However, at the last minute, he changed his mind.

"I really didn't want to appear at the funeral service, because if any of Dollar Bill's people show up, seeking to revenge his death, it'll undoubtedly turn into a shooting gallery." J.R. had told Reese, Cocky, and Jamel.

"I'll position at least 60 shooters outside of Crowe's, so we'll be more then ready if anything should pop off." Reese replied, before making the call.

Thankfully the funeral service was without incident, thought most of the people who'd attended, especially seeing J.R. and his crew present.

Once the service was over, J.R. exited the funeral home with Steve O's mother holding on to his left arm, and his mother, Yolanda, holding on to his right arm, all the while making eye contact with the one enemy he hadn't anticipated seeing….*Carmine*! Wearing a black & white pin striped suit, the cop walked up to J.R. and said, "I never thought an occasion that calls for mourning, would also be cause for celebration." Carmine smiled.

"You say that to say what?" J.R. asked, shaking the two

women's grip on his arms.

"I say that to say, *it's over*!" The cop gave him a serious stare.

"I always knew you was nothing more then a *key stone cop*, posing as this mighty *Whitey* detective." J.R. laughed in his face. "If you were nearly as street smart as you lead folks to believe, you'd know that this street shit *been* over with!"

Nodding his head up and down, the cop informed him, "Anyway, Joshua Reed Jr., you're under arrest for Accessory to Commit Murder. Instead of reading you your Rights, I'll just inform you that, *yours* is a crime punishable by death." The cop laughed, just so J.R., and all those watching, knew that it was *he*....who'd gotten the last laugh.

As the four detectives made their approach, to apprehend him, J.R. noticed that at least 30, of his sixty shooters who were on the scene, had their automatic weapons cocked and down by their sides! All J.R. had to do was give a nod, of the head, and Carmine, along with his four detectives would've all been dead!

Instead, he looked in his mother's eyes, then turned his attention towards Steve O's mother and apologized for the cop's presence, then he looked over at Reese and said,

"It's cool." Meaning their shooters could stand down, as he made his way towards the unmarked police vehicle, which was double parked in front of the funeral home. Before he got into the car's back seat, J.R. turned to face Carmine, who was less then two feet behind him, and said, "Fortunately for you, and your friends here," He smiled at the four detectives. "I'm no longer *that* nigga, whom I was, around the time you instructed my comrade to put the .45 hand gun back into my hands!"

Chapter Twenty.

May. 7th ,1992…

Prior to his arrest J.R. was certain that the Feds were investigating him, and his crew, for drug trafficking and possibly even murder. But apparently, they didn't have enough, or sufficient, evidence against him, considering he'd been locked up two years now and they didn't move in to take his case.

On the same token, he wasn't ready to celebrate, because he knew that being tried by the State posed an even more unpredictable outcome. Mainly because, he knew some cases where dudes were able to *buy* their cases, or rather their freedom, in the State Court, if their money was right. Yet, when, or if, the Government wanted a person bad enough the State Court could just as easily be influenced to crucify a nigga! And with all the media hoopla and attention surrounding *his* case, J.R. pretty much knew which category he would fall into. The *latter,* for sure!

On the day of his trial, he sat in the small holding cell, waiting to be escorted into the court room, at which time he reflected back on his conversation with his Attorney during a recent visit. "I've had an interesting conversation with your *father,* who thinks it would in our best interest to proceed with a Judge trial, opposed to a Jury trial." The lawyer informed J.R. "Truthfully, he brought out some good points, especially with all the media surrounding your case. Whenever the media is heavily involved, as well as the Government, the two sometimes have a tendency to influence the Judge. And under pressure, anybody can make mistakes! Even Judges!" The lawyer winked.

Acting not on the lawyer's advice, but because he knew his father would never lead him wrong, J.R. decided to take a trial by Judge.

Not having to go through the whole Jury selection process, the trial was ready to commence! And right from the start, J.R. could tell the presiding Judge was *against* him!

"*This is un-fucking-believable!*" J.R. told himself, seeing how the Judge continuously shot down any and every motion his lawyer presented. Yet, allowed the Prosecutor to make any and everything part of the record!

After countless *Objections* were made by J.R.'s Attorney, the Judge stopped the presiding and assured him, "It may *appear* as though I'm giving leeway to the Prosecution, but counselor, I assure you I'll take everything presented before me under careful consideration in reaching my verdict!" Meaning, he'd consider sifting through all the hearsay, allegations, and plain rhetoric, in which he was allowing the Prosecutor to *slip into* the record.

As for the media, they *ran* with it all!

Carmine was the State's first witness, and he testified that Joshua Reed Jr., also known as *J.R.,* was a ruthless drug czar and cold blooded murderer, who ruled the streets of Queens, among other areas of New York City, for a number of years! He also testified that, he personally arrested J.R., when he was only 16 years of age, for possession of a loaded firearm. "He had always been a violent individual, because even during that arrest he threatened to blow my head off, if he ever saw me on the streets." The cop testified, looking directly at the Judge. The same Judge who, prior to trial, said J.R.'s youthful offender record would not be brought up during the presiding.

"*Apparently someone forgot to tell that to Carmine.*" J.R. shook his head.

The Prosecutor called a number of witnesses who were at the Q-Club, the night of the shootings. All of whom, testified that they knew of J.R., some thought they'd seen him that night, yet none could say for sure if he was involved in the shootout.

"I did hear that the shootout was between J.R.'s crew and a rival crew from Brooklyn though." Testified a heavy set female, who had the nerve to wave at J.R. as she stepped down from the witness stand.

J.R. was surprised by how weak the case appeared, but then nothing could've prepared him for the State's last witness! A witness who would undoubtedly give the already bias, and partial, Judge the rope in which he needed to *hang* his man!

"Place state your name for the Court?" The Prosecutor addressed his star witness.

"Darnell Beasley."

"Is Darnell Beasley the name in which you're widely known by on the streets of New York City?" The Prosecutor asked.

"Nah." The witness smiled, looked over at J.R. who was sitting at the defense table, and added, "Everyone calls me *Dollar Bill!*"

"Okay Dollar Bill." The Prosecutor too, looked over his shoulder at J.R., smiled, returned his attention to the witness, and asked, "I'd like to direct your attention to the night of June 20th, 1990. Do you recall being at a night club known as the Q-Club, located on 150th Street, Jamaica, Queens that night?"

"Unfortunately, I do." Dollar Bill answered, rubbing the ugly scar on the right side of his forehead.

"I'm going to ask that you turn your attention towards the defense table, and tell me if you know, or even recognize the defendant in this case? If your answer is yes, to either question, I'd also like to know whether or not you recall seeing him at the Q-Club on the night of June 20th, 1990?"

"Yeah I know J.R." Dollar Bill gave him a hateful stare, then added, "And yes, he too was at the Q-Club that night."

"Your Honor," The Prosecutor looked towards the Judge. "Please let the record reflect that the witness has identified the defendant in this case."

The Judge wrote something in his notes.

Returning his attention to Dollar Bill the Prosecutor continued his questions.

"What were you doing at the Q-Club that night? I mean, were you there strictly for the purpose of having a good time?"

"Actually, I'm not into the club scene at all. I was there that night because one of J.R.'s workers, at cat name Calvin, brought it to my attention that J.R. wanted to meet with me, allegedly to squash an old beef between he and I." Dollar Bill screwed his face up at J.R., and added, "But apparently, I was being set up to be murdered."

"How do you *know* that this guy Calvin was one of J.R.'s workers?"

Dollar Bill looked the Prosecutor directly in his eyes and replied, "What would you label a nigga who expresses to you that J.R. had recently gave him 50 kilos of cocaine to get rid of?"

At that, the Prosecutor looked at the Judge wide eyed, at the same time making a *whistling* sound!

"So tell me, what proof do you have to support your theory that you were being set up to be murdered?" The Prosecutor continued his questioning.

"When I pulled up to the club, I noticed Calvin and two other cats standing out front, and as soon as I stepped foot out of my jeep, one of their people shot me from behind." Dollar Bill explained.

"Where were you shot?"

"In the back of my head. Fortunately, the bullet exited the right side of my forehead, without causing any major damage."

"Was the defendant one of the three individuals you saw standing in front of the club, when you pulled up in your jeep?"

"Yes. It was him, Calvin, and another dude who I never saw before." Dollar Bill lied.

"Were you by yourself that night?'

"No, I was with six of my partners." Dollar Bill answered.

"Were any of your partners hurt as well?"

"They're all dead!" Dollar Bill looked over at J.R. with murder in his eyes.

"Dead?" The Prosecutor feigned surprise, as if he didn't already know who all were killed in the shootout. "So *basically,* the defendant had an ambush set up for you and your six friends?"

"*You* can say basically, but for use of a better word, I'd say *exactly*!" Dollar Bill corrected.

"How can you be sure that Mr. Joshua Reed Jr., possessed a firearm that night, let alone shot someone?" The Prosecutor saved this question for last.

"Because, before I lost consciousness, I personally witnessed J.R. shoot my partner Jack, who was driving my jeep that night!" Dollar Bill lied to the Court.

"Thank you for your testimony Mr. Beasley. No further questions, at this time, for the witness Your Honor." With that said, the Prosecutor returned to his seat.

Before the Prosecutor could sit down, J.R.'s Attorney was already on his feet! Ready to tear holes into Dollar Bill's testimony!

"Wasn't it *you* who was setting up an ambush to kill my client?"

"Not at all, *Counselor*." Dollar Bill emphasized the word counselor, with a smile on his face.

"So, you mean to sit here and say that *all* of the witnesses, who I intend to put on the stand today, who *personally* heard you say that you made plans to kill Mr. Reed, are *all* liars?" The lawyer gave him a suspicious stare.

"I won't dispute that I've *once* harbored those feelings, or may have even expressed them to a few people. But I did not go to the Q-Club with intentions of killing *your* client, or anyone else." Dollar Bill answered.

"Isn't it true, that in exchange for your testimony in this courtroom today, the Prosecution has agreed to offer you a *deal* on your, pending, *multiple murder charges,* stemming from the robbery/ murder of an entire family of Cuban Americans?" The lawyer smiled, awaiting his response.

"Yes, I'm currently being *falsely* accused of those allegations. And yes, the Prosecutor did tell me that I could help myself by agreeing to testify against J.R. However, I never agreed to lie, nor fabricate the facts. Your client knows he tried to murder me." Dollar Bill stared the lawyer in his eyes, then added, "*Twice*, to be exact!" "In your words, when was the first attempt made?" The lawyer inquired.

"When he stabbed me *twelve times* with an ice pick, back when he and I were adolescents, in C-74."

"No where do I see a record of that incident ever occurring. Did you report to the Administration, in C-74, that my client was the person who stabbed you?"

"Hell no! Why would I have done something like that? That

would've been considered snitching!" Dollar Bill spat.

"So in essence, what you're saying is, you weren't a snitch *then*, your just a snitch *now*?"

At that, the entire courtroom burst out in laughter....even J.R.!

"I object!" Screamed the Prosecutor, who was up on his feet!

"Fuck you!" Dollar Bill barked on the lawyer.

"Sustained!" The Judge shouted, looked at J.R.'s lawyer, and said, "Counselor, I advise you to keep your *opinion* to yourself!"

"Did you not know, that a number of my client's friends were *also* murdered at the club that night?" The lawyer resumed his questioning.

"If they were, it certainly served them right! Because their demise only implies that their plans to assassinate me *back fired*!" Dollar Bill smiled from ear to ear.

"So why was it that you and all six of your partners, were also in possession of firearms that night?"

"Why wouldn't I be packing? I mean, I *do* have enemies! Hell, you're representing *one of them* as we speak!" Dollar Bill replied sarcastically.

"Even though you were under the impression, that you were coming to the club to *squash* an old beef?"

"True indeed."

"If, as *you* say, my client tried to kill you once before, why would you be willing to meet up with him period? And why even concern yourself with squashing such an old beef, when the two of you obviously move in different circles? The two of you don't even reside in the same Borough, so please help me understand the relevance?"

"Because, and I don't expect you to know this *counselor,* but the streets of New York City *is* one big circle! Therefore, it was only a matter of time before his and my paths crossed, being that he and I are both *street* niggas!" Dollar Bill said with bass in his voice, then added, "I realize now though, that I was wrong to trust a snake!" He said, staring J.R. in the eyes. "For the last time *counselor*," He returned his attention to the lawyer. "I went to the club that night in good faith, and to let my former bandit know that I've come to the realization that he and I were particles of the same cause, trying to achieve the same $effects$. So, in other words *counselor*, I was willing to meet your client that night to let him know that it was time for strength to *respect* strength! But apparently, he felt differently!" Dollar Bill sat back, cracked his knuckles, looked around the courtroom, then up towards the Judge, and asked, "Are y'all *finished* with me?"

"*I can't believe this dude!*" J.R. looked at Dollar Bill incredulously!

The Judge, on the other hand, believed every *word* of what he'd heard! What he obviously disregarded was J.R.'s alibi witnesses, who testified that on June 20th, 1990 J.R. wasn't even in the Country! Let alone Queens!

Before the Judge rendered his verdict, he asked that J.R. stand up and face him.

"Based on the testimony I've heard, the fact that an officer of the law swore under oath that you not only have been carrying guns since you were a youth, but you also threatened that same officer's life! The reputation you've garnered over the years, and the evidence before me, clearly demonstrates that you, Mr. Joshua Reed Jr., are a true menace to this Society! You have chosen a trial by Judge, and by the powers invested in me, I find that you, Mr. Joshua Reed Jr., are guilty of the charges that the State have brought against you, and have proven beyond a reasonable doubt!" The Judge announced, then informed him, "You will re-appear before me, seven days from today, for the purpose of sentencing! Court is now adjourned!" With that said, he banged his gavel.

Seven days later, J.R. was sentenced, by the same Judge, to 25 years to Life in State prison!

His father wasn't, at all, surprised by Judge's ruling, nor the harsh sentence. He had his own reasons for being *relieved* that the Feds didn't pick up J.R.'s case, or bring additional charges against him……………

Chapter Twenty One.

January 27th, 1994…

"I *hope* I didn't block your wife's visit?" Janice asked, giving her nephew a tight hug before the two of them sat down at the visit table.

"Of course not." J.R. smiled, considering it always pleased him to see his mother's sister. "Regina only comes on Fridays, and Sundays." He said, knowing how his aunt liked to pop up during the week, he reserved all five days for Janice.

"So, how are you holding up?" Janice asked, concern written all over her face.

"I'm maintaining." J.R. smiled.

"Well that's good to know. I'll just be glad when you get out of this place!" She said, looking down at her hands. When she looked up, all J.R. could do was smile, seeing that there were no tears in her eyes. Years prior, all she did was cry during their visits. "I brought you a food package." Janice informed him. "Which you probably don't even need." She smiled, judging by how healthy J.R. appeared.

"I can always use the extra food!" J.R. laughed out loud. "All I do is eat, sleep, exercise, and read." He informed her.

"What type of stuff

have you been reading lately?"

Knowing how religious his aunt was, J.R. made sure to include the Bible when he replied, "African history, American history, law books, as well as research the Bible and the Qu'ran."

"That's all well and good, especially since reading is fundamental, but you know what I'm talking about?" She gave him the eye, the same way she use to do when he was a child.

Laughing, he said, "I just told you I've been *researching* the Bible."

"Researching?" She repeated, as if offended by that. "What about Prayer? Have you been making time for Prayer?"

"The *question* is, how's my favorite aunt doing?" J.R. asked, changing the subject. "I'm your *only* aunt. I'm *fine*. Now answer my *question*?"

"You know I'm still striving to get a better understanding of how life, mathematics, and religion all coincide. So no, I haven't actually been Praying." J.R. admitted.

"Well if you've been *properly* researching your Bible, as you say, you'd know that *Man* must put his faith and trust in the Lord, if he wants to clearly understand *life*. It is the Lord who has the power to give you everlasting life. To fear God is wisdom, to depart from evil is *understanding*."

"Aunt Janice listen, " J.R. began.

"No J.R. *you* listen," She stopped him. "You're my nephew, whom I love dearly. All I ask is that, you trust and believe that my sincerest desire is that in the midst of this, *your*, tribulation and affliction, you are able to see God's love for you. The Bible says; a Man's steps are of the Lord, so *how* can a Man understand his own way? Yes, all the ways of Man are pure in his own eyes, but it is the Lord who weighs his Spirit!" Looking her beloved nephew in his eyes, Janice went on, "J.R., you've experienced, first hand, what Man deems as pleasure, You've lived on the wild side. Yet, you've also survived, whereas many others have gone on. Now, is the time to ask yourself, was it *really* pleasure in which you've experienced? Was your walk on the wild side *really* worth it? All you have to do is look around you, at the strife in which your endeavors have caused you! Just as I'm sure you're well aware of the saying; *if you keep doing what you've been doing, you're going to keep getting what you've been getting."* Still looking him in his eyes, Janice smiled and said, "God has so much better, in store, for you. The worst thing you can do with your life, is mess it up. The word of God says; I've set before you Life & Death, *you* choose! Choose *Life* that you may live, and your seed." Janice explained the word.

"I did make my choice, now I *living* with the repercussion." J.R. replied.

Janice, however, continued on, as if she hadn't even heard his remark. "Jesus Christ said; I didn't come to condemn you, *but*, to save you! Because that's how much God loves you! He sees, and knows, the mess you've made of your life! The disappointment! The people you've hurt! Mistreated! And, even *your* hurt! But, in spite of all the *wrong* you've done, or the mess you've made, God says; I do *not* condemn you! But believe in Me, surrender to Me, and be saved! J.R. if you continue to place your pursuit of riches and fortune above your need for an encounter, and, or a relationship with God, you'll only continue to operate in death!" As the two of them stared into each others eyes, Janice's were not only red, but, overflowing with tears. "You tell me you're an innocent man, and I *believe* you. Just as I *believe* that God can and will deliver you from your circumstances. But, you too, have to *believe* J.R., as well as repent for your sins. Again, I love you with all my heart, and will continue to Pray for you, but it's not enough, because you too have to Pray, for yourself, lest you end up perishing in your own iniquity."

Pleading through her watery eyes, Janice continued, "A wicked, negative lifestyle leads to nothing *but* destruction. Although that lifestyle may be paved with a few thrills, here and there, it'll never be enough to fill that void or make you complete. Proverbs 27:20 says; hell and destruction are *never* full! So the eyes of Man are *never* satisfied!" A few minutes of silence passed between the two of them, before J.R. got up from chair, came around the small table, and gave his aunt a hug, followed by a kiss on her cheek. Kneeling down beside her, he whispered in her ear, "I love you too. And trust me, I do not disregard, or take any of your words in vain. I know what you speak, is truth, as well as with my best interest at heart. Although I've committed countless sins, in my life, I guess my greatest sin, today, is too much pride! Whereas I've heard that God has the power to change a Man's heart and ways, if only he believes, I find myself, daily, trying to change my own heart, ways, and thinking! I realize I'm not doing the Lord a favor, by prolonging belief, faith, and trust in Him. But on the same token, I've *never* been a hypocrite, regarding anything I've ever believed in, or endeavored to accomplish. Therefore, I can't and won't become one *now*. In fact, I do read my Bible, and if I understand it correctly, Ecclesiates 5:5 says; *it's better to 'not' vow, then vow and 'not' pay*!" J.R. quoted the scripture.

Janice just sat there looking her nephew in his eyes, shook her head, then said, "You can say what you want, but you better not take *too* long!" Getting up from her chair, preparing to leave, she informed him, "More than likely, I'll be back up here to see you one day next week." She had a habit of not telling him a *precise* day.

"As always, I'll be looking forward to seeing you. And I love you." J.R. kissed her good bye, before the two of them went their separate ways.......

November 5th, 1994....

"So, here we meet *again*!" K Smooth smiled, as he and Nadine exchanged hugs at her victory party.

"With a lucky charm named Kenneth Shannon, my next victory party may very well be held in the White House!" Nadine returned his smile, gave a wink, then walked off to thank as many of her supporters as she possibly could.

"*Another four years!*" K Smooth thought to himself, not

knowing if he could endure the cold freezing winters of Albany, New York. Even though he knew it would be a cinch for Nadine to be re-elected as Governor. Not only because she'd done such a spectacular job, in her first four years, but also because none of her opponents were even qualified for the seat.

Nadine found that she still had an overwhelming support from young voters, the Black churches, the Italian's vote, various Organizations, and even Mark Wright lent his support once again. The only thing she'd dreaded about her job as Governor, was living in Albany! During the winter months the cold was almost unbearable! Thank God, she had Kenneth to keep her warm! She thought to herself with a smile.

"*You are clearly my God send*!" Nadine told herself, as she watched Kenneth mix and mingle with their guest, from across the room.

She had only been joking, when she'd told Kenneth that their next victory party may very well be in the White house, because truthfully, Nadine had lost all desire to run for public office again! "*This is definitely it!*" She told herself, meaning her second term as Governor. Mainly because, she desperately wanted to settle down, get married, and have some children before it was too late! Yes, she held the highest seat in New York State, and made decisions that only *she* could make. However, she also knew that no office, position, or Man given power, could stop here biological clock from ticking!

Nadine just hoped, and prayed, that Kenneth Shannon wanted the same things!

"*I guess I'll find out soon enough*!" She told herself, again looking in his direction only to find him looking in hers……..

Chapter Twenty Two.

August 12th, 1997…

After seven years of being incarcerated, J.R. had already exhausted his State, and Federal, remedies in the Court system. Although there was always a way for him to get back into the Courts, he had come to realize that in spite of all the *errors* made by the trial Judge, the Courts simply weren't trying to grant him any relief! Mainly because his case had *nothing* to do with Justice, and *everything* to do with Politics!

J.R. realized that it was time he faced the fact that he'd be spending the rest of his life in prison, because if he couldn't get no love from the Court system, he seriously doubted he'd receive any from the Parole Board!

As the weeks passed, he couldn't get his mind off the suggestion in which his father had made, during one of their visits.

"*You've been incarcerated for nearly eight years now, and your case is a clear example of how dirty our so called Justice system plays the game, especially when or if Politics are involved. That is partially why, I've once told you that playing to win means 'planning' in terms of long range. I'm very proud of you, my son, because although your alleged actions in the streets have prejudiced you from receiving a fair trial, they are the same actions in which made our desired outcome a reality. The Reed 'and' Shannon family(s) are not only well off, but will 'be' well off for generations to come! Kenneth's estimated worth, alone, is somewhere around four hundred million dollars! Whereas, our family is sitting on nearly 'twice' that amount!"* Joshua smiled. "*There is so much I want to reveal to you, but, right now is not the time. However, in due time you, and Kenneth, will know the entire story. In the meantime, do not give up on your freedom. What I need for you to do is, sit down and put together a short, position, and straight to the point 'letter' addressed to the Governor of this State. I, personally, know Governor Nadine Shepard, and she's a honest and fair young lady. Your case no longer receives any media coverage, it has pretty much died down. Just as, this is the Governor's last year in office, so you do not have much time left to reach out to her. From my understanding, your lawyer has already reached out to her, once your remedies in the Courts were exhausted, so has Janice, Reverend McCarthy, Mark Wright, countless other friends and family, as well as Kenneth. Now it's 'your' turn to reach out to her.*"

Sitting in his cell one night, J.R. began to write his letter to the Governor.

"*To: The Honorable Governor Nadine Shepard, September 1, 1997*

First, and foremost, I'm sincerely grateful for you taking the time to read my letter, because I can only imagine how busy a woman of your status and position 'must' be. Therefore, I'll strive to state my case, cause, and concerns as briefly as possible. It's been brought to my attention, recently, that a number of my friends, family members, Church, and Attorney have all reached out to you, in my behalf. In hope that you'd take interest, or at least, look into my case, cause, and fight for liberation, considering I've already exhausted all of my remedies in the Courts, to no avail. Whereas, I'm very appreciative to all those who have reached out to you, in my behalf, I realize that time has come for me to do likewise. Unfortunately, I didn't take the liberty to speak at my trial, acting on advice from my then Attorney, whereas I realize and understand, now, that an innocent man should 'always' exercise his Right to be heard. Not those fighting under the pretense of innocence, but, those who are 'truly' innocent. Such as myself!!! Unfortunately, at the time of my trial, I was pretty much a lay person, who was not at all versed in regards to matters of Law. Relying on an Attorney, and the Court system to do right by me. Fortunately, today, my eyes and mind, are both open to the Laws, Rules, Statues, and Criminal Procedures specifically relating to this State of New York. A fact, in which has also opened my eyes 'to' the fact that my conviction was not the result of the evidence produced against me, at my trial, because there were no sufficient evidence to support my conviction. If you, yourself, took a look at the record, my transcripts that is, I'm sure you'd find that I, like so many other young and 'now' old Black men, have been railroaded!!! Mainly due to 'outside' influences. No disrespect intended, but those 'outside' influences, most times then not, are actually 'your' constituents. Political influence, as well as Media influence. Both of whom, should not have any involvement 'inside' of our so called Justice system. I said, no disrespect to 'you', because I'm sure everyone in the City, and State, of New York have seen and/or felt your achievements, first hand. Yet, it is inevitable, that in spite of your many successes, accomplishments, actions, deeds, and overall work ethic in general, one fact will 'still' remain. And that is, no matter how hard, how long, or how much 'you' strive or endeavor to build up or fix, which ever Community, you're elected to oversee, as long as the Justice System in this State remains 'broken' there will never be any balance...not even in Society! Political and Media influences not only has the Courts, these days, making a mockery in, and of, itself, but, the 'two' really should not hold, or have, any weight upon the 'scales' of Justice!

Again, thank you, for your time, assistance and concern.

I remain,
Joshua Reed Jr."

September. 3, 1998....

When J.R. walked out of the Green Haven Correctional Facility, in Stormville, New York, a *free* man, he couldn't believe it! Nor could he believe *all* the people who were posted up, outside of the prison, to celebrate his release!

Among the many faces were, his father's, his mother's, his wife Regina, sister Pam, Spoon, their daughter Silver, Aunt Janice *who was in tears,* Steve O's mother, KeKe, Cocky, Reese, Jamel, Mark Wright, and Reverend McCarthy.

"So, how does it feel to be free?" Joshua asked with a smile, at the same time giving J.R. a hug.

"It's a little too soon to describe the feeling!" J.R. laughed.

After serving eight years, of his 25 year sentence, he was *finally* free! Looking about the crowd, J.R. noticed that K-Smooth's face was not among them. Yet, he knew he couldn't be mad, being that he knew it was none other than K Smooth who had leaked his letter, to the Governor, to the *Media*! "*How ironic!*" Thought J.R., realizing that the same Media, who had played a major role in securing his conviction, turned right around and played a major role in his being released!

Although it's been over 13 years since he and K Smooth had any direct contact, J.R. knew for quite some time that his childhood comrade was sleeping with Nadine Shepard. Yet, it had never crossed his mind to capitalize off of such a fact, by reaching out to K Smooth during his trial, or incarceration. Therefore, J.R. knew he could honestly say that he'd played his part, making sure their paths remained an unassociated one! Throughout his bid, J.R. had received much love and respect, from other convicts, throughout the penal system. However, the love and cheers from other inmates, at Green Haven, was also

overwhelming when the Governor granted his Pardon!
Ordering that he be released, immediately! Seeing J.R. leave gave so many of the other inmates 'hope', especially the Lifers, who'd also exhausted their remedies in the Courts.

The *welcome home party*, for J.R., was crazy! It seemed as if *all* of New York City had tried to gain entrance! Sitting in the VIP area, awaiting his *surprise* gift, from his father, who was also sitting at the table, along with his wife, Pam, Regina, Spoon, Cocky, Reese, and Jamel.

"You do know that a surprise isn't really necessary," J.R. said to his father with a smile, happy to just be home, amongst his people.
"It's too late, one of them has already arrived." Joshua replied with a smile, at the same time looking over J.R.'s shoulder.

Following his father's stare, J.R. couldn't contain his smile, seeing K Smooth standing bchind him! He too, was wearing a smile.

The two childhood comrades embraced, in a *brotherly* hug, for what seemed like an hour! At least, that's how the rest of the dinner party assessed it!

"When the two of you boys get through hugging, I'd like to have a word, in private, with the both of you." Joshua informed them with a smile.
The two of them looked at each other *both* recalling the last time they'd heard that!

"I wonder what the *talk* will be about this time?" K Smooth laughed.

"There's only one way to find out!" J.R. replied, as the two of them followed his father into another area of the club, which was actually secluded.

Once the three of them were alone, Joshua looked into the eyes of the two young men whom *both* he considered sons, before he began to speak.

"I realize that at the young age of 31, the two of you have undoubtedly seen and been through, more than, the average person will experience in a life time. I'm just pleased to not only still be around, but also to see this justified *end.* A desired *end* which I've anticipated from the beginning." Looking at J.R., his eyes welled up with tears when he added, "Unfortunately, nothing worth having comes without some degree of suffering. You've had to endure being in a cage for eight years, while your mother and I had to *witness* you caged for eight years. And son, I do apologize. Just as I must apologize for some of the secrets I've been compelled to keep, so not to distract either of you in the midst, nor from the productivity of our plan."

"Pop, you don't even have to go there." J.R. interrupted him, with a smile on his face. "I'm certain I speak for K Smooth as well, when I say you do not owe either of us an apology, or explanation for *anything*."

"I *second* that!" K Smooth laughed, even though he was serious.

"Just hear me, please." Joshua pleaded, determined to reveal the secret in which he'd been keeping from them. "Prior to having our discussion, at the house out in White Plains, I had plans for the two of you. Meaning, I was *already* planning in terms of long range. In fact, the *stage,* for the two of you to accomplish all in which you have, was *set* shortly after the two of you were born!" Joshua revealed. "I first met Nadine Shepard when she was 15 years old, and I had recently gotten out of Sing Sing prison. Her mother, Lorraine Shepard, had just had a heart attack, and her untimely death led to Nadine residing with her grand father, Keith Shepard, who ultimately adopted her. However, I too, stepped up to the plate to support her, guide her, as well as pay for her education. Also, I used all within my power, to help turn her dreams into her accomplishments." He said, looking K Smooth in his eyes, before informing him, "You do *know* that my daughter loves you very much?" Joshua smiled.

Then turning his attention to J.R., he added, "Her recent actions alone, should reveal to you just how much your *sister*, Nadine, loves you as well."

THE END!!!!!!

Epilogue....

J.R. lied awake in bed, as his beautiful pregnant wife slept peacefully beside him, *thinking* how fortunate he had been to survive a 'life' in which usually resulted in 'death', or a *mandatory* life sentence. It had once been his opinion that fate, and fate *alone*, chose and controlled a man's destiny! However, his father's plan, actions, and intentions caused him, these days, to re-evaluate his earlier opinion.

Putting his own plan together, J.R. knew he had some unfinished business, of his own, to conclude.

""Mister, you wouldn't happen to have a dollar, or two?" The dirty, smelly, junkie who couldn't have been no more then 19 years old, asked the white man whom he knew to be a cop.

"The *only* thing I have for a dope fiend is a steel toe boot, and a .38 shell! Which do *you* prefer?" Camine laughed, causing the other two detectives to laugh as well, as the three of them turned to head back towards their gray police van. Once again, satisfied that all dealers and junkies, had either took flight or scattered upon his arrival on the block. All, except the 19 year old junkie, who, with lightening speed, suddenly attacked his victim!

Carmine didn't even realize what stuck him, when he'd felt the sharp pinch in the back of his neck! Spinning around, gun drawn, he found the young junkie smiling from ear to ear, with a bloody syringe in hand!

"I guess now you have *three* things!" The young junkie laughed, being that he was diagnosed with full blooded AIDS!!!

Reaching up to touch the back of his neck, where he'd been stuck, Carmine immediately felt the blood. The blood from the contaminated needle, as well as his own, he was sure!

Carmine knew he'd have to live with the young junkie's final words, whatever life he'd have left, when the junkie revealed, "By the way, *J.R.* told me to tell you that he will always be *that* nigga!" Right before Carmine raised the .38 Special, and shot him, at point blank range.........

Carmine had been J.R.'s onc piece of unfinished business in the *streets*, however, he had another piece of unfinished business in the *penitentiary*! In fact, he couldn't believe it when he'd gotten the call, informing him that Dollar Bill had recently landed, in general population, at Green Haven.

J.R. had served the last five years of his bid at Green Haven, therefore, he knew exactly who he needed to reach out to!

"What a pleasant surprise!" Barkim smiled, walking into the visiting room, at Green Haven, to find Regina sitting at the table designated for him. Giving her a friendly hug, he said, "When they told me that I had a visit, I just knew my girl was trying to sneak up on me, to see if she could catch me out there with this other chick!" He laughed.

"I'm so sorry, I know one of us should have informed you that I would be coming to check you, when you called the house last week, but there's certain things J.R. isn't going to discuss over the telephone." Regina apologized, as well as explained.

"For good reason." Barkim smiled, then becoming serious he added, "In that case, speak on it Sis, I'm listening."

"He wants you to *see* Dollar Bill."

Barkim nodded, then said, "I heard dude came through, but I haven't seen him yet, because they have him housed on the West yard. From what I've been told, he hasn't been assigned to a job yet, so he's liable to be moved over to the east yard any day now." He explained, letting Regina know he pretty much *already* been on him. "However, if they don't move him over to *my* side, I guess I'll be moving over to *his* side!" Barkim smiled.

He and J.R. had formed a bond when they'd been in G-Block together.

Truthfully, at the time, Barkim wasn't looking to make any friends, especially *new* friends, being that he was pretty much a loner. Nonetheless, he, like most of the prison, had heard a great deal about J.R., and his actions on the streets. Yet, he'd also heard a group of young wanna be thugs plotting to *extort* J.R.

Not only did Barkim pull his coat, to the plot, he also gave J.R. a shank to handle his business! To say that Barkim was impressed, by the *four* examples J.R. made that day, was indeed an understatement!

Shortly afterwards, the two of them began eating 'set ups' together, working out together, and holding each other down, which J.R. continued to do even after his release. Barkim was serving 125 years to Life, for five murders! He'd initially came into the prison system with 75 years to Life, but ended up receiving the additional '50' as a result of two murders he *allegedly* committed in the penitentiary!

Two weeks following his and Regina's visit, Dollar Bill was found lying, faced down, in one of the shower stalls in the East Yard's recreation field, in a pool of his own blood! He had been dead, at least two hours, before an inmate desiring to take a shower discovered his body……

Pam's Beauty Salons and Fitness Clubs had continued to expand. Besides New York, New Jersey, and Connecticut, she now had locations in Boston, Philadelphia, and Baltimore as well. Her and Spoon were also the proud owner's of a chain of restaurants, throughout the Tri State area, called "The Silver Spoon", named after her daughter and husband.

Joshua and Yolanda were pleased with the accomplishments in which both of their children had made. Not to mention, their extended family, consisting of KeKe, Kenneth, Steve O's family, Cocky, Reese, and Jamel! All of whom were present at K Smooth and Nadine's wedding ceremony!

Once her second term, as Governor, had run it's course, Nadine announced to the Public that would not be seeking election in any branch of Legislative office *ever* again. Of course her fellow Democrats weren't to thrilled with her decision,

"That's there business!" She'd told K Smooth, because her decision was final! As for K Smooth, her decision was fine by him!

Nadine had met her father's wife, Yolanda, once, when she was about seventeen years old. She had always known about Pam, and J.R., but the three of them didn't formally meet until a few weeks following J.R.'s release. At which time, Nadine was no longer in office!

The wedding ceremony was a private, family only, affair, for obvious reasons, which she and K Smooth didn't even have to *explain* to their guest. The only photographs taken that day, were of the Bride & Groom….and their huge expensive wedding cake!!!

Til Death Do Us Part......

I Solute You, My "True" Comrades, That Is 'Those' Who Have Stood Firm, As Well As 'Those' Who Have Fallen, Not The Masses Of, Nowaday, Cowards, Who Consider Themselves Ballin!!!!!! That Is 'Those' Who Have Played The Game, As It Has Never Been Played, Not, Those Who Have No Respect For The Codes, But, Only Seek To Get Paid!!! That Is 'Those' Who The Masses Of Nowaday Cowards Portray, Not, Those Who Will Sell Out Their Comrades, To Remain "Free" Another Day!!! My Comrades, And I, Have Formed A Bond, (Since The Early Age Of Eight) We've Made Our Struggles One, Even If It Meant Sharing 'One' Plate!!! Our Trials & Tribulations Became Our Stepping Stones, Because, From Them, We've Learned. Love, Fear, And Respect (We Welcome From The Streets) Because, It Is What We've Earned!!! *Whether Through Manipulation, Intimidation, Or The Gun, We've Ultimately Accomplished Our Desired Mission, And That "Mission" Was Not Only To Put Ourselves, But Also, Our Families...In A "Better" Position!!!!! For A Period, My Comrade, And I, Weren't Allowed To Speak, Being Discreet, Yet, I Watched 'Him' Take Over The System, Just As, He Witnessed 'Me' Takeover The Streets!!!! Unfortunately, We've Lost A Beloved Comrade (Steve O), Who Will 'Forever' Live Within Us...The "True", His Name And Thoroughness Manifested Through Us, Because, 'That' Is How" Real" Comrades Do!!!! My Comrades, And I, Have Been Down For Each Other, Til The End, Matter Of Fact, From The Start, When The Words Were Being Tattooed Above Our Hearts, The 'Five' Words In Which We've Lived By.........*Til Death Do Us Part!!!!

(*Remember That!)*

Dewey Hill Entertainment & Publishing
PO Box 32316
Charleston, SC 29417
www.deweyhillpublishing.com
Phone: 1-(866) 827-8477

Order Form

My Brother's Keeper by Alfred Adams, Jr.	$14.95
Till Death Do Us Part by Alfred Adams, Jr.	$14.95
Book Title	$14.05
Shipping/handling (via U.S. Priority Mail)	$ 4.95
Total	$20.00

Purchaser Information

Name:______________________________Reg.#:____________________

Address:____

____

City:__________________________State:________Zip:______________

Total Number of Books Ordered:_________

For orders shipped directly to prisons, Polka Dotz & Stripez Publishing deducts ***25% off*** the sale price of the book. Cost are as follows:

Till Death Do Us Part by Alfred Adams, Jr.	$11.25
Shipping/handling	$ 4.05
Total	$15.30